HOTTER AFTER MIDNIGHT

HOTTER AFTER MIDNIGHT

CYNTHIA EDEN

BRAVA

KENSINGTON PUBLISHING CORP.

http://www.kensingtonbooks.com

BRAVA BOOKS are published by

Kensington Publishing Corp.
850 Third Avenue
New York, NY 10022

All Kensington titles, imprints and distributed lines are available at special quantity discounts for bulk purchases for sales promotion, premiums, fund-raising, educational or institutional use.

Special book excerpts or customized printings can also be created to fit specific needs. For details, write or phone the office of the Kensington Special Sales Manager: Kensington Publishing Corp., 850 Third Avenue, New York, NY 10022. Attn. Special Sales Department. Phone: 1-800-221-2647.

Brava and the B logo Reg. U.S. Pat. & TM Off.

ISBN-13: 978-0-7582-2602-0
ISBN-10: 0-7582-2602-0

First Kensington Trade Paperback Printing: May 2008
10 9 8 7 6 5 4 3 2 1

Printed in the United States of America

For Jack.
I couldn't have done it
without you!

Chapter 1

The vampire on her couch had a serious blood phobia. Dr. Emily Drake tapped a ballpoint pen against her lower lip as she listened to the vamp describe his little problem.

"I just . . . can't drink it. I tried taking the blood straight from a source." He glanced over at her, his brown eyes wide. "Ya know, like from someone's neck."

Emily nodded. Yeah, she had a pretty good idea. She scribbled a quick note on her pad. *Scared to take directly.*

"But the minute my teeth actually touch someone's skin—" He broke off, and a shudder worked the length of his too-thin body. "I feel like I'm gonna be sick."

Hmmm. Emily could only imagine how the guy's "source" had to feel. "Tell me, Marvin, have you tried going to a blood bank?" In her experience, some vampires just couldn't take drinking warm blood from a human's veins. They needed the blood cold, ice cold, and bagged—like some gruesome monster takeout.

He nodded and closed his eyes. "Been there, done that, Doctor. It just doesn't work for me." He exhaled heavily, and Emily had to fight to control the curve of her lips. Vampires didn't breathe, didn't need any air, didn't need anything but blood to live. But some habits were sure hard to break.

Even for the dead.

"I'm going to die." A pause. His eyes opened, gazed at her office ceiling. "*Again.*" His hands lifted in the air, began to gesture furiously as he announced, in a slightly shrill tone, "I've been a vampire for six days—*six days!* And I'm going to starve to death. I'll be the first vampire in history to starve because he's afraid of blood! I'm going to wither away, dwindle to nothing. There will be no bones left, no ashes. Just—"

Oh jeez, this guy was quite the drama queen. Emily leaned forward. Vamps were all alike. Always with the *I–I* talk. You'd think they were the only supernatural creatures who had any problems.

Not being able to drink blood *was* a pretty serious problem for a vampire. And that was why Marvin Scamps had come to see her. She had a reputation for being able to help creatures like him.

Emily pulled off her glasses, rubbed the bridge of her nose as she thought a moment, then said, "Have you tried mixing the blood with something else?"

He shot off the couch, began to pace the room, his skeletal body tight, his hands knotted into fists. *"It's blood! I can't drink blood! I can't—"*

Emily took a deep breath and lowered the shield she'd erected in her mind. Slowly, carefully, she opened her thoughts up to the creature before her.

Blood. Horrible, red, sticky blood. Dripping down my throat. Gagging me. Oh, the taste. Weak, stale. I hate it, hate it—

Oh yeah, the guy had a bad blood issue.

Emily probed deeper into Marvin's mind, pushing past the fear, the disgust. There had to be more to Marvin's phobia. There always was. If she could just find a memory to show her . . .

Emily's special gift in this world was her ability to touch the minds of others. She could peek inside their thoughts, feel the sting of their emotions, and that extrasensory ability made her the best damn psychologist in the state of Georgia. But, well, not everyone got to benefit from her little "bonus" power. Her gift only worked with supernatural beings—the *Other*— and that was why Emily was known as the Monster Doctor.

Of course, that wasn't her technical title. Couldn't very well post that in gold lettering on her door.

"I can't live this way!" Marvin's voice was a full scream now. He stood in front of her window, gazing down at the street below. His shaggy blond hair brushed against the window-pane.

She refrained from pointing out that, technically, Marvin wasn't living. Damn. She wondered who'd been the brilliant guy to transform him. Marvin really didn't seem to be cut out for being undead.

But it was her job to help him.

And she was very, very good at her job.

"Come here, Marvin." She didn't like the way he was eyeing the street below. There was no way he'd survive a jump from twenty-three stories. Only a level-nine demon or one very strong shifter could survive a fall like that.

His palms pressed against the glass. "If I can't drink the blood, I'll die."

Eventually. "You have a month," she told him, pitching her voice low, trying to soothe him. "A vampire needs to feed only once every full moon." And when he'd been transformed, he'd taken blood then. That gave him about three weeks before his next feeding.

Emily opened her desk drawer and pulled out her Rolodex. She took out a gray business card and held it up. "Take this."

Marvin glanced back at her, brows knitted suspiciously. "What is it?" He crept toward her, lifted his hand.

"A name and a number." She handed him the card, met his gaze levelly. "A very private name and number. There have been others like you, Marvin. Others who needed . . . help to feed."

He flinched.

"Worst-case scenario—you call that number when the hunger gets too much for you. Tell the guy who answers I referred you."

"Wh-what will he do?"

"He'll give you a transfusion." The alarm on her watch began to vibrate softly against her wrist.

Their session was over.

"A transfusion?" For the first time since he'd walked into her office, hope lit his face. "The blood can be pumped into me, so I don't have to drink it?"

Emily nodded. "If necessary." But that wasn't a permanent solution. "Marvin, you're a vampire. It's your nature to drink blood." He couldn't fight his basic nature forever. "Sooner or later, you'll have to feed."

He swallowed.

"But in the meantime, stop worrying so much." She tried a smile. "You've got a backup plan now, so you know you aren't going to starve."

His lips lifted in a faint grin, showing the hint of his fangs. "Yeah, I do, don't I?" His fingers curled over the card.

Her leather chair creaked softly as she pushed to her feet. "You and I are going to work through this." He just had to trust her enough to let her fully into his mind so that she could help him to fight his fear. "I want you to come back next week, same time."

"A-all right."

Marvin grabbed his battered leather coat and headed for the door. "Thanks." He opened the door, heading into the empty lobby. It was after eleven P.M. and Emily's assistant, Vanessa, had left just as Marvin arrived for his appointment.

Marvin looked back over his shoulder and said, "I'll see you next week."

She pushed her glasses back on her nose as she followed him into the lobby. "Don't worry. Everything is going to be—"

A loud knock sounded on her office door.

Marvin jumped.

Emily frowned. She didn't have any other appointments scheduled for the night. No one else should have—

A fist hammered against the wooden door. "Dr. Drake?" A man's voice. Deep. Hard. Slightly annoyed. The doorknob rattled.

Good thing Vanessa always locked up when she left.

The vampire edged closer to her. "Do you . . . know who that is?"

No, she sure as hell didn't. But she was going to find out. Straightening her shoulders, Emily marched forward, flipped the lock—

"Dr. Drake, I know you're in there!"

—opened the door, and found herself staring at a tall, dark stranger, a stranger with a badge clipped to the top of his faded jeans. *A cop.*

Alarm bells rang in her head. Anytime a cop paid her a call this late, well, it was never good.

The cop blinked at her, blinked a pair of sky blue eyes, and lowered the hand he'd raised to slam against her door.

Emily felt her stomach tighten as she stared up at him. A shiver of foreboding slid over her. This man, he was danger-ous, *very* dangerous. Her psychic gift told her that, and every instinct she possessed as a woman screamed the same warn-ing.

The cop was tanned a deep, dark gold. His hair was pitch black, a little too long. He had a hard, square jaw and a long blade of a nose. His cheekbones were high, glass sharp, giv-ing him a slightly predatory look. His lips were thin and cur-rently curved down in a frown of annoyance.

The cop was a big guy. Tall, well over six feet, with wide shoulders and thick muscles that stretched the black T-shirt he wore. He was also glowing faintly.

Shit.

She knew what that hazy, shining light around his body meant.

The cop wasn't human.

And there was only one kind of creature that carried a glow like a second skin.

The guy was a shifter.

Shit. Shit. Most people knew the legends about the shifters. Some folks called them *Weres.* They were creatures who could change their forms, shift into beasts.

Her empathic ability let her see their second form, allowed her to see the soft, shining glow of the beasts the shifters carried. Sometimes those beasts took control. Shifters had been known to go mad, to attack, to kill—

"Are you Dr. Drake?" His gaze darted over her shoulder to Marvin, narrowed.

"Ah, yes, yes, I am." Oh damn, but she didn't trust shifters. *Never trust anything that was born with two faces . . .* that was her motto.

What kind of shifter was the cop? She'd met plenty of his kind in her time. Met shifters who could become panthers, snakes, even one who could become an owl. What was the cop?

Something fairly safe like an owl or a snake?

Or something dangerous . . . like a bear, a dragon, or God forbid, a wolf? The wolves were the worst. Uncontrollable, aggressive, with strong psychotic tendencies—

The cop grunted, then said, "I need you to come with me." He reached out his hand to her.

She stared at his hand, at the long, broad fingers that reached for her. The hair on her nape rose. Go with a shifter? What, did she have the word *stupid* written on her forehead? She made no move to take his hand. Instead, she asked, "And just who might you be?"

"Detective Colin Gyth." He withdrew his hand, used it to pull out a black wallet, flashed her an ID card for all of two seconds.

"Ah . . . I need to see that again." Oh no, *never trust a shifter.*

His black brows lowered and he tossed her the wallet.

Emily took a moment to study the picture and ID information. Hmmm. It all looked legitimate. But what did the detective want with her?

"Uh, Dr. Drake?" Marvin's quiet voice.

She'd almost forgotten about him. Emily stepped back from the doorway, gave him a wan smile. "It's all right. You can go now."

He eyed the cop. "You sure?"

She nodded.

"Well, okay, then." Colin Gyth didn't step back when Marvin approached the door, and the vampire wound up brushing against him as he crossed the threshold of the office.

Colin's nostrils flared slightly and he turned his head, watching carefully as Marvin headed toward the elevator. He didn't speak, not until the shining, mirrored doors had closed behind Marvin's pale form. "He a client?"

Emily didn't answer, just stared back at him.

Colin sighed. "Sorry, none of my business, right?"

It sure as hell wasn't.

"Look, Dr. Drake, my captain sent me down here to get you. We've got a top priority case that—"

"Your captain?" Her heart began to beat faster. She knew a guy who worked on the Atlanta PD. He'd been one of her first patients when she'd opened her practice.

"Yeah, Danny McNeal. He wants you to look at a crime scene."

Danny. She kept her face expressionless. It was a skill she'd perfected years ago. When you could tell a person's innermost thoughts, it helped to be able to cloak your response. Cause sometimes, the thoughts that she picked up scared her to death.

Hmmm. So Danny had sent him. That relaxed her a bit, but . . . "I'm not a forensic psychologist, I can't help with any kind of—"

His hand reached out, snagged hers. "He told me to come get you."

His hand was warm. Strong. Colin's scent, rich, masculine, wrapped around her, and a strange ball of heat began to form in her stomach.

His blue stare held hers. "And, lady, I'm sure as hell not leaving this building without you."

She wasn't what he'd expected.

Colin Gyth glanced at Dr. Drake—*Emily*—from the corner of his eye as he pulled his Jeep to a stop in front of the two-story house at the end of Byron Street.

He'd heard of her before, of course. Heard rumors, whispers about the Monster Doctor. But rumors, in his experience, usually didn't amount to jackshit.

So, after getting the order from his captain, he'd done some quick research on Emily.

According to her driver's license, Emily was thirty-one, five foot five, and weighed one hundred thirty pounds. He'd learned that she'd been born and bred in Atlanta. Went to college at Emory and got her degrees there. She had a Ph.D. in psychology, with a dual focus on clinical studies as well as neuroscience and animal behavior. Her mom was a teacher at a local elementary school, and her dad was deceased.

The good doctor had never been in trouble with the law. She paid her taxes, owned a house in one of the historic suburbs, and was single.

She had long, midnight black hair—hair that was currently pulled back in a rather painful-looking bun. She wore black-rimmed glasses that made her wide, green eyes look even bigger.

Yeah, he knew the basic facts about her, but he hadn't known how . . . pretty she actually was. And pretty was a good word for her. The woman wasn't cute, she wasn't drop-dead gorgeous, but she was pretty. Nice heart-shaped face, a chin that was a little too pointed, high cheekbones and perfect bow red lips.

And her body. Very, *very* nice. Round, firm breasts. Long, shapely legs. When she'd climbed into his Jeep, her black skirt had hiked up two inches and he'd been given a glorious glimpse of her thighs. The woman had a killer pair of legs.

And he'd always been a sucker for great legs.

"I-is this the place?"

He stiffened at the sound of her voice. That warm, husky Southern drawl. He could imagine hearing that voice late at night, when they were in bed.

What the hell? Colin shook his head. Now was not the

time to start fantasizing about the doctor. He was on a case. And really, the lady wasn't his type. He'd never gone for the brainy broads. He liked the party girls. The here-today-gone-tomorrow-no-questions-asked girls.

And as for the doc, well, damn, she asked questions for a living.

Definitely *not* his type.

He cleared his throat, dragged his gaze from her legs, and glanced at the brightly lit house. Teams of cops were scouring the yard, shining flashlights, interviewing neighbors. "Yeah, this is it."

He wasn't sure why McNeal had ordered him to pick her up. But, hey, he'd been around long enough to learn that when the captain gave an order, you followed it.

He shoved open his door, started to walk around and let the doc out, but she jumped from the vehicle and headed for the house.

A uniformed cop stepped in front of her, holding up his hand as she approached the house's open front door. "Hey, lady, you can't go in there—"

"Yes, she can." McNeal's gravelly voice. The captain tapped the cop on the shoulder as he appeared directly behind the young guy in the entranceway.

The patrol cop gulped, mumbled an apology, and seemed to slink away.

"Hi, Danny." A hint of warmth crept into Emily's voice.

Colin's eyes narrowed as he stalked behind her. Just what was her relationship with the captain?

Danny McNeal was one of the toughest sonofabitches he'd ever met. The guy was in his early forties, completely bald, and built like a linebacker.

And, as far as Colin knew, the guy wasn't a shifter, a demon, or any other sort of monster.

Just your average bad-ass human.

So how did the guy know the Monster Doctor?

When McNeal hugged Emily, Colin stiffened and a hot

lick of something that sure as hell couldn't be jealousy ripped through him.

No, it couldn't be jealousy. He'd just met the woman less than thirty minutes ago. He didn't have a claim on her.

The captain's hands seemed to linger around Emily, and Colin got the impression that there was some genuine affection between the two. *Were they lovers?*

McNeal's gunmetal gray eyes met his. "Colin, give us a minute."

His jaw clenched as he nodded, then he stepped back a few feet. He could have stepped back twenty feet, it wouldn't have made any difference. McNeal might think he was getting some privacy, but thanks to his enhancements, Colin had hypersensitive hearing.

"I need your help," McNeal murmured.

Colin turned his back on them, watched the cops searching the area.

"There's a body inside," his captain continued, his voice little more than a whisper of sound. "I need to know if he's human or . . ." He let his sentence trail off. There was a moment of silence, then he said, "I know you can tell if someone's *Other* just by being near if the subject is alive, but will you be able to tell when he's dead?"

Oh shit. Every muscle in Colin's body tightened. *Other* was the general term for any magical being, a catch-all phrase that had evolved years ago.

His eyes squeezed closed and he began to sweat. *The doc could tell if you were Other just be being near you?* If that were true, then he was seriously screwed.

No one on the force knew about him. And if anyone found out, if the captain were to learn—

"I can tell," Emily finally spoke, and her voice was just as quiet as McNeal's. "If the death is recent, some of the spirit will still be there."

Damn. Damn. Damn. His eyes snapped open. The woman could tell if a dead guy was human or *Other.* Then she had to know about him.

But why hadn't she said anything? She'd gotten into his Jeep, as calm as you please, driven for miles, and never said a word about him being—

"The guy died less than two hours ago."

"Then I can tell."

"I'm also gonna need an idea of what did this."

What, not *who*, Colin noticed. He'd seen the body earlier, and he knew exactly why his captain was suspecting that the killer hadn't necessarily been human.

"I'll do my best," Emily promised.

McNeal grunted. Then, "Colin, come here!"

Colin glanced back over his shoulder, carefully avoiding Emily's stare. He'd deal with her later.

McNeal motioned toward the door. "Show her the vic."

He sauntered up the steps, brushed his body lightly against hers as he passed. "Hope you've got a strong stomach." It was all the warning he'd give her. He didn't think she'd be able to handle the body inside too well. Colin could still smell the stench of vomit from the first two green cops who'd found the victim.

He led her inside, past the gleaming parquet flooring in the foyer, past the spiral staircase, and straight to the body.

Or what was left of it.

"*Oh my God!*" She sucked in a sharp breath. Stumbled to a stop near the puddle of congealed blood.

He glanced at her face then. The color had bleached away. And her eyes, so big, so wide, were full of horror.

The impulse to touch her, to comfort her, rushed through him. His hand lifted.

She fell to her knees beside the body.

His fingers balled into a fist, dropped to his side.

A faint tremble shook her. She stared at the man's body. Gazed at his face, at the eyes that were wide open, staring at the ceiling in abject terror, at the mouth that was contorted in a final, silent scream.

Then her focus shifted to his neck, to the neck that had been ripped wide open.

"I-I need to see Captain McNeal." She rose to her feet, swaying for a moment.

Is the guy human? His teeth snapped together as he bit back the question. It was his damn case. He needed as much information as he could get, and he didn't want the doc and the captain keeping him in the dark.

He had a killer to find, and whether the guy was just a crazy-ass human or something more, he needed all the information about the perp he could get.

He lifted his hand, motioned for McNeal, and watched as his captain hurried across the room.

"Ah, Colin, can you excuse us for a minute?" He reached for Emily's arm.

Colin stepped in front of him, effectively blocking his move. "I wanna hear what she's got to say." His eyes met McNeal's.

A muscle flexed along McNeal's jaw. "I'll let you know the doctor's opinion—"

Not good enough.

Emily pushed past him, stopped beside the captain.

Colin slanted a quick glance at her, then said, "I wanna know what the Monster Doctor thinks."

She jerked, a slight but telling movement.

So did the captain.

McNeal's eyes narrowed. "How much do you know?"

"Enough." Most folks didn't know about the creatures that lived right next to the humans, didn't know about the dangerous world that existed in the shadows.

People thought monsters lived in horror movies. Thought that life was about birthday parties, Christmas trees, and summer vacations.

But he knew better. Hell, he'd lived most of his life in the darkness that everyone else feared. He knew the smell of evil, had seen firsthand just how perverted the world could be.

Yeah, he knew about the monsters.

After all, he was one of them.

McNeal glanced around at the other cops. At least five

other officers—three men, two women—were in the room. He jerked his thumb toward the kitchen.

Emily nodded her understanding and led the way to the white swinging door.

No cops were inside. The kitchen had already been cleared.

McNeal waited until the door swung shut behind Colin, then he growled, "This doesn't go past the three of us, got that, Gyth?"

Colin nodded.

"Good." McNeal leveled his stare at Emily. "Well?"

"He was human."

A grunt. "Good. At least I don't have to worry about the ME finding two hearts inside the guy. . . ." He blew out a hard breath. "After a couple of times, those explanations get harder to make."

Yeah, he just bet they did. Colin kept his attention on Emily. "So, Doc, any ideas about what might have done that to him?"

She nibbled her lower lip for a moment, then said, "It could have been an animal attack, maybe a dog—"

But the captain was shaking his head. "The owner of the house has one of those fancy security systems with cameras trained on the doors. We've got a picture of the perp—a guy in a black hood who was smart enough to keep his damn face hidden—and there's no animal with him."

Emily's eyes narrowed.

"So what do you think, Doc?" Colin pressed. "What kind of thing could have done this?"

Her head cocked to the side and she studied him with that too-knowing gaze of hers. "Well, Detective," she finally murmured, "the way I figure it, there are three prime suspects."

He didn't speak, just waited for her.

She held up one finger. "A vampire."

A second finger. "A demon."

Third finger. "Or"—she stared straight into his eyes—"a shifter."

"A shifter?" McNeal whistled softly. "What kind of shifter would do that?"

Her shoulders lifted in a faint shrug. "A bear. A panther, any kind of wildcat really, or . . . a wolf." Her green eyes were still on him. Watching, weighing.

Judging.

With an effort, Colin managed not to squirm.

McNeal made a faint *hmmming* sound. "Is there any way to tell for certain?"

"The ME might be able to tell if it's a shifter." She pulled off her glasses, polished them absently on her shirt.

Colin blinked. Oh, he liked her without the glasses. She looked softer, sweeter, *like*—

"He can look for animal hairs. Compare the radius of the bite marks to let us know what we're looking at."

Colin raised his brows, impressed. The doc might specialize in mind games, but she knew a bit of forensics too.

Her gaze drifted to the white door that stood between them and the den, between them and the body. "There is so much rage here," she whispered softly. "I can feel the echoes."

And just how the hell could she do that?

The doc was a bigger mystery, and a hell of a bigger threat to him, than he'd originally thought.

"You have to find this guy." She swallowed, straightened her shoulders and seemed to shake off a heavy weight. "Before he does this again."

Colin stiffened. "Again?" He repeated softly. So far, they just had one body. Sure, the killer had obviously been in a fury—there was blood everywhere, pooled near the victim, smeared on the walls, the furniture, but that didn't mean they were dealing with a serial—

"He'll do it again." She sounded absolutely certain.

McNeal swore beneath his breath. "You sure?"

"Yes."

Colin stepped toward her, stepped right in front of her so that barely an inch separated them. "And how do you know that?"

"Because now he's gotten a taste for the kill." Her gaze held his. Her breath blew lightly across his skin. Her scent, the light, fragrant scent of roses, filled the air around him. "Once a creature like this gets a taste, there's no going back."

The good doctor sure as hell sounded like she knew what she was talking about. But he hoped, hoped with every fiber of his being, that she was wrong.

Because if one of his kind really was off on a killing spree, then the humans were screwed.

Chapter 2

She couldn't get the dead man out of her head.

Emily stared blankly at the flickering TV screen, a bowl of Dutch chocolate ice cream in her lap, a spoon gripped tightly in her fist.

She'd left the crime scene long ago. Been driven back to her office by one of the patrolmen on duty. She'd thanked the fellow, very politely, then gotten into her car and traveled home. And she'd been shaking the whole time.

Dammit. It wasn't as if that had been the first dead body she'd ever seen.

She'd found her grandmother after her heart attack, and her father after his suicide.

She stabbed the spoon down into the rapidly melting chocolate. No, it hadn't been her first dead body, but the sight had still hit her like a punch in the gut.

Jesus. There had been so much blood.

And she currently had four vamps as patients, so it wasn't as if she weren't used to dealing with blood. Every time she touched their thoughts, images of blood took center stage.

But tonight, that man . . . he'd been different. The vamps she saw treated blood like it was sacred. To them, blood was life.

Yet when she'd seen the crime scene, the blood had meant nothing more than death.

I have to stop thinking about the body. Emily took a big

bite of the ice cream, feeing the cold, delicious chocolate slide over her tongue.

Her toes curled into her carpet. Oh, that was better. That was—

A flash of headlights lit up her living room.

What in the hell?

She pushed the bowl of ice cream onto her coffee table, rose quickly, and turned toward her window. Through the thin curtains, she could see a vehicle pulling into her driveway.

The purring of the engine reached her ears, followed by the faint crunch of gravel beneath the tires.

Her gaze darted back toward her TV stand, locking briefly on the VCR clock. *Two-thirteen* A.M.

Who would be coming to visit her at two A.M.?

A car door slammed. Footsteps rapped against her sidewalk.

The image of a blood-soaked room flashed before her eyes. The image of death, of a man's final, terrified scream.

Her doorbell rang.

Emily crept toward the door, moving almost soundlessly over the carpet. She pressed her hands against the wooden door, leaned forward, peered through the peephole, and saw—

Detective Colin Gyth. He was standing just on the other side of her door, illuminated by the porch light.

Her breath expelled in a nervous rush. Okay. She should probably be glad that a cop—*instead of a robber or some kind of crazed killer*—had come to see her in the middle of the night. But Detective Gyth . . .

He just wasn't your average cop.

And the guy made her very, very uneasy.

She opened the bottom lock but kept her security chain in place as she opened the door two inches. Enough room for them to talk, but nothing else. "Detective Gyth?"

He stepped closer. The light dipped across his face, making him look somewhat sinister.

Oh yeah, like she needed that visual right then.

"I need to talk to you."

She'd figured that out, considering the guy had driven all the way to her place—*and really, just how had he known where I lived?* He must've had her checked out, she realized. Probably when Danny had first told him to contact her.

"Dr. Drake?" He lifted his hand, touched his palm to the door. "Let me in."

She didn't want to. Every instinct she had screamed at her. Letting Gyth inside would be a very serious mistake.

"I don't want to cause a scene"—his dark voice was pitched low—"but if I have to wake your neighbors to get inside, I'll do it."

Her chin lifted. "I don't like being threatened, Detective." She started to push the door closed. She had only two immediate neighbors. One was out of town—the family had gone on a vacation to Disney World. The other, well, there was no way Shirley was home yet.

"Wait!" His palm shoved against the door, effectively halting her movement. His eyes met hers. "Would you *please* let me come inside?"

Umm, now that sounded like it must've hurt. But she still wasn't budging. "What do you want?"

"I told you, I need to talk to you."

Yeah, and so did all of her patients, but she wasn't inviting them inside her house in the middle of the night.

"It's about the case."

He had her attention.

"All right." Her fingers fumbled with the chain. "You can come in *for five minutes*. Got that? It's late, I want to sleep, and you can just come in for—"

He pushed open the door, stepped inside, his big body forcing hers back. His thumb lifted, rubbed against her bottom lip. Then he brought his hand to his mouth and licked the tip of his thumb. "Mmmm . . ."

She stared at him, eyes wide, mouth agape. He hadn't just—

His lips tilted into a smile. "I love chocolate." His gaze dropped down to her lips. "Mind if I have another taste?"

Emily stepped back, ramming into the wall. Her heart was suddenly beating too fast. Her palms were damp, and that tight, hot feeling was back in her stomach again. And all he'd done was touch her lips.

Oh no, she could not want this man.

Getting involved with a shifter would be pure idiocy.

She swiped her hand over her lips, trying to rub away any ice cream that might be left. Didn't want to leave any temptation for him.

"Hmmm. Guess that's a no, huh?" Colin sighed, glancing back toward her living room.

"It's a definite no." Despite the little voice in her head that wondered, just for a moment, what it would be like if he kissed her.

Emily inhaled sharply. It was late, she was getting loopy, and she was most definitely not finding the shifter attractive.

"Is it because of what I am?" He asked the question as he turned his back on her and sauntered into her living room.

"What?" She shook her head, hurriedly slammed and locked the front door, and followed on his heels. "I thought you came by to discuss the case."

"Umm." Not really an answer. He made himself comfortable on her sofa, put his boots on her coffee table. "Nice. Real comfortable place you've got." His stare swept around the room, noting the bookcases, the light yellow walls, the big-screen TV. "I like it."

Well, that was just great.

Damn. She should have never let him in.

"You and I have a problem, Doc." He turned that bright blue stare back on her as she stood at the edge of the couch, glowering down at him.

Emily stared at him silently, waiting.

"You know what I am." His voice roughened slightly as he made this announcement.

She didn't deny it. What would be the point?

His eyes narrowed fractionally as he studied her expression. "That's not good for me. Not good at all."

A flicker of nervousness shot through her. She wasn't sensing any sort of physical threat from the cop, but maybe she just wasn't looking deep enough *into* him.

His hand snagged her wrist.

And her pulse skyrocketed beneath his grip.

"How much do you know?"

Emily swallowed, tried to figure out just how much she should reveal.

His hold tightened around her.

He was the one sitting down, the one forced to look up at her, but Emily had the feeling she was the one in the vulnerable position. "I-I know you aren't human." Her voice came out softer, huskier than she'd intended.

She hoped Colin would leave it at that. Hoped he wouldn't probe any deeper.

"Ah, baby, I already knew that."

She tried to tug her hand free, but his grip was unbreakable.

"You're the Monster Doctor, the one all the local ghouls go to see." A faint trace of amusement underscored his words. But his eyes were watchful, intense, showing no echo of humor.

Her jaw clenched. "Let go of my hand."

He smiled at her, and his fingers fell away from her wrist.

Emily immediately sprang across the room, putting several feet between them. *Nice, protective space.* "Look, if you aren't here to discuss the case, then I want you to leave." She turned her back on him, heading toward the front door.

"How do you do it?"

His words stopped her.

"How do you tell who's human and who isn't?"

She heard the soft rustle of the sofa cushions as he rose.

"That's a pretty interesting talent you've got there. And I'm just dying to know exactly how you do it."

Emily cast a longing glance toward the front door. "I'm afraid you're just going to have to live with your curiosity, Detective." Because she sure as hell wasn't going to reveal her innermost secrets to a stranger. *Yep, letting the guy inside had been a definite mistake.*

"Hmmm." His breath blew against the nape of her neck. Emily jumped, startled to find him so close to her. The guy hadn't made a sound when he'd crossed the room.

"I'd like to see your hair down," he muttered, and his fingers brushed against the bun she'd yet to unwind.

She jerked away from him. "And I'd like to see you leave. Guess which one of us is about to get her wish?"

His hard lips curved into a smile, a smile with a hint of real warmth. "Tough lady, aren't you?"

She'd had to be.

His smile slowly faded. "But trust me, I'm a hell of a lot tougher than you could ever dream of being." And in a flash, he had her pinned against the wall. His strong, hard body pressed against her, his muscular thighs pushed between hers, shoving up her skirt, and his right hand locked around her wrists as he forced them against the wall over her head.

Her breath left her body in a startled gasp.

"Now let's try this again," he growled. *"Just how much do you know about me?"*

His anger hit her then. Hot, fierce. Oh yes, the detective was enraged. He was also . . .

Afraid.

If the other cops find out what I am, they'll kick me off the force. Make me leave. No one will trust me. They'll all think I'm some kind of fucking animal, just like the guys back in Grisam did.

Mike tried to kill me. Because he knew. He knew, just like she knows.

She knows . . .

His thoughts hit her, hard, pummeling right through her mind.

She thinks I'm an animal . . . a monster, a—

"I-I don't!" The words were torn from her. His thoughts were flying into her mind so quickly now. Too quickly. She tried to raise her shields, tried to block the onslaught of sudden images—

Colin, covered in blood, holding his shoulder, staring up at a pale man with a face full of freckles. "Why? *Why?*"

Colin, staring up at a burning house, his fists clenched, his face twisted in hate.

Colin, changing, shifting—

"*Aaah!*" She slammed her shields up. She didn't need to see any more. Didn't want to see what he'd become.

"Emily?"

She'd squeezed her eyes shut.

"I'm not going to hurt you."

Yes, she believed him. A hard rage was riding him, but Colin was still in control. She lifted her lashes, peeking up at him. "You don't have to worry," Emily told him, completely sincere, "I'm not going to tell anyone about you." She'd been keeping secrets for people—patients, friends, strangers she met on the street—for years now.

He grunted. "And I'm just supposed to believe you?"

"Yes, you are." This close, she could see the flecks of gold in his eyes. And they were nice eyes. Not nearly as cold or hard as she'd originally thought.

"Sorry, Doc, but I don't trust you for a minute."

Fair enough. She hadn't trusted him either, until she'd gone tiptoeing through his thoughts.

Course, if he found out about her little journey, he'd probably just be even more pissed off.

"Do you know what I am?"

Emily nodded. No point in denying it now. "You're a shifter."

His fingers tightened around her wrists, not quite, but almost hurting her. "How the fuck do you know that?"

"Ah . . . can you ease up there a bit, Gyth?"

His brows beetled.

"The hands," she elaborated. "Little too tight."

He eased his hold. "How do you know?"

"I always know." That was true. "I can tell with a look." Sometimes she could tell just by hearing a voice or catching a scent on the wind. When it came to the *Other,* she was definitely wired for them. "Your kind—you carry a glow with you. Like a bright shadow that follows you everywhere." The shadow of the beast.

He winced. "Can others see this damn glow?"

Not as far as she knew. "I've never known anyone else who can see the things I can." And she'd looked. Searched desperately for years. Especially back at the beginning, back when she'd thought she was crazy.

"Shit."

Yes, that pretty well summed up the situation. Emily wiggled her fingers. "Mind letting me go now?"

His nostrils flared and his gaze dropped to her lips. "Yeah, Doc, as a matter of fact, I do."

The woman smelled like sin. Like a delicious combination of roses, rich chocolate, and seductive female flesh, and he really, *really* wanted to taste her.

His canine teeth were starting to lengthen, an unfortunate side effect of his shifter blood. When he got angry or aroused, the beast tended to wake up.

And the good doctor had succeeded in both royally pissing him off and turning him on.

She wasn't wearing her glasses now. Her eyes looked soft, sexy.

His head lowered toward her.

"Wh-what are you doing?" She stiffened against him.

The lady had a Ph.D. He figured she had a pretty good idea of what he was about to do. Slowly, deliberately, he brought his lips to hers.

Her mouth parted on a startled breath.

Perfect.

His lips brushed hers, his tongue thrust inside the wet warmth of her mouth.

Oh, damn, but she tasted good. His tongue slipped past the edge of her teeth, rubbed against hers. Stroked. Teased.

A faint moan rumbled in her throat and *she kissed him back.*

Her breasts brushed against his chest. The nipples were tight, pebbled. He wanted to touch them, but he didn't think the doc was ready for that.

He sucked her tongue slowly, drawing out the kiss, wanting to make every second count. His cock was rock hard for her, pressing tight against the tempting cradle of her sex.

What he wouldn't give to have her naked beneath him right then.

Colin forced himself to break the kiss, forced his head to lift. Her lips were red, wet from his mouth.

She glared up at him, and her breath sounded ragged to his ears. "Are you satisfied now?"

Not by a long shot. But he had a good idea of just how the doc could satisfy him.

Her bedroom had to be down the darkened hallway. He could take her in there, strip her, and—

"Not going to happen." She exhaled slowly, shaking her head. "So you can just forget about that. A kiss is one thing, shifter. Sex is a whole other game."

He blinked. "Ah, now, baby, what makes you think I was—"

"Hands off, *now,*" she snapped, not answering his question, but instead narrowing those gorgeous green eyes of hers.

He liked her eyes. Liked the dark, emerald green. Course, those eyes were starting to shine with a rather furious glint.

Reluctantly, he dropped his hands. Colin inhaled her delicious scent one more time, then he stepped back, completely freeing her.

Her hands dropped to her sides. "Future reference note." Her chin jutted into the air. "If I want you to kiss me, I'll tell you. I'm not a big fan of the He-man routine."

"Ah, so you're already thinking of our future."

Her lips thinned.

"That's fine, Doc. When you want to be kissed, you just let me know." He'd be more than happy to oblige her.

"What I want is for you to go." She pointed toward the door. "Now."

Colin didn't think that was what she really wanted. He could smell her arousal in the air, and her nipples were still tight with desire, thrusting against the white T-shirt she wore. But he nodded.

He'd accomplished most of his goals by coming to see the doc.

He'd discovered that she knew he was a shifter, and she'd given her word that she wouldn't reveal his secret. For now, he'd take her at her word. Wasn't like he had much choice in the matter. He'd try trusting her, and for the doc's sake, he sure as hell hoped that she didn't betray him.

So he'd gotten her to lay her cards on the table, and he'd finally gotten to taste her. For nearly three straight hours, he'd wanted to feel her lips beneath his. Now that he had, well, he wanted to taste her again.

And he would. Soon.

He stalked toward the front door, flipped the locks.

"You never wanted to talk to me about the case, did you?" Her voice stopped him.

Colin glanced back at her. She still stood against the wall, but her arms were crossed over her chest now and her left foot tapped out a hard rhythm on the floor. "I don't want to talk about that yet." Not until he'd gotten his report from the ME and he'd talked to McNeal about the possibility of bringing Emily on the case in a more official capacity.

If she was right, if the killer really was *Other,* then he figured the PD would need all the help it could get in solving the case.

And who better to hunt a monster than the good doctor?

"Would you work with us?" he asked as he began to make his plan of attack. McNeal had brought her on originally; he'd probably okay pulling Emily completely onto the case.

"Work with you?" Her foot stopped tapping. "I already did. I told you what I know and—"

"Lady, I have the feeling you know a hell of a lot more

than you told me." About the case, about him—but he'd deal with all that in due time.

Her expression never altered. "What is it you want from me?"

Once he'd gotten the official okay, he wanted her to be— "A profiler. I want you to give me a workup on this guy, want you to tell me exactly how he thinks, how he lives." So that he could catch the bastard before he hurt anyone else. "Can you do that?"

She nodded.

"Then I'll be seeing you soon, Doc." And they'd start tracking a killer.

Hmmm. Not a usual date, but with the doc, he had a feeling he'd have to take what he could get.

They'd been inside the house for twenty minutes. The cop had gone in, like he owned the place, and he'd been inside with her *for twenty minutes.*

A slow rage began to build inside him. This shouldn't have happened. This should *never* have happened.

Her front door opened. The cop appeared. He looked back at the woman, muttered something, then marched down the steps.

His body tensed as he watched them. He'd hidden himself well; they wouldn't be able to see him in the darkness. He was—

The cop froze. Lifted his head. Looked slowly around the yard.

"What is it?" Her voice. Dr. Drake stepped onto the porch. The light cascaded over her. For an instant, with that shining light all around her, she almost looked like an angel.

But he knew she wasn't an angel. No, not an angel. Never an angel. The doctor was a demon. Just like the others.

The cop was looking right at his hiding spot now. The guy took a step forward.

"Gyth? Is someone out there?" Dr. Drake crossed to the cop's side.

A trickle of sweat slid down his cheek. He realized the crickets around him had stopped chirping. The night was quiet, too quiet.

Now wasn't the time, he realized, inching deeper into the brush.

He'd come back for the doctor another night. Wait until she was alone.

Then he'd destroy the demon.

After all, hunting demons was his job.

Colin stared into the dark, twisted trees on the vacant lot across the street. For an instant, he'd sworn he'd heard something, *someone*.

He spared a quick look at Emily. She was gazing at the trees, a faint furrow between her brows.

"I want to check that place out," he told her, and pulled his gun from the holster at his hip. "Stay here."

He didn't wait to see if she obeyed, just took off, moving slowly, stealthily across the street. Maybe he was wrong, maybe he was just too damn tired, but he had to check the place out.

Because his instincts were screaming at him, and he never, *ever* ignored his instincts.

The faint scent of cigarettes teased his nostrils as he crept closer. Yeah, someone had been here all right.

But why?

The moonlight barely trickled past the trees, but he'd always had excellent night vision. Another little shifter side effect. So he could easily see the ground and the bent grass where someone had knelt, *where someone had watched*.

A growl rumbled in his throat.

His fingers tightened around the butt of his gun and—

A twig snapped behind him. He spun around, gun drawn, leveled, aimed, and ready to fire—

Right between Emily's eyes.

"Dammit!" He lowered his gun. "Didn't I tell you to stay put?"

Her gaze followed the movement of the gun, then slowly lifted back to his face. "Yes, but I'm not a dog. I don't generally 'stay' when I'm told."

He realized the doctor was annoyed. Good. Matched him perfectly. "Future reference note," he muttered, quoting her earlier words back to her, "when I give an order, there's usually a damn good reason for it. And next time, you'd sure as hell better listen to me."

Her lips tightened. "I thought you might need some help."

"*What?*" Jesus. He was the cop! He didn't need the mind doctor to back him up.

And he was a shifter—that fact alone meant he knew how to guard his own ass.

She muttered something beneath her breath, something he didn't quite catch but sounded a lot like "asshole shifter."

"Shit. Just stay behind me, all right?" He wanted to check out the thick patch of bushes up ahead. He strained, trying to listen for any telltale sound that might indicate the watcher was still there. But he heard only the call of crickets, the faint rustle of the leaves in the breeze.

He crept ahead, keeping his gun up. Emily's soft footsteps whispered behind him.

With his right hand, he pushed back a mass of bushes. Saw only dark earth.

He looked up, gazing straight ahead. There was no sign of anyone else. He couldn't hear anyone, and he had damn good hearing.

Looked like their watcher was gone.

Pity. He would've liked to have found out exactly why the sonofabitch was hanging outside the doc's place.

He spun back around, frowning down at Emily. In the darkness, he knew she couldn't see much of him, probably little more than the rough outline of his body. "You got any enemies I should know about, Doc?"

With his enhanced vision, Colin could see every detail of her face and body. He could easily recognize the sudden tension on Emily's face.

"Doc?"

She swallowed. "No."

He'd interrogated enough perps to know when someone was lying to him. But he decided not to push her. Not yet.

Colin pushed his gun back into its holster. "Well, looks like one of us managed to catch someone's attention." He stalked back to the circle of bent grass. Kneeling, he inhaled and caught the same stale scent of cigarettes he'd noticed earlier.

Someone had been hiding in the darkness, watching her or him. But why?

He sure as hell intended to find out.

But first—first he was going to discover just what sort of enemies the mysterious Dr. Drake had.

Chapter 3

"You wanna do what?" Danny McNeal shot forward in his worn leather chair.

Colin stared levelly back at him. "Hey, you're the one who brought her in." He paused, then said, "Now that the doc's in the game, I want to keep using her."

McNeal rubbed his right hand over his gleaming head. "I don't think you know what you're dealing with here, Gyth."

Oh, he had a pretty good idea.

"So what, one night you ran up on a vampire or a demon in the park? You saw they were real and now you think you're some kind of hotshot who can go out and fight these things?"

Not exactly.

"Well, I've got news for you." McNeal was glaring at him now, bushy brows lowered. "These things will eat you up and spit you out—literally."

Not without a hell of a fight. "I know what I'm doing," Colin told him, struggling to keep his voice level. He didn't think the situation was a game, but he sure as hell wasn't about to reveal his true nature to the captain.

Been there, done that, with shit for results.

McNeal grunted and spun his chair to face the small window in his office. The captain didn't have much of a view. The window overlooked the back alley and two nearby buildings. But if you strained, you could just make out the green grass of the park in the distance.

"Have you got a report yet from Smith?"

He'd been in the medical examiner's office all morning. "She's not done with the autopsy yet, but her preliminary judgment is that Preston Myers was attacked by an animal."

McNeal turned slowly back to face him. His fingers drummed on the arms of his chair. "We know that's not the case."

Yes, but proving it would be a whole different matter. "She thinks the vic was attacked by a dog or a wolf." Colin tossed a manila envelope onto McNeal's desk. "But judging by the bite radius, I'd say it could just as easily have been a vampire."

"Shit." McNeal squeezed his eyes shut. "Why couldn't this asshole have stayed out of my town?" He huffed out a breath, cracked open his eyes, and studied Colin. "You think Dr. Drake was right? You think this bastard will kill again?"

Colin nodded. He had no doubt that the killer would strike again. The crime scene had been a bloodfest; that much rage, that much hate—no one could stay in control with that dangerous mix brewing inside.

Yeah, he'd kill again. Unless they stopped him.

"She's got the credentials," McNeal muttered. "The press will buy that we're bringing her on as a profiler." He leaned forward, grabbed a newspaper from the edge of his desk, and waved it in front of Colin. "Did you see what those idiots printed today? The guy's had one kill and they've already given him a name."

The black and white letters were stark: NIGHT BUTCHER CLAIMS VICTIM.

Oh Jesus. That was the last thing they needed. *Night Butcher.*

"No details of the body were released." McNeal tossed the paper into the trash. "But some jerkoff managed to peer into the house with one of those high-powered lenses, and he caught a shot of all the blood."

"He's gonna like the name, you know," Colin warned. He'd seen it before. Seen perps who got a high off the killing, but got an even bigger rush from the media attention that turned them into fucking celebrities.

"I know." McNeal's jaw clenched. "And I also know we've got jack for leads."

It was time to seal the deal. Colin leaned forward. "That's why we need the doc. She's been treating guys like him for years; she knows how they think. She can help us, I *know* she can."

The captain stiffened slightly. "I don't think she's been seeing guys *quite* like this one." His lips thinned. "I don't think the doctor makes a general practice of treating killers."

"No, but we both know who she does treat."

A reluctant nod. Then, "How do you know she'll even agree to this? Emily doesn't like attention, and when the press finds out, they'll splash her name on every page of their rags."

So she was Emily now. His eyes narrowed. There was familiarity there, a lot of it.

"Get her permission, and we'll talk again—"

"I've already gotten it."

"Do you now." Not a question. McNeal narrowed his eyes, and Colin realized he'd just stepped on the captain's toes.

Shit. He spoke slowly, carefully, as he said, "She agreed Friday night. Before I went to you with this plan, I needed to make sure the doc would be onboard." And she'd agreed. Now it was just up to McNeal.

McNeal stared at him in silence a moment, two, then finally nodded. "Well, then I guess I'd better make a few phone calls and get her officially attached to the case." He reached for his phone.

Colin took the hint. He rose, headed for the door, then paused, unable to contain his curiosity. "Captain, just how did you and Dr. Drake meet?"

The phone receiver was cradled at McNeal's ear. For a moment, his lips curved in a somewhat taunting smile. "When you're ready to tell me your secrets, Detective, I'll tell you mine."

*   *   *

"I want more than just sex."

Emily lifted a brow as she studied the succubus stretched out on her couch. "And what exactly is it that you do want, Cara?"

Cara pounded her small fist against the leather cushions. "I want someone to want me, *me!* Not some hyped-up dream of a sex goddess!"

Ah, now here was the tricky part. "Well, umm, you know, you actually . . . are pretty close to being a sex goddess." A succubus was created to entice men, born with a high level of pheromones. Just the scent from one of Cara's kind had been known to drive mortal men wild with lust.

Of course, normally, the driving men wild with lust bit worked out well for the succubi. They derived a shot of magical power from the sex act. That power enabled them to alter their appearances, to live longer—heck, most succubi thought it was a pretty good deal all around.

Cara was definitely not like most succubi.

She sat up on the couch, pushing back her long, blond mane. "I'm tired of men looking at me and only wanting one thing."

Emily didn't speak. She'd learned it was best sometimes to just sit back and let the patient talk.

"I'm tired of random men, tired of guys who can't remember my name a week after we've met."

Her brows wrinkled at that. What kind of moron would forget a woman as gorgeous as Cara?

"I want someone who knows that I like sunsets, that I swim every morning before dawn, that I like damn blueberries on my pancakes—" Cara's face was starting to redden. "Dammit, I want someone to *know* me!"

And not just the sex goddess.

"What's wrong with me, Dr. Drake?" Cara's hands balled into fists. "I'm not like the others, am I? They're all happy. My friends love the power they have over mortal men. They laugh about it, but I—I—" She broke off, floundering. Then she swiped her hand under her left eye, rubbing away a lone tear that had fallen. "Shit, I guess I'm just a freak."

Reaching for her tissue box, Emily said very softly, "No, you're not." She offered the tissue to Cara. "You just . . ." Now here was the hard part. Cara might not be ready to hear it, but she needed to realize, "You just want someone to love you."

The tissue fell from Cara's fingers. "But men don't love women like me."

Cara had been coming to see her for nearly a month now. In that time, Emily had discovered that beneath the succubus's perfect exterior, there was a smart, kind, caring woman. A woman who'd been born into a life that didn't necessarily match up with the person she was. And it was time Cara changed that life.

Men don't love women like me. Gazing straight into Cara's glistening blue eyes, Emily softly asked, "Don't they?"

Emily had just shown Cara Maloan out when her intercom beeped.

"Hey, boss, you got a call on line one." Vanessa whistled softly. "A guy by the name of Colin Gyth. *Very* sexy voice."

Colin Gyth. Emily hurried around her desk. "Ah, okay." It'd been nearly three days since she'd heard from Colin. Not that she'd been counting or anything. "Put him through."

Inhaling deeply, she waited a moment for the telltale click that signaled the call transfer. Then she picked up the handset. "Emily Drake."

"Hi, Doc."

Heat bloomed between her thighs. Vanessa was right, the guy did have a sexy-as-sin voice. She'd forgotten the deep timbre of his speech.

Damn. What was wrong with her? Was she honestly getting turned on just by Colin's voice?

Cara's problem is that she has too much sex in her life. Maybe my problem is that I don't have enough.

Maybe she'd just been alone too long. What had it been?

Five, six months since she'd broken up with Travis? Or rather, since Travis had broken up with her.

I don't know you, Emily. You won't let me know you. And I'm tired of ramming my head into a wall just because I want to get close to you.

She jerked off her glasses. That had been bad, very, very—

"Uh, Doc? You there?"

"Ah, sorry, yes." Emily coughed. "What can I do for you, Detective?" She really, really hoped he hadn't just heard that little quiver of excitement in her voice. In talking with the guy for less than two minutes, she'd gone from professional psychologist to needy woman.

Maybe she could use some therapy of her own.

There was a brief pause on the other end of the line, then Gyth's deep voice announced, "You can tell me that you meant it when you said you'd help out on this case."

Now that got her attention. Her back snapped straight. "Yes, yes, of course, I meant it." *He was calling about business.* Time for the professional psychologist to get her ass in gear.

"Good, cause the big boys just gave me the go-ahead to bring you in as a profiler."

A profiler. Her fingers tightened around the phone. *Working a murder investigation.*

"The press is already crawling all over this case. Once you're officially in, they'll get your name." He sighed, then said, "So prepare to start seeing a lot of yourself on the six o'clock news."

For a moment, she hesitated. She hadn't given a thought to the press. Hadn't even considered that they'd learn of her. "Can't we keep my involvement quiet for now?"

"The DA wants to make sure the public feels like we're doing everything possible to catch this guy. He wants to release data about our profiler to make everyone feel better."

"O-okay." Surely there was no way that anyone would discover her past. It had been so many years since—

"Relax, Doc, dealing with the press will be the easy part.

Catching the killer, that's the challenge." There was a rumble of voices in the background, then he asked, "Hey, when are you gonna be free this afternoon?"

"I'm free now." Maloan had been her last patient of the day. No night clients were scheduled.

"Good. I'll be there in twenty minutes."

"Twenty minutes? But—"

"You need to start on the profile, right? Well, I'll take you back to the crime scene, then you can come meet Smith."

"Smith?"

"The medical examiner."

Oh. Her stomach tightened. She didn't have a good track record with MEs.

He laughed softly. "Don't worry, Doc. I'll be with you every step of the way."

Not exactly reassuring.

A thin line of yellow police tape blocked the door at 208 Byron Street. Colin pulled out a knife, slashed through it, and opened the door.

The smell hit her when she stepped inside. The stale, cold odor of death. The coppery scent of blood.

Emily swallowed. The house was dark. Shadows loomed across the floor. "Can you do something about the lights?"

He tapped a button on the wall. Light flooded the foyer and the den.

She inched forward, keeping her attention on the ground. Colin had told her that the killer had entered through the front door. So he'd come this way, walking slowly, carefully into the house.

The thick carpet swallowed her footsteps as she entered the den. The killer had crept into this room, found Preston Myers. And attacked him.

The stark outline of Preston's body still marked the floor. The stain of his blood covered the brown carpet.

Her gaze rose to the nearby wall. Dried blood marred the surface. *So much blood.*

"This guy was in a fury," she murmured, bending to inspect the carpet. Her hand lifted over the outline, hesitated.

"Is this your first murder, Doc?"

She hadn't heard his approach but wasn't really surprised to hear his voice sounded from right behind her. Shifters often made no sound when they moved.

Her fingers were trembling. She balled her hand into a fist and glanced back at him. "Yes." But not her first blood soaked scene.

For an instant, her mind flashed back to that last bloody room. She saw the man's body, slumped on the floor. His brains and tissue were on the wall, blood surrounding him.

Her father's death hadn't been pretty, and sometimes, late at night, she still woke up screaming.

Emily drew in a deep breath. She had to focus on Preston, not the past.

Standing, her stare swept the room, lingered on the pictures decorating the mantel, on the chess set in the corner, on the books lining the built-in shelves near the doorway.

From all appearances, Preston Myers had been a normal guy. *Completely human.*

So why had he been attacked? Why had the killer chosen him?

"It doesn't make sense," she muttered. "SBs stick to their own kind."

"Uh . . . SBs?"

"Supernatural beings." In her experience, SBs always stayed with their own for mating, for fun, and for killing.

To cross over like this and to murder a human, to so blatantly attack—

Her gaze narrowed as she glimpsed a familiar face in one of the photos.

Hell.

She marched closer to the mantel. Snatched up the picture.

"Hey, Doc, what's—"

Her fingers tightened around the small frame. "Have you run a background check on Preston yet?"

"My partner's working on it." His eyes narrowed. "Why, Doc? What do you know?"

She held up the picture. "I know that one of the guys in this picture is a demon."

One black brow shot up. "A patient?"

"No." She would never have agreed to treat Niol. The guy gave off black waves of energy that made her far, far too nervous. Her nail tapped just over Niol's unsmiling face. "But I've met him a few times. He owns a bar near here, a place called Paradise Found."

"Then I guess I'll be paying him a visit." He smiled at her. "Good thing I brought you over. You might not have gotten any more details about the killer, but you sure did just speed up the—"

"Oh, I know more about the killer," she interrupted, frowning at him, feeling slightly insulted. What did he think she'd been doing? Daydreaming over a dead body?

He pulled out his notebook. "Then tell me."

Emily licked her lips. "This wasn't an impulse kill. Nothing's disturbed. Nothing's taken. The guy came to the house with the attack already planned out. He knew where the security cameras were, and he knew how to hide from them. That probably means he's been here before, that he knew the victim."

She pointed to the blood on the wall. "When there is this much violence, this much rage, it's usually very, very personal."

"Yeah, I figured that." So far, Colin wasn't sounding particularly impressed.

She dropped her hand, squared her shoulders as she faced him. "The killer had to be strong to overpower Preston. The victim was what, six foot two? One hundred eighty pounds? He would have fought back, would have fought as hard as he could." Her lips tightened for a moment. "But then, supernaturals are always stronger than humans, aren't they? Preston never had a chance."

"No," Colin agreed, his voice quiet. "He didn't."

* * *

When they left the house, they found a reporter waiting for them. A blond woman with close-cropped hair stood on the walkway, a black microphone clutched in her hands. A cameraman stood behind her, his face partially obscured by the bulk of his equipment.

"Detective Gyth!" The woman's face lit with hungry enthusiasm. "Darla Mitchell, News Flash Five. I have a few questions for you."

"Shit." The word was a bare breath of sound, but it reached Emily's ears, and for a second, she almost smiled at the disgust she heard.

But then Darla shoved the microphone into her face. "Dr. Drake, my sources say that you've joined this case as a profiler."

"Ah . . ." *Her sources?* She'd been on the case for less than an hour. How had the woman already found out about her?

Colin stepped in front of Emily. "The Atlanta PD has no comment at this time."

Darla tried to squirm around him. "But what about Dr. Drake? Does she have—"

Colin grabbed the bobbing microphone, leaned close, and snapped, "No comment."

"Fine!" Darla snarled. "Cut it, Jake!"

Emily stepped to Colin's side just as Jake lowered the camera.

A hard glare twisted Darla's pretty face. "You can't keep information from the public forever, you know, Gyth!"

"When I have information, I'll give it to you." He smiled. Okay, well, he flashed a lot of teeth. Not really a smile so much as a baring of fangs.

Darla growled at him, then spun on her two-inch heels and stomped back to the News Flash Five van.

The cameraman studied Gyth and Emily. Then he sighed. "She's been pissed since Channel Three scooped her on the Butcher story." His eyes narrowed on Emily. "Dr. Drake . . . I've heard a lot about you."

A tingle of awareness skated down her spine as she stared into his golden eyes.

He was Other.

He smiled at her, and for just a second, his eyes shifted, the gold changed into a midnight black.

Demon eyes.

She felt his power in the air then. Weak, low-level power, maybe a two or three on the demon scale.

"If there's anything I can do for you, Doctor, or if you decide that you want to talk to News Flash Five, give me a call." He handed her his card.

"Jake!"

Sighing, he glanced back over his shoulder. Darla stood beside the van, arms crossed, eyes glittering.

"Well, guess I'll talk to you both another time." With a little salute, he hoisted the camera and hurried toward the van.

"Looks like the vultures have already started circling." Colin shook his head and marched down the sidewalk.

She followed on his heels. "Gyth, did you know they were going to be here?"

He jerked open her door, narrowing his eyes. "No." Then comprehension lit his face. "What, you think I brought you here as some kind of setup?"

Well, the thought had crossed her mind. "You said I'd be on the six o'clock news soon. Looks like you were right."

His fingers tightened around the metal door. "I said you'd be on the news because the DA is going to hold a press conference about the case in the next few days. You'll be at the conference."

Emily climbed into the Jeep. "So, for the record, you didn't know Darla was going to be here?"

He slammed the door. "No, I sure as hell didn't."

She blew out a hard breath as he circled the Jeep and jumped into the driver's seat.

"And just so you know, Doc, you aren't to talk to reporters alone, ever." He slanted her a simmering glare. "So you might as well just throw away the card that slick passed you."

"I think I'll just hold on to it." It wasn't the first time that one of the *Other* had passed a card to her as a signal that he wanted something.

"Fine." He cranked the engine, sending the vehicle roaring to life.

Emily glanced down at the card in her hands. JAKE DON-NELLEY, CAMERAMAN, NEWS FLASH FIVE. His contact information was in clear, bold letters at the bottom.

She flipped the card over.

> *Have information on the case. Meet me at Paradise Found. 10 P.M.*

"Ah, Gyth?"

"What?" He braked at a traffic light and glanced her way.

"I don't think that guy wants to ask me questions." Holding up the card, she showed him the note.

His brows snapped together. "What in the hell?"

A horn blared behind them. Colin swore and stomped on the gas.

No, Jake doesn't want to ask her questions. But it sure looks like he might have a few things to tell her.

Colin turned into the parking lot of an old convenience store, braked, and spun to confront her. "Let me see that card."

This time, she handed it over.

He whistled soundlessly. "*Sonofabitch.*" His gaze rose to capture hers. "Why'd he give this to you?" Suspicion laced his words.

She glanced away, shrugged.

"Emily . . ."

She jerked. He'd never called her Emily before. Usually, he just called her Doc in that slightly mocking drawl of his. Hearing her name on his lips now seemed strangely intimate.

"Why'd the guy give you the card instead of me?"

Her lips parted—

"Shit." His fist rapped against the steering wheel. "The guy's *Other*, isn't he?"

"Yes." There didn't seem to be much point in denying it.

"So what is he? Shifter? Warlock? Psychic?"

"He's a demon." Most people didn't really understand demons. They thought demons were servants of the devil—evil, winged creatures with tails and talons. But the truth was that demons were a whole other race of humans, possibly descended from the original Fallen. On the outside, demons looked just like humans, except for one small detail: the eyes. All demons had completely black eyes. Cornea, lens, retina—everything was black.

But although the demons looked like humans, they were incredibly different. Most demons had psychic powers. Some were amazingly strong, while others were barely gifted. But even those with the light touch of the gift were able to cloak their eye color so humans would not see them for what they really were.

Emily's extrasensory power let her see past the glamour, let her see past the magic to the true nature of the creatures. She usually kept her mental shields up around them, though, because she'd once made the mistake of going up against a level-nine demon. The guy had nearly blasted her into a coma.

Before she'd passed out and slammed face-first into the floor, she'd managed to fight back and burn out the guy's magic. Turnabout could be a real bitch . . . as the demon had learned.

"A demon," Colin repeated softly. "Like that guy you mentioned, Niol?"

No, she didn't think Jake was like Niol at all. She hadn't sensed any evil in Jake.

Like people, some demons were good and some were evil. The demons who were good, well, they tended to keep to themselves. But the ones who were evil—those were the badasses people knew from history, the ones who'd first made folks think they were servants of the devil.

A demon who had incredible power and no conscience, well, he was truly a being to fear.

"I don't think he's like Niol," she told him softly.

Colin tucked the card into his pocket. His eyes remained locked on hers. "And how do you know that?"

Time to lay her cards on the table. "Because I'd feel it if he were." Sure, she hadn't gone shieldless with the guy to get a full mind probe, but she also hadn't sensed any of the dark, seething black power in the air that usually signaled a dangerous demon.

He seemed to stiffen before her. "Feel it? How?"

"I'm an empath, Colin. My gift is that I sense things. I sense the *Other*. I can sense their feelings, their thoughts."

Yeah, he'd definitely tensed up on her. "You're telling me that you can read my thoughts?"

The temperature seemed to drop about ten degrees. "I'm telling you that *sometimes* I can tell the thoughts of supernaturals." She'd known he wouldn't be thrilled by this news; that was why she hadn't told him the full truth the other night. But now that they were working together, now that her talent was coming into play, well, she figured he had the right to know.

Colin grabbed her arms, jerked her forward against his chest. "So this whole time, you've been playing with me."

The sharp edge of his canines gleamed behind his lips. "No, Colin, it's not like that—"

"You've been looking into my head and seeing how much I want you?"

"Colin, no, I—" *Seeing how much I want you.* Had he really just said that?

His cheeks flushed. "While I tried to play the dumb-ass gentleman."

Since when?

"Well, screw that." His lips were right over hers, his fingers tight on her arms. "If you've been in my head, then you know what I want to do to you."

Uh, no, she didn't. Her shields had been firmly in place

with him all day. Her heart was pounding so fast now, the dull drumming filled her ears. She licked her lips, tried once more to tell him the truth. "It's not like that—"

Too late. His mouth claimed hers, swallowing her words and igniting the hungry desire she'd been trying so hard to fight.

Chapter 4

Damn, but the doc tasted good. Colin thrust his tongue past her soft lips, loving the feel of her mouth against his.

His cock was hard for her, arousal pumping heavily through his body. Her scent surrounded him, and the warm weight of her body pushed against him.

His fingers tangled in her hair, tangled in that bun that had been driving him crazy, and he pulled the silken strands free. And he kept kissing her, kept tasting her, thrusting his tongue deep.

The beast within him began to roar as his hunger built. Higher, higher . . .

Colin shifted, trying to get closer to her. His knee rammed into the gearshift, but he truly didn't give a fuck. Her breasts pressed against his chest, the nipples tight. *She wanted him.*

Good, because he was going crazy wanting her.

And she knew it. She'd been in his head, stealing his thoughts, seeing how badly he wanted her.

Christ, what was it about her? Every time he was near her, his body went into overdrive, and he needed—he needed—

Her.

The lust he felt mixed with the anger simmering in his veins. His lips grew rougher on hers. A faint moan trembled in her throat, but she didn't fight him. Her small hands lifted, wrapped around his shoulders.

Elation surged through him. His right hand lowered, slid

down her body, and pressed against the curve of her breast. His fingers stroked her, cupped the warm weight of her flesh.

Emily shuddered against him, and the rich scent of her arousal filled the air.

Colin realized he was seconds away from taking her, there, in the car, with an abandoned store behind them and a road full of cars in front of them.

What in the hell was wrong with him?

Slowly, he lifted his head. Emily's breath was panting out, her bow lips reddened and wet from his mouth. He licked his lips, and he still tasted her.

Shit. He was in trouble. Serious trouble.

Her hair had fallen around her shoulders. Dark as night. Straight and silky. Her glasses were tilted slightly on her nose, and she looked so sexy it took all of his control not to kiss her again.

Down, boy. Now wasn't the time. Later he'd get the doc alone, and he'd get his fill of her.

His kind were notoriously sexual. He'd never found a partner to match his needs, but the doc, well, maybe she'd prove to be the exception. Course, he'd have to break her in easy, get her used to him, then he could let his full hunger reign.

"So what am I thinking now, Doc?" *That I can't wait to get you naked. To have you beneath me, screaming my name as you climax.*

Emily blinked, took a deep breath, and seemed to realize that she was still clutching his shoulders. She dropped her hands, then jerked back against her seat. "Th-that shouldn't have—"

"It happened." He stared at her. Watched as she tried to finger-brush her hair. "And it's gonna happen again." He'd gotten his second taste of her, and he was even hungrier now. No way was he going to walk away from her.

But she was shaking her head. "We're going to work to-gether, we can't—"

"Yeah, we can." His fingers lifted, brushed back a lock of

her hair. He didn't care about the dumb-ass rule of mixing business and pleasure. So they were working together on the case. Big damn deal. Just made it easier for him to see her.

Emily stiffened.

"So tell me, Doc, what am I thinking now?" His voice was a whisper and his stare dropped to her shirtfront. Her nipples were pushing against the fabric. He wanted them in his mouth.

"I-I don't know." Her hands were tight fists in her lap. "I tried to tell you earlier, I don't usually jump in someone's head without permission."

Ah, so the lady had a no-peeking policy, huh? Some of the tension within him began to ease, and with an effort, he managed to lift his gaze back to her face. "You're telling me you've never used your gift on me?" That would make things so much easier.

Emily looked away.

Ah, shit. "Doc?"

"Once, okay?" Her head snapped toward him and her green eyes glittered. "When you came to my house that night. But it wasn't deliberate. You were projecting, blasting me with your memories. I jerked up my shields as soon as I could."

Blasting me with your memories. "What memories?" His back teeth clenched as he gritted, "Just what did you see?"

For a moment, she was silent. Then, "You. You were shot, bleeding."

His right shoulder ached at the memory of the pain. "What else?" 'Cause he knew there was something else. The doc still wasn't looking him in the eyes.

"A fire."

He tensed. "What about the fire?"

"Look, I just saw a house on fire, okay? You were there, looking up at this big, white house that was being eaten by flames."

The flames had burned so brightly that night. Orange flames. Hotter than hell. And so hungry. They'd destroyed the house and everything inside.

"You don't have to worry," Emily muttered, pushing back her glasses. "I'm not going to deliberately look into your head."

Well, that was reassuring. But . . . "Why not, Doc? Did you try that before on someone and find out more than you bargained for?" Had she probed a lover's mind only to discover the man wasn't as she'd thought?

"You could say that." Her lips turned down. "The guy nearly put me in a coma."

What?

"I was eighteen, hanging in the wrong place with the wrong guy. I thought I knew him, that I could trust him. So I lowered my guard, and I found out that I'd been dead wrong about him from the beginning." She exhaled. "After that, I decided it'd be a hell of a lot safer for me to make absolutely certain that my shields were in place. I probe the thoughts of my patients—and only my patients."

When he opened his mouth to question her, she said, "They give me their permission. I *never* touch thoughts without permission." Her mouth tightened and she said, "Unless somebody's projecting so loudly I can't shut them out."

Like he'd been doing. He huffed out a hard breath. Good thing there weren't any other folks like the doc running around Atlanta. Otherwise, he'd be screwed.

"And I *never* lower my shields all the way," Emily spoke again, her voice softer now. "I always keep some protection in place."

Colin grunted and cranked the Jeep. He wanted to ask Emily more about the coma, ask her about the guy who'd nearly put her under, but he figured he'd pushed enough for one day.

Besides, he needed to get her to the station. They needed to talk to Smith, needed to find out if the ME had gotten any more information for them.

After they talked to Smith, he'd drop the doc off at her place. Then he'd go meet the cameraman. And he'd find out exactly what Jake Donnelley knew about his case.

"Uh, aren't you forgetting something?"

He glanced at her. Found her eyes narrowed on him. "What?"

Her lips thinned. "An apology."

"Ah, Doc, you don't have to apologize to me. I understand now." She wasn't jumping in his brain. As far as he could tell, she still didn't know the full truth about him, and that was very good news. "Just stay out of my head, and we'll get along just fine." More than fine if he had his way. In fact, they'd be—

The doc growled. Actually growled. *Oh, he liked that.* The beast within emitted a hungry growl of its own.

"I'm not talking about me giving you an apology," she snapped. "I meant you owe *me* an apology."

"What would I owe you an apology for?" He hadn't jumped in *her* head.

"I don't remember asking you to—to—" The doc broke off, flushing.

And the light dawned. He hadn't jumped into her head, but he'd jumped her.

"I told you before, Gyth." That pointed chin lifted and she stared straight at him, even as a blush stained her cheeks. "If I want you to kiss me, I'll ask."

Ah, yes, the doc wasn't a fan of—*what had she called it?*—the He-man routine. Well, if the lady wanted an apology . . . "Sorry, Doc, guess my basic nature just got the best of me." His basic nature, his anger, and the hard lust he seemed to feel every time he got near her.

"Yes, well, shifters are reputed to be highly volatile and, umm—"

"Sexual?"

She blinked.

"Yeah, we are." Unfortunately, most shifters tended to be male, so it wasn't like there were a ton of like-minded women strolling the streets.

But when he'd held the doc, for a bit there, "It seemed like your basic nature took control, too, huh?" She'd been kissing him back, rubbing that sweet little pink tongue of hers against his, pushing her body against him, clutching him tightly with her hands.

"Maybe it did," Emily said softly, and his respect for her shot up. A woman who could admit her need—just what he wanted.

He wished they didn't have to go back to the station. Wished they could just keep driving, preferably back to his place so that he could find out more about Emily's needs.

Even though he could still taste her, he knew his lust would have to wait.

The case came first. It had to. But once the killer was caught, oh yeah, once the killer was tossed in a dark cell to never see the light of day again, then he could focus completely on Emily.

In the meantime, he'd keep mixing his business and pleasure every damn chance he got.

She wanted Colin Gyth. Wanted a shifter. All right, she could admit it.

Emily hurried to keep pace beside Colin as they maneuvered through the police station. A few officers called out greetings to Gyth as they passed. He didn't stop for anyone, just kept walking with that I'm-a-badass stride of his. She was having to double-time it to keep up with him.

He pushed open a door leading to a stairwell. A dark, narrow stairwell.

"Ladies first," he murmured.

"Thanks." She brushed past him, and his scent—the warm, rich scent of masculine flesh—teased her nostrils.

Her heart beat faster, her breath hitched.

Oh yes, she had a serious problem where the detective was concerned.

So what was she going to do about it? About him?

The stairs ended in front of a rust-colored door. Emily knew what waited for her on the other side of that door.

It was time to stop fantasizing about the detective and get to work.

Straightening her shoulders, she pushed open the door and began to walk across the shining white tile. Her high heels tapped lightly against the floor.

Colin pointed to another door. A metallic door with a narrow strip of a window.

"Go on, Doc. Smith's waiting."

She stepped inside.

Damn, but she *hated* that smell. It had been seven years since she'd been inside a morgue. But the place still smelled the same.

Emily inhaled and tried to control an automatic gag impulse. God, the place reeked. Chemicals. Bleach. Decay. The scents of death.

Fluorescent bulbs glowed overhead, revealing the stark environment of the morgue. A small desk sat in the far corner. A covered body rested on a table. And a shining tray of sharp instruments stood waiting near the body.

"Hey, Gyth, couldn't wait any longer, huh?" A tall, thin, incredibly gorgeous black woman stepped from behind a row of filing cabinets. Her hands were covered in white, latex gloves and a blue face mask dangled around her neck.

"Hi, Smith." He flashed her a smile. "You know, it's been at least"—he glanced down at his watch—"five hours since I've been down here."

"Hmmm." Smith didn't smile back at him, and she didn't sound too happy. Her gaze drifted to Emily. "And you've brought company."

"This is Dr. Emily Drake. She's profiling the Myers case."

Smith nodded. She held out her hand, and a smile finally curved her full lips. "Nice to meet you."

"Ah, you, too." This was the ME? The woman could have been a double for Tyra Banks.

Smith's smile dimmed a bit as she turned her attention back to Gyth. "Seriously, you *need* to stop harassing me about this case. I'm working on the body as fast as I can. Myers wasn't the only guy to get murdered lately, you know."

"Yeah, but he was the only one killed by the Night Butcher."

Her jaw dropped. "The what?"

"The Night—"

Smith held up her hand. "I heard you. Jesus, you mean the press has already named this guy?"

Colin nodded. His hand came to rest at the small of Emily's back and he gently pushed her forward.

She could feel the warm weight of his touch through her shirt. She stiffened, trying to ease away from the strong press of his fingers.

"Don't guys like him usually have to kill a couple of times before they get nicknames?" Smith shook her head. "He could be a one-hit wonder, right, Dr. Drake?"

"Ah, maybe." But she really doubted it.

Smith's dark eyes narrowed. "You think this guy's a serial?"

Not in the strictest sense of the word. The rules for serial killers didn't really apply to the *Other* when they crossed that thin line that separated right and wrong for them. "I want to study the case more before I make a determination of that." Nice, safe answer.

"Night Butcher." Smith muttered the name again, shaking her head. "What a dumb-ass name." She headed for the gurney, the gurney that held a body covered with a thin white sheet. "The poor SOB wasn't butchered. He was bitten, clawed."

Emily lowered the shield in her mind just a bit. She wasn't sensing any supernatural powers from the doctor, but on this case, she didn't want to take any chances.

She felt the whip of Colin's shifter life force against her, but as for Smith . . .

Nothing.

The ME was completely human. Not even a half or a quarter breed.

That meant they needed to handle this case very, very carefully.

"You said he was bitten?" Emily questioned as she stepped toward the covered body. "You mean the killer showed cannibalistic tendencies toward the victim?"

"The guy wasn't eaten," Smith said, tapping her gloved fingers against the sheet. "But there were marks on the throat, like the attacker bit him. Bit his throat half open and then clawed it the rest of the way."

Oh, not a good visual. Unfortunately, it was exactly what had happened. The image of Preston's dead body flashed before her eyes.

Vamps and shifters had never been known to eat prey. Drink blood, yes, but actually eating human prey? She'd known only a few demons who indulged in consuming flesh.

"A man didn't do that." Smith stopped her tapping and looked straight at Gyth. "No man *could* have done that."

He didn't say a word.

So Emily had to take the ball. "Then what do you think attacked Preston Myers?"

Smith's midnight-black gaze never left Colin. "I think it was a large dog, maybe a wolf."

He shook his head. "You know that's not possible, Smith. The cameras—"

"I know! Dammit!" She jerked the mask off her neck and tossed it into the garbage. "But nothing else makes sense. I found animal hairs on the vic. I sent them off for analysis. We should have a full match on them soon. The bite radius on the vic's neck—there's no way that came from a human mouth. And the lacerations—" She paused, shook her head, "They don't fit the profile of knife wounds or ice picks. They're jagged, deep as hell."

A wolf shifter had powerful, deadly claws. Far longer and stronger than a normal wolf's.

"This is the weirdest damn case I've ever seen." Smith turned her attention back to Emily. "And I'll sure be interested in finding out exactly what you think about this killer."

Well, Smith wasn't going to be among the select few who got to view her full report. Emily knew Danny would want her data to go to his select superiors—the superiors who he knew would "understand" the special details of the case.

Smith pulled off her gloves and held her hand out to Emily.

"I'm glad Gyth brought you on the case, Dr. Drake. I sure hope you can catch this bastard."

Emily's hand met hers. "Yeah, me, too." She cleared her throat, glanced back at Colin. "Is there an office I can use here? I want to start going over the files."

"Yeah, we've got a place for you." He jerked his thumb toward the door. "Come on, I'll show you. It's barely bigger than a closet, but that's the way all the offices are in this place."

Nodding to Smith, Emily stepped back. "Good to meet you."

"Same here." The ME watched her as she crossed the room. Just as Emily stepped over the threshold, Smith called out, "Dr. Drake, just one question."

Emily glanced back. Beside her, Colin seemed to tense. "Yes?"

"You didn't seem particularly surprised to hear about the animal hairs on the vic." Her head cocked to the side. "Why is that?" Suspicion was rich in her voice.

Emily hesitated.

"I'd already told her," Colin said, shrugging casually. "I mentioned that bit about the dog or wolf hair on the ride over." He flashed her a smile. "Sorry to steal your thunder, Smith."

The ME's shoulders relaxed. "Ah, it's okay, Gyth." She laughed softly, the sound a little rusty, and she admitted, "I was worried there for a minute, though."

"Worried? Why?" He asked.

Smith didn't look at Emily as she said, "I thought the doctor might know more about the perp than she was letting on."

Yes, that was the truth. Emily tried a smile of her own, but her lips felt stiff, the movement too false. "I just have suspicions at this point, Smith. Nothing more."

She glanced down at her watch. Five o'clock. There was time to start reviewing the case files, time to get more than just suspicions before she had to meet Jake.

Time to start tracking the shifter.

* * *

The woman had been huddled in the shoebox-sized office for the last three hours. He could see straight through the windowed walls, could see right inside to her hunched figure.

The doc was poring over the files. Crime scene photos were spread on the table before her. Typed notes lay to her side.

She was tapping a pen against her lips as she read, tapping, tapping . . .

"Well, well, is that her?"

The gravelly voice sounded at his side. Colin didn't bother glancing to his left. He'd know that broken drawl anywhere.

His partner was back.

"Yeah, that's her." She pushed the notes aside, reached for a photo. Held it up, stared.

"Hmmm. Kinda pretty." A chair shrieked a protest as Todd Brooks sat down.

Colin swiveled his chair very slowly to face him. Todd was the pretty-boy of the precinct. Brown hair perfectly cut. Too perfect teeth. And big, brown, You-Can-Trust-Me eyes that he'd used on more than his share of suspects.

The idiots couldn't trust him, but they never realized that fact until it was too late.

Brooks reeled 'em in, convinced them he was their best friend. He got their confessions, then those eyes lost their warmth.

And the real man began to show.

Normally, Colin almost liked the guy. Todd didn't ask stupid questions, he minded his own business, and he was a damn good shot.

The guy was also a notorious ladies' man. He'd slept with nearly every female cop in the precinct.

But he'd sure as hell better not be planning on letting his gaze drift to the doc.

"She's off-limits, Brooks." Better to go ahead and make that clear.

His partner just shrugged. "So she's working the case. Big deal. We can still—"

Colin leaned forward. "No, I don't think you get it. *She's off-limits.*"

Those puppy-dog eyes blinked, and the light seemed to dawn. "Ah, got her marked already, huh, partner?"

No, he hadn't marked her. Not yet. That would come later. *Shifters always marked their mates.*

Colin stiffened. Where the hell had that thought come from? The doc was *not* his mate.

Sure, he wanted to have sex with her, wanted it damn bad, but *she was not his mate.*

No fucking way.

"Pity." Todd's brown eyes drifted past Colin's shoulders. "I sure would have liked to have gotten her on *my* couch."

"Stop thinking with your dick, Brooks." Captain McNeal stood behind him, his brows beetled low.

Brooks clenched his jaw. Then lifted one brow. "You knew he was there, didn't ya?" His voice was whisper soft.

"Hell, yeah." He didn't bother lowering his voice. His gaze lifted to meet the captain's. "Having a late night?"

"I was waiting to talk to Dr. Drake." When Brooks turned to face him, McNeal shoved his index finger into his chest. "Don't screw around with the doctor, Detective. We need her."

"I'm not the one you've got to worry about," he muttered.

"What's that supposed to—"

"Captain McNeal? Gyth? May I speak with you both?" Emily asked, her seductive voice cutting straight through the rumble of noise in the precinct.

"Ah, sure, Em—Dr. Drake." McNeal nodded to her but stabbed his finger against Brooks's chest once more. "Don't mess with her."

The captain pushed past him and Brooks exhaled heavily. Then he took a step forward. "Hey, I should hear what she's got to say, too."

McNeal didn't glance back at him. "Colin will brief you tomorrow. Go home, Brooks."

Colin easily read the disbelief on his partner's face. This was *not* the way things were usually handled at the PD. "*What?* But I'm assigned to this case, I need to know—"

McNeal stopped, turned slowly to face the angry detective. "You need to know what I tell you. She hasn't worked up a full profile yet. When she does, you'll know."

He clenched his jaw, shot a fuming glance toward Colin. "You'll fill me in?"

Colin nodded. He'd tell him as much as he could. He had a feeling the captain wouldn't let him reveal all the facts to Brooks, but he actually saw that as a good thing. Brooks probably wouldn't believe them when they started talking about the *Other,* and he sure as hell wouldn't know how to track one of them.

"Fine." He inclined his head toward the captain. "Then I'll follow your orders and get the hell out of here." His glance drifted to Emily. "But first I want to meet the doctor."

The captain grunted but stepped back so that Brooks could make his way over to Emily. She watched him with lowered brows as he approached, her lips slightly pursed.

Colin crossed to Emily's side, deliberately positioning himself next to her.

Brooks held out his hand. "Dr. Drake, I've heard a lot about you." He flashed his pretty-boy smile. "I'm Colin's partner, Detective Todd Brooks."

Emily took his hand, held it for all of three seconds—*yeah, he counted*—then pulled away. "Nice to meet you, Detective." Her hair was still loose around her shoulders and the lenses of her glasses glinted faintly in the light. Her stare fell on Danny. "Will Detective Brooks be joining us for the briefing?"

"Ah, no, he—"

"I've got orders to head home tonight," Brooks murmured. "But I'll look forward to discussing the case with you soon."

She nodded.

Brooks gave a little salute. "Night, guys." Then he turned on his heel and headed for the exit.

Emily stepped back into her makeshift office. Colin and

Danny crowded in behind her. When Colin kicked the door closed, the bustle of noise from the station immediately quieted.

"So what do you have for us, Doc?" he asked, his gaze dropping to the crime scene photos spread across her desk.

Her hand lifted and she tucked a stray strand of hair behind her ear. "I've got a basic profile going so far. You're probably looking for a male—but you already knew that. Shifters are predominately male. And in this case, the killer had to be damn strong to overpower Preston. Another point for a man. The level of raw violence is also an indicator that the perp is male."

Yeah, Colin had already guessed they were looking for a guy. "Keep going."

"The killer's young, probably in his mid-twenties to late thirties, and it's a good bet that he lives in the area."

"How do you know he's not a drifter?" the captain asked, and Colin knew he was hoping the killer was a one-hit wonder who'd just been passing through.

"He knew the house," Emily explained. "Knew the neighborhood. Knew how to get in and out without being seen. This guy *knew* Preston. He's not an out-of-towner who just popped in and randomly decided to murder the vic." And stranger crimes didn't usually have this dangerous level of rage.

"Well, shit." McNeal looked even more disgruntled than usual. "There've been some rumblings upstairs about this guy being a serial." He leveled a hard look at the doc. "You told me before you thought he'd do it again."

"Yes, I did." Her lips pursed. "But so far, this guy doesn't fit the strict definition of a serial."

"You mean because he hasn't killed three people?" Colin asked.

She nodded. "The FBI requires three victims before the label of serial killer can be applied. So far, we've only got one body."

The doc was holding back. He could feel it. "But?"

"But I think he's killed before." She touched the security photo of the hooded figure entering the Myers house. "This guy is confident. He had his plan in mind, probably for days before the actual attack. And there were no hesitation wounds on the victim's body." Her tongue snaked out, licked her bottom lip. "He went straight for the kill. This guy's no amateur, no first-timer feeling his way. He knows exactly what he's doing."

"But until we find more bodies, we can't say he's a serial," McNeal muttered.

"Right."

Colin didn't think that was a particularly bad thing. The public tended to panic when they got news that a serial killer was on the streets, and a panicked public could be very dangerous.

"If he is a true serial killer, he won't attack anyone else right away. He'll wait and have a cooling-off time. Could be for a few days or it could be years." She began to straighten the photos, putting them into a nice, neat pile. "Course, since the guy's a shifter, the normal serial rules might not apply at all."

"What rules would apply?" This came from the captain, who was no longer leaning back against the wall. He'd shot to attention as Emily spoke, and now he stood at the edge of the table, arms crossed over his chest.

"Well, if we're right and he *is* a shifter, then here are a few generalities for you." She didn't glance toward Colin as she spoke. "The guy's about five times stronger than a human male. He's highly sexual, got an extremely high IQ, and he's damn good at manipulation."

Colin stiffened at that. "Manipulation?" He didn't particularly like that term.

Her head turned slowly, and she met his gaze. "Shifters are born looking human, but they carry beasts their whole lives. They have to hide their animal natures, have to pretend to be just like everyone else, and usually, by the time shifters reach adulthood, they're damn good at pretending."

You have to pretend, or else the humans will kill you. Hunt you and kill you.

Emily glanced back at McNeal. "He's used to lying, used to hiding, used to blending in with the crowd."

"If this guy is so damn good at blending in," McNeal muttered, "then how the hell are we going to find him?"

Good question, and one that Colin didn't have a ready answer for. Sure, he was chasing down leads. He was planning to go see just what Jake Donnelley knew about the case, but flushing out a shifter? That wasn't going to be easy. Not by a long shot.

"We have to go into his world," Emily said softly. "Preston was involved with at least one demon that I know of. He could know other SBs. Maybe we can get one of them to talk to us."

Well, hell, the doc had just voiced his own plan.

McNeal shot him a quick, searching glance.

Colin nodded. "That's my general plan." Emily had just beaten him to the punch.

The captain grunted. "You can't take Brooks with you to question them. The guy doesn't understand the circumstances of this crime."

Yeah, he knew Brooks was out. The guy was a decent partner. Smart, tough, and dependable. Hell, the guy's main flaw seemed to be that he was always chasing a new lady.

Brooks was a good-enough guy, but he had no clue about the existence of the *Other* in the world. No idea that the creatures from the horror flicks he loved so much were actually real.

His partner lived in the human reality, the black-and-white world where bad guys pulled guns or knives on you—not the world where shape-shifters could rip you apart or demons could incinerate you.

"Take Dr. Drake with you."

Colin jerked at the order, sure he'd misunderstood. "Ah, run that by me again, Captain."

McNeal's lips thinned. "You heard me, Gyth. You need

someone to go with you when you interview the *Other*. You need her. Hell, without her, you won't even be able to tell the difference between the humans and the—"

"It's not safe for her," Colin snarled, cutting across the captain's words. Take Emily with him to interview demons, shifters? Hell, no.

"You keep her safe."

"I—" He floundered. Well, sure if Emily was with him, he'd do everything in his power to protect her. But he didn't want to put her at risk. Anything could happen on the street, and if someone were to hurt the doc on his watch . . .

His nails began to stretch into claws.

What the fuck?

Colin balled his hands into fists and jerked away from McNeal and Emily. He hoped they hadn't seen the change. Hoped they hadn't noticed the razor-sharp claws that sprung from his fingertips.

Jesus. That had never happened before. He'd never had the change come on him so damn fast when there wasn't a physical threat nearby.

What in the hell is happening to me?

"Colin?" Emily's voice. The soft drawl was laced with concern.

Great.

"She doesn't go." He didn't look back at her. At the captain. His normal control wasn't back yet, and he was having to fight the lure of the beast.

McNeal grunted. "Don't be an asshole, Detective. You need her and you know it."

The faint creak of the floorboards grated against his ears. *Emily is inching closer to me.*

Get your control back, man. Get it back now.

He spun around, came face-to-face with her.

Her green eyes widened and her lips parted on a startled breath of surprise.

With the beast so close, all of his senses were heightened. Her scent filled his nostrils, and the light whisper of her breathing filled his ears. He could even hear the faint drum of her heart. Beating fast, so fast.

"Are you all right?" Her brows drew together as she stared up at him.

And he wondered just what she was feeling. Was the doc using her mojo? Was she tapping into his emotions? Before she'd told him that he projected, and he bet the beast was projecting a hell of a lot of raw emotion straight at her then.

"I'm fine," he gritted, and it was the truth. The beast had just tried to slip its leash for a moment, but the animal was chained again.

Emily had lifted her right hand toward him. It hung in the air, hovering just above his chest. As he watched, her fingers slowly lowered and she pulled back her hand, stepping away from him.

"A civilian can't work the street." And his captain should damn well know that. "She's not armed. She won't be able to defend herself."

"But she'll know exactly who you need to talk with, won't she, Detective?" The captain looked about as satisfied as a man could get. The jerk.

Yeah, she'd know who he needed to interview. She'd make his questioning go a hell of a lot faster.

But the idea of taking her with him . . .

It didn't sit well with him. Not one damn bit.

"You need me, Gyth," Emily told him softly. And yeah, she was right. He needed her for the case.

Needed her in his bed.

Right then, he wasn't pleased with either fact.

His eyes narrowed on her. "If we do this, you do what I say, exactly as I order." Keeping the doc under his control wasn't gonna be easy. Hell, this was the same woman who'd gone traipsing after him as he searched that old vacant lot near her house.

I thought you might need my help.

Dammit, taking her out on the streets with him would be hell.

"Do you think you can do it, Doc?" he asked, taking a step toward her. Their bodies were close, so close he could feel the warmth of her skin against him. "Do you think you'll be able to take orders from me?" *To actually follow those orders?*

Her jaw clenched and her green eyes blazed with fire. "Yes," she gritted. "I think I can."

Well, he might not like it, but it looked like he and the doc would be working the street together.

And since Jake Donnelley had asked for a meeting at the Paradise Found in—Colin glanced down at his watch—less than an hour and a half, it looked like their partnership was about to get started.

Shit, but he wasn't pleased with this situation. Not one damn bit.

His captain was glaring at him, giving him the old you'd-damn-well-better-not-screw-this-up stare.

Emily was gazing up at him, eyes slightly narrowed. Anger burned in her green eyes.

That couldn't bode well for the night.

He leaned in toward Emily, pitched his voice low as he whispered in her ear. "If we're doin' this, then you remember that I'm the one in charge. You listen to me, Doc. And you do exactly as I say."

She exhaled heavily. "I'm not an idiot, you know," she snapped, making no effort to lower her voice. "I know you're the one with the police experience."

Oh, that had been easy. Too easy, really.

Her index finger jabbed into his chest. "But don't forget I'm the one with the *Other* experience." Then, finally, *finally,* the woman decided to lower her voice as she whispered, "You might think you're the baddest thing out there, Gyth, but I've got news for you . . . I've seen things a hell of a lot scarier than a cop shifter."

His gaze shot to McNeal's. But the captain was just staring blandly back at him. His lips were curved with faint amusement.

He bit back the words that sprang to his lips. If Emily ever saw the beast he carried, he'd bet his life it'd scare her. Hell, when his ex-partner had seen his other form, Mike had run like hell. Then Mike had come back and tried to kill him.

Good thing he was hard to kill.

"So are we going to do this?" Emily stepped back. Reached for the files on the table. "Or are you too worried that my presence will screw up your case?"

Oh, he was worried. But they'd do it anyway. He'd play her game, play the captain's game, for now.

And he'd make damn sure he kept the doc safe. He'd stick by her side every moment.

He just hoped she meant what she'd said about following his orders. Because listening to him, doing exactly as he ordered, well, that could be the difference between life and death.

"Umm, glad that's settled then." McNeal stretched slowly. "I'm going to get out of here." He shot a quick, hard glance at Colin as he opened the door. "Let me know how the meeting goes."

His head inclined in a barely perceptible nod. He'd briefed the captain earlier about Donnelley's note. In hindsight, he now saw that hadn't been the best plan. It'd obviously made McNeal think the doc would have a connection with the suspects on the case.

The fact that Emily *did* have a connection with them only pissed him off more.

He hated being forced into a corner.

Colin waited until Emily bid the captain good night, waited until the glass door swung shut behind McNeal, then he reached for her hand.

His fingers locked around her wrist, and her pulse pounded fast and hard beneath his touch.

"You sure you're ready for this?" Once he took her onto the street, there would be no going back. Acting as a profiler was one thing. She could sit back in an air-conditioned office and scribble her notes, but going with him to talk to the *Other* . . . well, it could make her a target. A very big target.

Behind her glasses, her green eyes stared straight back at him. There wasn't even a hint of hesitation in her expression. "I'm sure."

"All right, then, Doc. Let's go find out what our cameraman has to say." Yep, it was time to go and meet Jake Donnelley. Time to go to Paradise Found.

According to Emily the place was the town's number one demon hangout.

As dates went, it wasn't his best.

Then again, it wasn't his worst either.

Chapter 5

Getting past the seven-foot-tall demon guarding the door of Paradise Found had been incredibly easy.

She'd handed the guy a twenty, and he'd let them slip right past without even a raised brow.

The guy had known they weren't demons. They didn't carry the "demon scent" that marked the beings of that race. No, Emily knew she just smelled human. She wasn't exactly sure how Colin had registered to the bouncer's sensitive nose.

"That was easy," Colin muttered, his eyes sweeping across the darkened interior of Paradise Found. "I would've thought it would be harder to get into one of the pits of hell."

Yes, and if the bouncer hadn't been one of her ex-patients, Emily was certain it would have been much, much more difficult.

Demons were real particular about letting humans into their playgrounds. And from what she'd learned over the years, they didn't feel a whole lot of love for shifters, either. But then, who did? Shifters were the black sheep of the *Other* family.

She'd been to Paradise Found before. Once she'd hung out there far, far too often.

The place still looked the same. Dim lighting snaked across the bar, hiding the demons in the darkness. The old dance floor was still as small, and as packed with humans as ever. Jesus, the place even smelled the same. Sweat, alcohol, and sex.

Very carefully, Emily unclenched her hands. When had she

balled her fingers into fists? Probably the second she'd stepped over the threshold and entered the bar.

Bad memories. There were a lot of bad memories here.

Her gaze drifted toward the long, black bar top. That's where she'd almost died, where Myles had tried to shove his power into her mind and make her into one of his damn human puppets.

"I don't see Donnelley." Colin paced in front of her, tension tight in his body. He was already attracting more than a few nervous stares.

Her hand touched his arm. "He's probably in the back." She motioned toward a row of booths heading down a thin corridor. "Let's look over there." Emily walked across the dance floor, easily dodging the crowd and letting her gaze scan the back row of booths. She could feel the supernatural energy in the room swirling around her. So many *Other.* Demons, vamps, charmers. She'd better keep her shields up. Keep them strong and—

"Hold on, Doc." Colin snagged her wrist, stopping her at the edge of the wooden floor. "Why do I get the feeling you've been here before?" His words were spoken into her ear. His breath blew against her.

She swallowed but didn't turn back toward him. Now wasn't the time to rehash her past. Hell, she'd be happy if she never had to rehash it. She'd been a kid, she'd made dumb-ass mistakes, case closed. "Colin, I—"

A man rose from the shadows of the back booth. Lifted his hand to her.

"There he is," her voice whispered out.

Colin's fingers tightened around her. "Remember, Doc, this is my show." A distinct warning laced his words.

"Like I could forget," she muttered. Jesus. How many times was the guy going to remind her? She got it. The investigation was his game. She was supposed to play the good little girl and sit back and let the big, bad guy do his job.

Well, she'd never been a good little girl.

Good little girls didn't get sent to—

"Come back to play with me, huh, Emily?"

Her head jerked up at the deep, rumbling voice, and Emily found herself staring into the midnight black eyes of Niol.

Shit. The dark waves of his power lapped at her, and a dull headache immediately formed behind her eyes.

The guy made her sick. Literally.

Come back to play with me. Not damn likely. But she'd better not burn any bridges yet. She and Colin needed to find out exactly why Preston Myers had a picture of this guy in his house. "Uh, hello, Niol."

Colin stepped up to her side. Bared his teeth. And kept his hold on her wrist. "I don't think I've had the pleasure." He held out his right hand.

Niol lifted one black brow. "No, Detective, I don't think you have." He took Colin's hand, his fingers tightening for the briefest of moments.

Colin kept his smile—*well, it really wasn't a smile, it was that same baring of fangs that he'd flashed at Darla*—on his face as he said, "I see you know who I am."

"But not what you are." Niol's gaze returned to Emily. "If you're with Emily, then that means you must be . . . special."

Colin didn't respond.

The dancers around them crept back, giving them plenty of space. *Probably running away from Niol.*

Niol crossed his arms over his chest. "But you're not my kind, are you, Detective?"

"Your kind?" Colin shrugged, a faint ripple of muscle, of menace. Then he brushed back his jacket, subtly revealing the butt of his gun. "And just what kind would that be?"

Niol laughed softly, and the sound sent a chill skating down Emily's spine. Oh damn, but this guy was trouble. Serious trouble. His power was so strong, she could practically see the black energy waves in the air around them. Even with her shields up.

"Ah, so you like to play games too? Just like our lovely doctor?"

"*Our?*" Where the hell had that come from? Her back teeth locked.

"We're not here to play games," Colin told him softly.

Niol's dark stare drifted down Emily's body.

Then Colin's.

"Pity." Niol pursed his lips. "I have a feeling I could have enjoyed myself with you two for a time." He centered his attention back on her. "But if your detective doesn't want in on the fun, then perhaps you and I could—"

"Don't even fucking think about it," Colin snarled, stepping forward. He'd dropped her wrist, clenched his hands into fists.

He was as big as Niol. As tall, as muscled.

As a shifter, he'd be Niol's match in physical strength. But as much as she'd love to see the demon lord get an ass kicking, now wasn't the time.

"He's just messing around, Colin." She glanced at Niol. Met that dark stare. Unlike other demons, Niol didn't bother disguising his black eyes. Didn't bother pretending he was anything other than what he was. *A very, very dangerous demon.* One that it didn't pay to cross. Keeping her eyes on Niol, she told Colin, "He doesn't mean it." *He'd damn well better not mean it.* She'd sooner live the rest of her life sexless than be with a guy like him.

Niol was watching Colin, calculation plain on his face. "So it's like that, is it?"

Colin jerked his head in a nod.

Niol licked his lips. "Pity," he said again.

It was a pity that she hadn't let Colin kick the jerk's ass. But they were at the bar on official business. She kinda thought McNeal would frown on a fight between his detective and the bar's owner. "Niol, we need to ask you some questions."

"We?"

What, had she stuttered? Emily glared at him. "Yeah, *we.*"

"Working for the cops now, are you? How disappointing." He sighed. "I'd hoped you'd come work for me one day. I could always use a woman with your talents."

Emily plastered a bright, completely false smile on her face. "Thanks for the offer, but I've got a job." Two, actually.

"You know, love, people still talk about the way you burned out that demon. Nearly died doing it, didn't you? But you took his power away, every last drop."

Her eyes narrowed and her head kept throbbing. Time to stop the painful walk down memory lane. "About those questions . . ."

Niol's full lips stretched into a smile, a smile that showcased his perfect, white teeth. "Let me save you some time, love. Yes, I knew Preston. He was a fairly wealthy guy who wanted to invest in my place. No, he wasn't my kind. And, no, I didn't kill him."

Emily blinked. Well, the guy wasn't playing dumb about the case. That was good. But was he telling the truth?

For an instant, she was tempted to lower her shields. Just a few seconds, that would be all she'd need . . .

From the corner of her eye, she caught sight of the long, gleaming bar.

She'd fallen against that bar, *fallen, hit the floor, screaming, clutching her head—*

Emily exhaled. *Bad idea. Very bad idea.* She couldn't drop her shields in this place; there were too many unknowns. She couldn't risk a burnout in the middle of a crowd teaming with *Other.*

Wouldn't be good for business.

"You say you didn't kill him," Colin drawled. "You got an idea who did?"

Niol shook his head. "Someone who hated him."

"You didn't hate him?"

Emily watched his reactions carefully. Niol appeared calm, perfectly in control. As if he got questioned about a murder every day.

"I didn't like him," Niol replied. "But hate? No, too strong of a word. I just . . . didn't really care one way or the other."

Yes, the guy was calm, controlled, *ice cold.* "Do you care that he's dead?" Emily asked.

His expression didn't change as he shrugged. "Now I've got to get another investor. It's an inconvenience."

An inconvenience. A man's death was an inconvenience to him.

Colin grunted. Slanting a quick look his way, Emily noticed that a muscle was flexing along the line of Colin's jaw.

He looked seriously pissed as he demanded, "Where were you last Friday, between eight and nine?"

"Niol?" A tall, model-thin brunette slipped behind the demon and wrapped her hands around his waist. "You made me wait," she whispered, stretching to kiss his neck.

"Sorry, love." He never glanced her way. "I had to play nice with the PD." His hand lifted, covered hers. "But I'm done now."

An obvious dismissal.

Colin pulled out a card, thrust it toward Niol. "If you happen to learn anything about the case or if you"—a deliberate pause—"*remember* anything you want to share, call me."

Niol pocketed the card. "I'll be sure to do that . . . if I learn anything else." His head inclined slightly. "As always, it's been a pleasure, Emily."

Right. She snorted. Why did he even bother pretending with her? Niol knew she could see right through his fake manners to the real nature of the demon within.

And that demon, he wasn't a gentleman. He was hard, evil. Deadly.

Pity the lady clinging to his arm so tightly and glaring at her didn't realize those important facts.

And now wasn't the time to warn her.

Niol and his companion stepped back, and in mere seconds, they had vanished, melting into the crowd.

"What a bastard." Colin glared into the throng of dancers, then turned his bright blue stare on her. "Think he knows more than he's saying?"

She didn't have to use her psychic powers on this one. "Without a doubt."

"Yeah, me, too."

Emily turned her attention back to the darkened booths. Was Donnelley still waiting on them?

"Was the woman a demon too?"

"No." She answered absently as she tried to search the shadows. Had Jake gotten frightened when he'd seen them talk to Niol? Had they missed their chance to find out exactly what he knew about the case?

"Then what was she?"

"Human." There'd been no shift in the atmosphere when the woman approached, no telling flow of power, no faint shine emanating from her body. Niol's companion was most definitely a human.

Did she know what he was?

"What did he mean, about you draining some demon's power? Thought you said you were an empath, that you just felt—"

He would *lock onto that part of the conversation.* Her eyes continued to search the booths as she said very softly, "I was defending myself, okay, Gyth? The bastard attacked me, shoved the full force of his power into my head." As a level nine, the demon had plenty of power to shove. "It was instinct. I fought back, tried to push the energy right back at him." And she'd managed to blast away all his power before she'd collapsed.

Emily finally looked at him, found him watching her. "It's not something I like to talk about." Explanation made, case closed. She didn't want to bring up the subject again.

"Understood."

Her shoulders relaxed. Good. Maybe she could get through the rest of the night without any more rehashing of one of the most painful moments of her life. Her stare swept the bar once again, then locked on the shadowy figure of a man.

A man who stood near the back booth. He motioned to her, waving his hand quickly in the air.

"Donnelley's there." Relief poured through her. She'd been afraid that Niol's dark presence had screwed up the meeting.

"I see him."

Course he did. He could probably see perfectly through the shadows while she had to strain and squint. Shifter skills. Sometimes they sure could come in handy.

A waitress brushed by them as they maneuvered to Donnelley's table. Emily caught the faint whiff of power around the woman. *A witch.*

Donnelley was bent low over the table, his hands fisted over the old, scarred wood surface. His jaw tightened when they sat across from him. "I gave the note to her, Gyth, not you." A Braves baseball cap was pulled low over his head, hiding his blond hair.

Colin leaned back against the black cushions. "It's my case."

"And my life!" A bead of sweat rolled down Jake's cheek. "Do you know what kind of risk I'm taking just by being here?"

"Why?" Colin jerked his thumb toward the dance floor. "Scared your buddies will turn on you if they find out you're givin' information to the cops?"

Colin sure didn't have much finesse.

"I wasn't planning on talking to *you.*" His stare darted to the left, the right. Then landed on Emily. "I wanted to talk to Dr. Drake."

Beside her, Colin shrugged. "So talk. We're both listening."

Jake licked his lips. Hunched even deeper into the booth. "Preston knew about us."

"Us?" Emily asked softly. She'd figured she'd better jump in, before Colin scared the guy to death with his hard-ass approach.

Sometimes a delicate technique was required. She'd spent years honing that technique.

"Yeah. You know, the *Other.*"

Well, that wasn't exactly news. But she nodded anyway, trying to look encouraging.

"His girl, she was a demon."

She could feel the sudden, alert tension in Colin's body. "What's her name?"

Jake sucked in a sharp breath. The weak beat of his power flickered in the air around them. "You didn't get this from me, okay?"

"Right." Colin tapped his index finger on the table.

"Gillian Nemont." He swallowed. "But I don't think you're gonna be able to talk to her."

Jake pushed to his feet and cast another nervous glance toward the front of the bar. "Shouldn't have come here," he muttered. For a moment, his face tightened as he looked back at Emily. "I thought we'd meet alone."

Colin stood slowly. "Sorry, we're a package deal." He positioned his body in front of Jake's, effectively blocking the demon's path. "And just why won't Gillian talk to me? Does she have a thing against cops?"

Jake shook his head. "No, if you can find her, she might talk, but . . ."

"But what?" Emily pressed.

One shoulder lifted in a faint shrug. "But I think she's hiding. I haven't seen her in at least a week, maybe two."

Jake stepped forward, obviously intending to make his exit, but Colin didn't move. Colin stood a few inches taller than the demon, and he stared down at him, his head cocked to the right. "That all you got for us, Donnelley?"

Jake nodded. "Yeah, I wanted to make sure the doctor knew to look in the right direction for the killer, that's all."

"The right direction?" Emily repeated, frowning slightly at his phrasing. "And just what is the right direction?"

"A human didn't do this," Jake said. "It's one of us. I knew it when I saw the body."

"Well, damn." Colin whistled softly. "You're the guy who got the shot of Preston, aren't you? You're the one who took the picture of his body and got it splashed across every newspaper in the city."

Jake lifted his chin. "I'm a reporter, okay? I was doing my job."

"Huh. Here I was thinking you were just the cameraman."

Jake's golden eyes flashed black. A ripple of weak power swept through the air. The power would have been enough to cause a human to stumble back, maybe even to fall.

Colin didn't waver from his spot. One black brow rose. "Is that all you've got?"

"You don't want to see what I can do," Jake snapped. Then he lifted his hand and shoved past Colin.

Emily sighed. *That did so not go well.* No wonder Danny wanted her to accompany Colin. "Not much for tact, are you?" He glanced at her. "The guy tried to use his magic on me." Shifters were immune to demon magic. Actually, a demon's magic worked only on humans.

"You know you just showed him that you're *Other.*" And that worried her. Had Jake deliberately tested him?

His lips tightened.

"If you don't watch it, Gyth, your little secret might get out."

"He's not gonna tell anyone. If he did, he'd have to reveal his own history."

Yeah, he was right. Jake would have just as much to lose.

The crowd in Paradise Found was even bigger now, even louder, and as they maneuvered back to the entrance, Emily was aware of the stares on them, aware of the whispers.

She breathed a sigh of relief when they finally stepped back outside. The night air was slightly cool, and the sky was a starless black, illuminated only by the glistening moon.

They walked in silence for a moment. Emily replayed both Niol's and Jake's conversations in her mind. She wasn't sure she trusted either man.

"We need to find this Gillian," Colin said, stepping off the sidewalk and turning into the alley. His Jeep was parked just around the corner. Just a few hundred feet away. "Brooks ran Preston's background check. We both talked to the neighbors, family. *No one* mentioned this woman."

"Maybe he was keeping her secret. It's not exactly easy to announce to the family that your new love is a demon."

"Yeah, he coulda kept quiet about her." He paused beneath a flickering light hanging from the back door of a club. "That black eye thing—it's a demon trait, isn't it?"

She nodded, and realized that she seriously needed to brush the guy up on *Other 101.* Despite being an SB, he sure didn't seem too aware of their world.

Probably because he'd been hiding from that world, trying to fit in with the humans.

"Why doesn't Niol change his eye color?"

"Because Niol doesn't give a damn. He doesn't care if people realize he's different." Hell, as far as she could tell, Niol actually got off on jolting humans out of their safe worlds.

And, of course, he got off *with* humans too.

The fluorescent light hanging over Colin made a faint humming sound, then faded into darkness.

A chill skated down her body. Emily glanced around the alley. She didn't see anyone else.

She lowered the shields in her mind, aware of a sudden shift in the atmosphere.

No, she didn't see anyone, but she could *feel* a presence.

Emily opened her mind, sent her powers questing out. A blast of hot, burning rage hit her, driving straight into her mind, driving her down to her knees as she cried out in sudden pain.

Level-ten demon. Shit.

"Emily?" Colin reached for her, catching her by the arms and pulling her onto her feet. "Baby, what's wrong?"

Her teeth were chattering. "S-someone's h-here . . ." She shook her head, clenching her jaw.

What the hell? He kept his left hand wrapped around her. He could hear her heartbeat; the frantic drumming filled his ears.

He didn't hear anything else, though. Didn't hear the telltale crunch of gravel beneath shoes. Didn't hear the whisper of clothing that would alert him to someone else's presence in the alley.

His senses were fully open. If an assailant was in the alley, he should know it.

Colin reached for his weapon. He didn't sense anyone, but the doc sure did, and he wasn't about to take any chances. He slipped off the safety, wanting to be ready.

Four men jumped from the shadows. They wore full black

ski masks, jackets, pants, and boots. The masked men lunged for him and the doc. Colin shoved her back against the alley wall and turned to face them, lifting his gun. "Get back," he ordered, "I'm a cop—"

They attacked.

Sonofabitch. They fell on him at once, hitting and punching, driving him back to the ground. He fired a shot, but he must have missed, because they didn't stop, not for an instant. He felt an icy pain slice into his right hand. Felt blood pool into his palm as his gun dropped from his suddenly nerveless fingers.

He didn't know who these guys were, but they'd just picked the wrong guy to fuck with.

Colin was pinned on the ground, his bloody fingers scraping against the rough gravel. One of the assholes was driving his boot into Colin's ribs.

Another one was going for the doc.

Screw this.

The beast within roared its rage. Colin's nails lengthened into razor-sharp claws. He slashed out with his hands, catching two of his attackers; he cut open the leg of the asshole who'd been kicking him and then drove his claws into the second bastard's stomach.

"Get the hell off me!"

Colin turned at Emily's shout. She was pinned against the wall. A man, tall, hulking, had his hands wrapped around her arms. He was leaning into her, and she was kicking against him, ramming her high heels against his shins and trying to head-butt him.

If he hadn't been so furious, he might have been impressed with her.

Then the man's hands shot to her throat.

Colin forgot about everything in that instant but the urge to kill.

He was behind the man in less than a second. Grabbed him, lifted the bastard up, tossed him headfirst into the alley wall.

Emily gasped for breath, her hands rising to her throat.

Colin spared her a glance. Her hands were shaking, her body quivering lightly.

He crouched over her attacker. He wanted the guy's blood. Could almost taste the kill.

He touched Emily. Wrapped his hands around her throat. Tried to hurt her.

The beast was screaming its rage, and Colin could actually hear the howl in his ears.

Destroy. Attack.

Kill.

The beast was hungry, so hungry.

His claws lifted over the man.

"Dammit, watch out!" Emily shot past him, arms raised, and drove straight into the last assailant.

Colin spun around. He'd forgotten the other man. For one blind, reckless moment, he'd completely forgotten the guy.

They were on the ground now. Emily was sprawled on top of him, and Colin could see the faint glimmer of a knife next to the fallen man's hand.

Well, damn.

The doc had just saved his life.

"Bitch!"

Colin's eyes narrowed. He took a step forward just as Emily drove her knee into the asshole's crotch. He jerked, yelling in pain and twisting away from her.

Colin grabbed Emily, pulled her to her feet. The perp on the ground was curled into a fetal position, squealing.

He whistled softly and glanced at Emily. "And here I thought you were the delicate type." She'd lost her glasses, and her hair fell loosely around her face. His hand lifted toward her cheek. He wanted to push back her hair, to touch her, to—

"What in the hell?" Emily grabbed his wrist. Her eyes widened. "Gyth, you've got claws!"

His body tensed. He'd forgotten about his partial shift. He could only be grateful for the darkness, otherwise Emily would see the blood on his hands, embedded in his claws.

"What kind of shifter are you?" There was a note of hesitation in her voice, a note of almost . . . fear.

Damn. That was the last thing he needed. He didn't want the doc to fear him. Not now.

"Colin?"

He couldn't tell her. Couldn't risk it.

Colin spun away from her, glanced back down at the guys on the ground. "Who are you bastards and why the fuck did you attack us?" Okay, not the standard police interviewing technique, but he wasn't exactly feeling all nice and professional. His ribs were hurting like hell thanks to Mr. Kick Happy. Colin swiped his hand against his lip, feeling the wet warmth of blood. His lip had probably gotten busted when they tackled him to the ground.

The guys were rousing, sending narrow-eyed, glittering stares his way. *What in the hell?* He'd taken them down, hard. They shouldn't be getting up this soon, no damn way, not unless—

"They're demons," Emily told him, confirming the suspicion that had been filling his mind.

Well, shit.

Things were suddenly much, much more dangerous. He wasn't an *Other* expert like the doc, but he knew demons healed fast.

"They're low level." She stood beside him. Their backs were near the wall of the alley. "Maybe a one or a two."

He didn't really know what that meant, and he made a mental note to quiz the doc on *Other* lore sometime later. Once they'd gotten out of the alley and far away from the jerks who were trying to kill them.

"Stay behind me," he ordered, now eyeing the perps with deep suspicion. They could attack again at any moment.

The guy who'd made the mistake of going after Emily climbed to his feet. A deep gash swept across his forehead, and blood trickled down his face. "Catching on now, cop?"

The others pushed to their feet. Crept up behind the one ballsy enough to talk. Colin figured him for the leader.

"He cut me, Scott." The snarled words came from the guy bleeding out a river in the back.

Colin held up his hands, let them see the claws springing from his fingertips. "And I'll do it again." He'd cut the demons apart if they came at him or if they tried to attack Emily. He'd been pissed enough before when they'd first jumped him, but now that he knew they weren't human, all bets were off. He'd use every bit of his shifter strength to make them wish they'd never stepped into the alley.

"Let's kill 'em!" Same demon talking. The bastard who was currently bleeding out in the alley. He was a tall guy, lean but muscled.

"You can try," Colin said. "But I don't think you'll succeed. Especially considering the fact that I just kicked your asses." And he'd be more than happy to do it again.

Emily's nails dug into his back. "Someone else is here. Someone a hell of a lot more powerful than these guys."

The night just kept getting better. "I don't see anyone," he muttered, and it was true. The night was dark, but with his enhanced vision, he could see perfectly in the alley. He could even see the snake tattoo swirling around the left wrist of the bastard he'd clawed. *That'll help identify you later, asshole.*

"He's here," she repeated softly. "And—"

"Stay the fuck out of our business, cop!" This snarl came from the leader, the guy who'd been called Scott. "Tonight was a warning. You and the doctor won't get another."

Our business?

"Stick to your own kind!" Now snake tattoo was shouting his own warning. "Leave the demons alone."

Oh yeah, like that was going to happen. If anything, these idiots had just made him all the more determined to plunge straight into their world.

"Who sent you?" Emily asked, and she sure as hell didn't sound like she was frightened. She sounded royally pissed. "Who told you to jump us in the alley?"

Scott stiffened.

"Was it Niol?" She pushed. "Is he the reason you're threatening us? Did he tell you—"

A siren sounded nearby.

The men cursed, then turned, fleeing down the alley just as the swirl of blue and white lights lit up the scene.

Two uniformed cops jumped out of the vehicle, guns drawn. "Hands up, now!"

"Shit." Colin lifted his hands and watched in disgust as the demons disappeared into the shadows. He'd find those bastards again, he'd make certain of it. "Listen, I'm a cop. Detective Colin Gyth, badge number 2517." He made no move to reach for his ID. The cops looked more than a little nervous to be confronting him in the alley, and he wasn't about to give these green guys a reason to become trigger happy.

Emily had her hands lifted up too. One of the patrolmen approached her, pulling her away from Gyth.

"Come with me, ma'am."

Hot rage still coursed through Colin's body. He took a deep breath, inhaled the stench of the alley, the sweat from the cops. He needed to regain his control, needed to cage the beast.

His claws began to recede. Slowly, slowly.

"Show me your ID, Detective." The patrolman still held his gun on Colin.

Carefully, Colin reached inside his jacket and pulled out his ID. The cop took it, stepped back. "Don't move." He crept toward the car, and Colin heard him radio in his information.

"We were attacked! The guys who jumped us are getting away!" Emily still sounded pissed as she raged at the cop.

He glanced toward the end of the alley. *Correction: they'd already gotten away.*

"Okay, Detective, you check out."

Colin lowered his hands. "I need you to start a search in the area. Four men just attacked us." *And warned us to stay the hell out of demon business.*

Not gonna happen.

"They were wearing black ski masks, shirts, pants." Which would make identifying them damn hard. "But one guy had a snake tattoo on his left wrist. And the leader was a man named Scott." Not much to go on, but it was all they had.

"Four men attacked you?" This from the cop who'd taken Emily away.

"That's what I've been trying to tell you," she snapped.

The patrolman dutifully radioed in the information Colin had given him. "Are either of you hurt?" he asked.

Emily shook her head.

Colin remembered the icy flash of pain he'd felt in his hand when one of the bastards had cut him. The wound had already stopped bleeding, and his ribs only ached in a brief echo of pain. "No." He'd be completely healed long before any EMT could arrive to help him.

"Why'd they jump you?" The cop who'd radioed in their information cast a level stare Colin's way.

Because I'm getting too close. Colin shrugged. He had to be careful now. He couldn't very well reveal that the demons didn't like him sniffing around their territory.

Ah, but his presence had sure made someone nervous.

And that was good. Very good.

Emily crossed to his side. She'd picked up her glasses, and she was rubbing the lenses against her shirt.

"Is he still here?" he asked her, pitching his voice low so that the patrolmen wouldn't hear him. She'd said the watcher was a strong *Other*, and Colin wondered if the guy had stayed around to catch the rest of the show.

She shook her head. "No. He left right after the patrol got here."

Colin grunted. *Figures.* "Well, Doc, looks like we've managed to catch someone's attention." He flexed his fingers, feeling the newly healed flesh stretch lightly.

"Yes, I guess we did." She gazed at the dark end of the alley. "Are we going to heed their warning?"

She'd put a nice, subtle emphasis on the *we*. "What do you think?"

She pushed her glasses onto her nose. "I think I don't like it when jerks in black ski masks jump me in an alley."

He fought the curve of his lips. "Yeah, I don't like that too much either."

"I also think it's good that someone's nervous out there." She lifted her chin, still gazing into the darkness. "It means we're on the right track."

His lips tightened. "It's a dangerous track, Doc." And he didn't like her being in danger. When that bastard had put his hands around her throat—

"Despite what you think, Gyth, I'm not some delicate flower." She finally looked at him. There was determination in her eyes—determination and, unless he was mistaken, excitement.

He realized the doc liked the thrill of danger. She enjoyed the hook of adrenaline that came from staring straight into fear.

Oh, but he could really like this woman.

"No, you aren't delicate," he agreed, remembering the way she'd attacked the guy who'd tried to jump him from behind. The bastard was probably still tasting his balls.

The doc was a hell of a lot stronger than he'd originally thought, but the fact remained that she *was* human. And the guys who attacked him, the demons, they could easily kill her.

As for the shifter, the "Night Butcher," well, he'd be even worse. A human would never stand a chance against a guy like that. Emily would never stand a chance.

"You're not going to shut me out," Emily said, and he wondered for an instant if she'd used her powers to read his mind. "Threats from two-bit demons aren't going to make me run."

Threats might not, but what if those demons got ahold of her? What if they caught her when he wasn't around, when he couldn't protect her?

But she burned out a demon once, he reminded himself. *She burned out the guy who'd tried to attack her—*

And nearly wound up in a coma.

No, the doc wasn't cut out for fighting demons or shifters.

But she was in this thing now. The demons knew about her involvement.

"It's only going to get rougher from now on," he warned. The closer they got to the killer, the more dangerous the situation would become.

"I know." Simple, clear words. No hint of fear.

He held out his hand to her, palm up. She glanced down at his offered hand for a moment, her brows wrinkling. Then slowly, very slowly, she placed her palm against his.

His fingers instantly curled around hers. "You ready for everything that's going to happen?" And he wasn't just talking about the case. About the danger. He was talking about them. About the hot tension he felt every second he was with her.

Emily gave a brief nod. "You're going to need me, every step of the way."

Oh, he didn't doubt that. His body was already hard with need for her. The leftover battle-ready tension still coursed through him.

But she was right about the case too. Whether he liked it or not—and he most definitely did *not*—he needed her special gift to unmask the killer.

Together, they'd keep hunting the Night Butcher. Be partners, of a sort.

He'd make absolutely certain he watched her back. At all times.

The uniforms were talking quietly behind them. The siren no longer blared into the night, but the blue and white lights still lit the alley with a swirl of color.

He wanted to get the doc alone. Wanted to get her out of that damn smelly alley. Wanted to get her home, where she'd be safe.

Where he could hold her, strip her. Take her.

He'd leashed the beast when the uniforms arrived. Managed to stop the shift. But the adrenaline in his body was running thick and hard through his veins, and it was feeding the monster. Making it stronger. Making it want, making it need . . .

Emily.

His fingers tightened around hers. It was definitely time to call it a night. While he still could. "Come on," he muttered, "let's get the hell out of here." They could talk to the cops more later.

Emily glanced back along the alley. A small shiver worked its way over her body. Colin fought the urge to pull her against him, to warm her, to hold her.

Don't want the uniforms to see me do that. Gossip spreads in the PD like wildfire.

"The other person I sensed—" Emily bit her lip for a moment. "He was strong, Colin. Very strong."

"Was he a demon?" She'd mentioned Niol before. Had it been him? Had he been angry that they'd invaded his precious club? Had he sent his errand boys to try and give them a scare?

"Yes. A level ten, at least."

Again with the levels. He still wasn't sure what that meant, but he figured there was no way being a level-ten demon could be a good thing.

He needed to learn more about the demon world, and he needed to learn fast.

Colin started walking toward his Jeep, pulling Emily along with him. He couldn't see his vehicle, and he sure hoped the demons hadn't trashed his ride.

"Hey, Detective Gyth, wait, we need to—"

Colin threw a hard look over his shoulder. "I'll call the station," he snapped, cutting across the uniform's words. They'd been out in the open long enough. He wanted to get the doc to safety, and he wanted to get some answers from her.

"We need your statements, you just can't—"

"Yeah, I can." He kept walking. Giving a statement wasn't exactly his top priority right then. He needed to be careful what he revealed to the other cops. It wasn't like he could just say that a couple of demons had roughed him up.

The last time he'd tried talking about the *Other*, his partner hadn't taken it well.

No, Mike hadn't taken the situation at all well.

And when Colin had shifted, hoping to prove to his partner that his words were true, well, then things had truly gone to hell.

Because Mike, the guy who'd watched his back on the street, the guy who'd graduated by his side at the academy, had pulled his gun and tried to kill him.

Sometimes folks just didn't take well to the truth.

So lying was the only option.

It was a pity that a cop had to lie. But, well, lying was better than dying.

It was a philosophy that worked for him.

They rounded the street corner. The Jeep was waiting, not a scratch on it.

Colin exhaled a rough sigh of relief. He opened the passenger door for Emily, ushering her inside. He wanted to get out of that neighborhood, fast.

But he'd be back. He planned to come back and have a nice, long chat with Niol.

He didn't trust the demon, not for a minute.

Colin hurried around the Jeep and jumped inside. A patrol car cruised past him. Good. At least backup had arrived and they were searching for the perps.

Though it was doubtful they'd find the bastards.

He drove quickly through the night. Traffic was slim, the streets dark. Emily sat quietly beside him, but he could practically feel the hum of her thoughts.

He turned off the interstate, took a left at the stoplight.

"What the hell are you doing?" Emily had finally snapped out of her reverie. "This isn't the way to my house!"

No, it wasn't. Colin shifted easily and kept driving. "I'm not taking you home tonight." It'd be too dangerous. Those demons could be waiting for her.

Definitely not a risk he was willing to take.

Besides, he wanted her with him, wanted—

"Then where are you taking me?" From the corner of his eye, he saw her fingers clenching around the door handle.

"Relax, Doc."

"Where. Are. You. Taking. Me."

"My place."

"The hell you are!" He heard the faint scrape of her nails digging into the upholstery. "Turn this Jeep around and take me home."

"Sorry, Doc, no can do." Not that he wanted to, anyway. "In case you've forgotten, there are demons after us."

"I haven't forgotten—"

"And as an officer on the Atlanta PD, it's my responsibility to keep you safe." Oh, that sounded good. And it was true, mostly.

He *did* want to keep her safe.

He also wanted her.

So whether the doc liked it or not, she was going home with him.

And once they got to his place, well, what happened next would be entirely up to her.

Chapter 6

"You're playing He-man again," Emily muttered as she paced in front of the fireplace. She would not admit, *would not*, that she actually liked his place. Liked the homey, relaxed feel of the wooden house.

Colin had gone all king-of-the-jungle on her again. Hadn't asked if she wanted to spend the night at his place. No, he'd done the whole I'm-a-man-I'll-keep-you-safe routine on her. It made her want to scream.

"In case you've forgotten," she snapped, "I saved your ass tonight."

"And I saved yours." He was leaning against the fireplace mantel, his arms crossed over his chest. "Guess that makes us even."

"Even?" Not in her book. She hadn't kidnapped him.

"Relax, Doc. You can go back to your nice house tomorrow. But I can't let you leave tonight. It's too dangerous."

"And it won't be dangerous tomorrow?"

"Tomorrow those bastards might not be on the street. The uniforms could pick them up tonight." He stared at her, his blue gaze hard and determined. "Get used to the idea, Doc; you're staying here."

If she wanted, she could leave. She could stomp out of the house, use her cell phone, and call for a taxi to take her home. She didn't have to listen to Colin, but . . . dammit, he was right. It *was* safer for her to stay at his place for the night. Until they found out who'd sent those goons after them, it made sense to stick together, but she didn't have to like the situation.

And she definitely didn't like the idea of staying at Colin's house, *alone* with him.

Her heart was beating too fast, and a tight ball had lodged in her stomach from the moment she'd realized where Colin was taking her.

What would happen? What did she want to happen?

"Why don't you make yourself comfortable, Doc?" Colin inclined his head toward the couch. "I've got to go clean up." Then he was gone, disappearing down the hallway, quietly shutting a door behind him.

Emily frowned. The man had nearly ran from the room. Pretty much mid-argument. That was odd.

"Colin?" She stepped toward the hallway. The wooden floor creaked beneath her. "Colin, are you all right?" Now that she thought about it, there had been a tension on his face. And he'd looked the slightest bit pale.

He just fought off four men. It stands to reason the man would look pale and tense.

She crept forward. "Colin?"

A nagging worry filled her. What if he was hurt? Trying to hide his wounds?

She could hear the rush of running water. Emily paused next to a white door. The bathroom, she figured. She didn't want to burst in if nothing were wrong, but . . .

Something isn't right. Her instincts were on high alert. Her fingers curled around the doorknob. "Can you hear me?"

He jerked the door open. Stood gazing down at her, his chest bare, red water dripping from his fingers.

Red water. Blood. "Oh God, you're hurt!"

Colin stepped back, shoved his hands under the pouring water that sprayed from the faucet.

"Colin?" She grabbed his arm. Felt his muscles tense. "Dammit, where are you hurt?"

His hands clenched beneath the water. "The blood's not mine."

Not his? Emily yanked his hands up, stared at the now-glistening fingers. There wasn't so much as a scratch on him. She looked up, gazing into his eyes. He was close to her, so close that the warmth of his body surrounded her. Her eyes fell to his chest. Bare. Strong. Tight, with hard muscles. Covered with a light coating of midnight black hair.

Emily swallowed and realized that she was still holding his hands. Realized that her fingers had begun to stroke the back of his palms.

Realized that she wanted him.

Following Colin had been a mistake. "I-I should let you—" Do what? Finish stripping? The mental image that immediately flashed through her mind sent a wave of heat spiraling between her thighs. "Umm, I'll wait in the den." She was definitely sex deprived. One look at a man's chest and she was reduced to a stuttering mess.

Emily forced her hands to release his. The water still flowed behind her, and the sound seemed strangely loud in the small room.

She stepped to the side, intending to go, to collect her lost dignity as best she could.

"Don't run from me, Doc."

"I-I'm not running." Just walking—okay, creeping—away from the half-naked man who was making her very, very nervous.

His hands lifted, curled around the frames of her glasses, then slowly lifted them off her.

Emily blinked, trying to adjust her eyes to the sudden change. Colin stared down at her, and his eyes—they were filled with hunger.

For her.

"I'm not going to do it this time, Doc." He was staring at her lips now. Gazing at her with those hot, shining blue eyes.

Was it her imagination or were his eyes really, really bright right then?

His words registered after a heartbeat of time, and she didn't understand. "Do what?"

His arms snaked out, caught her around the middle, and pulled her ever closer to his body. She was trapped now, caged between the bathroom sink and Colin's equally hard body.

"Kiss you." He leaned forward, and his breath blew lightly against her. "I'm not going to kiss you. Unless you ask."

His lips were so close to hers. *So close.* But she hadn't come into the bathroom for this, hadn't followed him inside because she wanted *him,* had she?

"Come on, Doc. It won't be as hard as you think." There was nowhere for her to go, but Emily still tried to stumble back. She slipped against the edge of the sink.

Colin caught her before she fell. Lifted her up, sat her on the cold, granite vanity. Her legs were spread, and he inched forward, pushing right between them. The thick length of his aroused flesh pressed against her. The hard muscles of his thighs seemed to burn Emily through her clothing. She squirmed against him, and instead of working herself free, she just rubbed against him, rubbed against that heavy arousal.

Her sex clenched as a wave of raw hunger rocked through her. *No, this isn't what I planned.*

But it was exactly what she wanted.

"Do it." His voice was a rough rumble of temptation. His fingers were locked around her waist. She wanted him to lift his hands and cup her breasts. To push her shirt aside and take her nipples into his mouth.

"Ask for my kiss . . ." His breath blew against her lips.

She could already taste him. Her lips trembled, parted, and she heard herself whisper, "Kiss me." But she wasn't asking. She was demanding.

For an instant, his lips curled in a satisfied smile, but then the hunger in his eyes flared even brighter. His fingers tightened around her.

And his lips claimed hers.

He wasn't gentle. He wasn't cautious.

His lips took. His tongue probed, drove deep into her mouth. He tasted, seduced, *claimed.*

A growl sounded low in his throat. The sound was stark, animalistic. It should have scared her. *He* should have scared her.

But the sound just made her hotter. Made the liquid heat between her thighs pulse even more.

Her hands were wrapped around his arms, digging into the tight muscles of his biceps. Her mouth was open wide, her tongue rubbing, thrusting against his.

She loved the way he kissed her. Hard. Hot. Wild. Yes, most definitely wild.

He kissed her like he couldn't wait to get her naked beneath him. Kissed her like he had to have her.

Kissed her like no other man ever had.

His fingers brushed against the underside of her breasts. They rose slowly, then his hands were cupping her, his thumbs brushing against her nipples.

His mouth continued to feed on hers. His fingers—long, strong fingers—stroked her breasts, teased the aching peaks of her nipples.

She tore her mouth from his, moaning softly. She was still sitting on the sink. Her legs were spread wide. His thick arousal pushed against her. Her fingers itched to touch him, to stroke him.

This isn't like me. Emily fought to regain her control in the maelstrom of lust that was overwhelming her. She wasn't one to be driven wild with passion. Not her. Never her.

She was the calm one, the controlled one, the six-dates-before-third-base one.

But there was something about Colin, something that was driving straight past her barriers.

"I want to feel you," he muttered, the words hard, nearly indistinct. He caught the hem of her shirt, jerked it up and over her head. Colin tossed the shirt onto the floor. She heard the soft swish as it hit the tiled floor.

He was touching her now. Skin to skin. His warm fingers, slightly rough, were smoothing up her abdomen, inching closer to her breasts.

A thin black bra covered her. Her breasts pushed against the silky fabric.

Colin licked his lips.

Emily knew she should stop him. The logical part of her mind was screaming at her to push him away.

Not the time. Not the time.

Things were moving too fast between them. But, God, she wanted him to touch her.

She wanted to let go of her control for just a moment. She wanted to *feel*.

Yes, part of her was screaming that she should push him away, but part of her was also demanding that she pull him even closer.

His fingers slipped under the edge of her bra. Stroked, then found her nipples. The nubs were tight, hungry, and when he shoved the bra to the side and lifted her breasts in his hands, she could see the dark pink of her aroused flesh.

"I've got to taste you."

His head lowered toward her breast. His mouth opened; she felt the hot stir of his breath against her, then his tongue, God, his tongue swirled around the areola. A long, teasing lick that had every muscle in her body tightening.

"Oh, that's good." He drew in a deep breath, then his tongue rubbed against her nipple. "Damn good." He took her breast into his mouth, sucking strongly, drawing the peak deep inside and using his tongue, his teeth.

Her hands rose, fisted in his hair. She pulled him tighter to her, loving the demanding pull of his mouth.

Her hips were rocking against his cock. Riding him. She could feel a warm wetness on her panties. Damn. When was the last time she'd gotten turned on like this? So fast?

Never.

His left hand lifted, lightly pinched her nipple while his mouth kept working her other breast.

Oh Jesus.

She squeezed her thighs around him.

A hard coil of tension tightened inside her.

Colin lifted his head. Her fingers were still buried in the thick, black mane of his hair.

He kissed her, thrust his tongue deep. His right hand gripped her thigh, his fingers so close to her mound that she trembled in anticipation.

The drumming of her heartbeat filled her ears. Her breathing was coming hard and fast. Her body felt too hot, too tight.

And she realized with a sense of dazed shock that she was moments away from having sex with Colin.

His lips were glistening. And behind his lips, just for a moment, she caught a glimpse of . . . fangs?

Fangs?

She yanked her hands away from him.

"You want me," he rumbled, and she saw his nostrils flare. "I can smell your need."

Not the most flattering comment, but one that was damn true. She did want him. Wanted him so much she'd soaked her panties. Wanted him so much that she was minutes, hell, maybe even seconds away from coming.

Emily glanced down at her legs. His hands were on both thighs now, the warm weight of his fingers seeming to scorch her through her pants.

His nails . . . they looked longer than before. Sharper.

Of course they look longer. The man's a shifter, for God's sake. You know the beast likes to play during sex.

The beast was always close to the surface during sex. That was why shifters were so notoriously sexual.

She was about to have sex with a *shifter*. A shifter she still knew *damn little* about.

"I'll make it good for you, Doc." Colin growled the words as he lowered his head to her neck. She felt the rough rasp of his tongue on her throat, and a shiver skated over her. *Oh yeah, it'd be good between us. I don't doubt it.*

His mouth pressed against her, the sharp edge of his teeth grazing her skin.

"Stop!" Damn, but that word had been hard to say. And

instead of coming out as a shout, it sounded as a hoarse whisper.

Colin froze.

Emily drew in her breath, held it. Her body was still screaming for release, but her mind had finally taken control again.

She couldn't do this, not yet. There was too much she didn't know about the detective.

His hands tightened around her thighs. "You sure that's what you want?" His voice was gravelly, hard with lust and need.

She wanted him to drive that long, thick cock into her. She wanted to shut off her mind and just feel.

It was too late now. The voice of reason in her head was screaming at her, and she couldn't ignore the voice. Dammit.

The last time she'd ignored that little voice, she'd fallen for the wrong man and ended up unconscious on the floor of Paradise Found. Then she'd had a not-so-nice two-week stint in the hospital.

Colin was just as strong as Myles, she'd bet her life on it. Shifters didn't have demon levels, but they had their own power scale. She'd seen the way he'd taken down the demons who attacked them.

And when a guy was that strong, he was also very, very dangerous.

Her hands pushed between them. She crossed her arms over her chest, covering her breasts.

Colin drew in a long, hard breath. A muscle flexed along his jaw, and she saw the struggle for control flash in his eyes.

After one moment, two, he lifted his hands, stepped back.

"Like to tease, do you, Doc?"

His words lashed right to her heart. They should have pissed her off, but she knew that he was right. She had teased. Gotten them both ready, minutes from release, then pulled back. Emily wrenched her bra into place. "Things got"—*wild, hot*—"out of control."

Colin's hand ran through his hair.

Emily slid off the sink. Water was still pouring behind her. With slightly shaking fingers, she jerked the handle, stopping the flow.

"You wanted me."

She couldn't very well deny that. She'd been clawing the man, moaning, rubbing her body against his.

"You still want me." His knuckles grazed down her bare arm. "Don't you?"

Emily lifted her chin. "Sometimes we don't get what we want." *Because what we want may not be good for us.*

She swallowed, fought to hold tight to her own newly found control. How could she hunger so much for someone that she feared?

"Sometimes we do." But his hand dropped away. "Sometimes all it takes is a little waiting."

Emily scooped up her shirt. "I didn't mean for things to go so far." *So fast.* She hadn't realized need would explode with the touch of his lips, his hands, against her.

"Then how far did you mean for them to go?" It was then that she heard the icy edge in his voice that alerted her to his rage.

Well, hell, what had she expected? That the guy would be all thrilled that she'd stopped their lovemaking? Not likely. She jerked on her shirt.

"Tell me, Doc. I really want to know." He rolled his shoulders back, and the muscles in his chest rippled. "How far did you want to go? A few kisses? A few feels through your clothes? One lick on your breast?"

A flash of heat stained her cheeks. Oh yes, Colin was definitely pissed.

"So I'm good enough for a little light play but not good enough for a fuck?"

Okay, enough was enough. Emily's eyes narrowed on him. "I don't know you well enough for a fuck, Detective." She sure as hell didn't go around giving those out to strangers.

His lips thinned.

"And for the record, I'm not a first-date-screw type of

woman." Despite what she'd just done. Emily shook her head. "I want you, yes, I won't deny it, but I'm not screwing you tonight." No, she wasn't about to make herself that vulnerable to him, not until—

"Sonofabitch." Understanding flashed across his face. "You're scared of me."

Not of him so much as what he was. Time to cut to the chase. "What kind of shifter are you, Colin?" He had claws, sharp teeth. She'd seen both of those telling changes. Ruled out snakes. And it hadn't been the look of a bird or even a bear.

His hands fisted at his sides. "So that's what this is about. You don't want to screw a shifter."

"No." Her back teeth were beginning to ache from the whole grinding exercise she was doing. "It's not that."

"Isn't it?" There was a sharp bite to his words. "You've been acting skittish around me from the moment we met, from the moment you realized what I was."

"I'm not saying no because you're a shifter." Confession time. "I've actually been with a shifter before." The affair had been very, very brief and back when she'd been a grad student.

"Then what the hell is it?"

"You're going too fast!" Everything was going too fast. "I just met you a few days ago and—" Damn, why stop now? "I'm not sure I can trust you, Gyth. Shifters have a reputation." Some would say a very well-deserved reputation. "And while I don't know what beast you carry, I think he's strong, and he's dangerous. And before I crawl into bed with you, I want to *know* more about what's going on in your head." *And in the head of the beast you carry.*

Because there was a chance, a very definite chance, that Colin was one of the shifters that folks knew to give a very wide berth. A panther. A cougar. *A wolf.*

"You wanna know me?" The force of his feelings, his anger, his need, his . . . fear, lapped at her. "Then why don't you just take a peek inside my mind?"

Oh, she was tempted. It would be so easy. But . . .

It would also be wrong. Because once she stepped inside his mind, she wouldn't get a glimpse of just his life. No, if she went in, fully in, she'd see everything. Every secret. Every lie. Every fear. *Everything.*

And she didn't think that either of them were ready for that.

Emily shook her head. "That's not the way for us."

"Then what is the way?"

She stared up into his eyes. "To take some time."

"Shit." His hands slowly unfurled. "I'm not good at being a gentleman, Doc."

Yes, she'd rather figured that one out already.

"But I'll do it." He reached out, stroked her cheek. "For now." The rage had dimmed in his eyes, but the hunger remained.

His hand felt so warm against her.

His fingers trailed over her lips. "Just don't make me wait too long. I won't be a gentleman forever." Then he stepped back, clearing her way.

Emily snagged her glasses, drew in a deep breath, and was immediately wrapped in his rich, masculine scent. "Wh-where should I sleep?" Jesus, she was stuttering like some kind of schoolgirl.

"Well, I'd hoped you'd sleep with me." Yes, that was another point she'd managed to figure out on her own.

"But since I'm not . . ." Her brows lifted as she stared meaningfully up at him.

His lips hitched into a half smile. "Since you're not, you can take the bed and I'll take the couch."

"Wow. You are trying to be a gentleman, aren't you? I'm impressed." And she was also planning to jump on his offer. Bed versus couch. She'd definitely be selfish and take the cushy choice.

Emily brushed by him.

"It's the second door on the right, Doc." His hand slipped down her back, rested for the briefest of moments on the curve of her buttocks. "Have good dreams."

Since her dreams would probably all be about him, and he'd be naked in them, she figured her dreams would definitely be good, if extremely frustrating.

It was going to be a long night.

And she didn't even have dry panties to change into. Talk about sucking.

He gazed up at the doctor's house. All of the windows were black. Had been black all night.

She hadn't come home. He'd waited for her, waited hours to see her, and she hadn't come home.

Where was she? *Where?*

A slow rage had been building inside of him. Building, building . . .

The demon was out tonight. She was somewhere in the city, working her evil.

He couldn't let her continue. Couldn't let her keep attacking innocents.

He would stop her.

Evil had to be destroyed.

She had to be destroyed.

Soon. The doctor's time would run out.

The demon would die.

Chapter 7

"I think it's time for an *Other 101* lesson."

Emily glanced up from her files, brows raised, as Colin walked into her office.

Vanessa stood behind him, a rather sheepish expression on her face. "Sorry, boss, but when he found out you weren't with a client—"

"I decided to let myself in." He flashed her a smile and strolled toward the couch. "We need to talk."

"Well, that *is* what most people do when they come here," she murmured. She looked back at Vanessa, certain her assistant had heard the *Other 101* comment. Since Vanessa was *Other*, a hereditary witch, she figured it didn't really matter. Vanessa had been with her for five years, and Emily trusted her to keep quiet about the cases and people in her office. "It's all right, Vanessa. I can talk to the detective for a few minutes." Until her twelve o'clock arrived, anyway.

Vanessa's eyes narrowed, and Emily realized she wasn't quite as taken with Mr. Sexy Voice as she'd been when he'd called on the phone.

"Fine." Vanessa's plump lips had little white lines around them. "But next time"—she jabbed an index finger in the air toward him—"he'd better wait until I escort him inside."

"Sorry." Colin looked anything but.

Vanessa spun on her heel and marched out, shutting the door smartly behind her.

Perhaps a mild warning was in order here. After all, the man had come asking for information on the *Other*. "If I were you, I probably wouldn't make her angry."

He lowered himself onto the sofa. The leather creaked beneath his weight. "Cause she's a witch?"

Emily blinked. How had he—

Colin laughed. "Don't look so shocked, Doc. I might not have your handy little gift, but I am a detective. Trained to observe." He winked. "And I observed her reading a spell book when I walked inside the lobby."

Mental note. *Tell Vanessa to keep her private reading material at home.*

She cleared her throat. "Just what is it that you want to know?" She was trying to keep things professional between them, trying hard despite the fact that she'd awoken less than five hours ago to find him standing at the foot of her bed— *his bed*—wearing only a towel wrapped low on his hips and gazing at her with lust in his eyes.

She shifted her legs beneath the desk, feeling warmth rush through her at the memory. He'd told her he'd come inside for some clothes. But she could tell he'd wanted more than clothing. The thick bulge of his arousal would have clued in even the most naive of women.

And after a night of dreaming about him, she'd wanted more, too.

But Colin had turned away from her, grabbed a handful of clothes from his closet, then disappeared.

He'd taken her home less than thirty minutes later, and after he'd done a thorough check of her house, he'd left her.

He'd kissed her, then he'd left her. A hard, swift kiss that she could still feel.

"So this is where the magic happens, huh?" He wasn't lying on the couch, but sitting up, hands draped over his knees.

"I don't necessarily think of it as magic," she said carefully. Magic was a word generally reserved for the *Other*. They had magical powers. She was just a human who had a high psychic sensitivity to the *Other*.

"Umm." He cocked his head to the side. "Tell me about them."

"Them?"

"The *Other*." His eyes never left hers. "I realized last night that I know damn little about"—a brief hesitation, then—"my kind. And that lack of knowledge could get me into some serious shit."

Ah, yes, it could. "You've known others like yourself before, of course?" She'd figured it'd be better if they started with something he knew. They could begin with shifters and then build from there.

"I've met a few others. Haven't exactly had deep meaningful conversations with 'em, if you know what I mean. And I've seen some vamps, a few demons—"

"What?" The pen she'd absently picked up fell from her fingers. *Haven't exactly had deep meaningful conversations?* He made it sound as if other shifters were as foreign to him as vampires. "But your parents—"

"They died when I was a couple of months old." He shrugged as if it didn't matter to him, as if it were just some random event that had happened long ago and didn't have any meaning to him now. "I got put in foster care after that."

Her breath rushed out in a fast expulsion. "What did you think was happening the first time you changed?" To shift without someone around for guidance, God, it must have been a nightmare.

He turned his head. Gazed out the window. "I thought I was dying."

Emily said nothing. Just waited.

"My bones snapped, twisted." His lips thinned. "Do you know what it's like to hear the crunch of your own bones?"

No, she didn't. "B-but I didn't think the change was painful." She'd been told it sometimes felt like a mild sunburn spreading through a person's body.

"The first time it is. Damn painful. Like your insides are exploding. Everything reshapes, transforms. My nails changed first, grew into claws. Then my teeth—they got sharper, longer.

Then the fur grew." Colin stopped, shaking his head. He looked back at her, and she could see the painful shadows of his past in the depths of his eyes. "I tried to call for help, but by that time I didn't have a human's voice anymore."

"Once you'd changed, how did you feel then?"

"Like a freak."

Emily grabbed her pad, began jotting notes by rote. *Traumatic first shift. No knowledge of his kind.*

"I was an animal." His jaw clenched tight. "I didn't know what the hell had happened to me or how the hell I was going to change back. And for a while I thought . . ."

Her pen was poised over the pad. "What did you think?"

His eyes narrowed, dropped to the pen and paper. "I'm not one of your patients, Doc. I don't need an analysis."

Her fingers tightened around the cool metal base of the ballpoint pen. "I thought you might want to talk about—"

"About what? My screwed-up childhood? The ten foster homes I lived in? The first time I changed into a damn animal and thought I was going insane?"

Actually, yes. The pen scribbled across the pad. *Feared insanity. Serious hostility issues.*

"Emily."

She froze. Lifted her head to stare at him.

Colin rose and stalked toward her. He leaned over her desk, bracing his hands on the old wood. "I don't need you to poke around in my past and figure out why—" For a moment, his gaze dropped to the pad and his lips tightened as he said, "I've got *hostility issues.*"

She decided it would be best not to point out right then that he was definitely exhibiting said hostility issues. So she tried to be tactful. "Some people think the key to a successful future is facing a painful past."

"Then those people are fucking idiots. A painful past needs to be shoved in a cold, dark grave and left to rot."

Well, that was one perspective. Very carefully, Emily placed her pen down. "I shouldn't have started to—" She broke off, clearing her throat, and realized that she was embarrassed.

Slipping into psychologist mode was second nature to her. And Colin's pain, it had just called out to her. She licked her lips, tried again, "I shouldn't—"

"Shouldn't have started screwing with my head?"

Her eyes narrowed. "I wasn't screwing with your head, as you so kindly put it."

"Lady, you make a living screwing with people's minds." He leaned forward another inch.

She didn't like the way he was towering over her. Asserting his dominance. Showing that he was the big, strong detective and she was the psychologist who needed to mind her own business.

Her own temper began to spark. Emily shoved to her feet. "I was trying to *help* you, Gyth. In case you haven't noticed, you're carrying around a hell of a lot of baggage." And rage. Lots of rage.

She placed her hands deliberately on the table and leaned into him. Close enough to kiss. Or hit. And she was very tempted to do both.

Colin stared back at her, those crystal blue eyes of his glinting with emotion. "I told you about my past because I was talking to *you*, Emily Drake. Not the Monster Doctor."

Understanding filled her. "It's hard for me to stop being the Monster Doctor." Her voice was softer. She'd been working with the *Other* for so long, trying to heal their minds, and she'd nearly forgotten how to turn off the doctor.

"We're way off topic," he muttered, and stepped back, rolling his shoulders. "I didn't come here to drag up my shitty childhood."

Emily licked her lips and realized that she'd very nearly screwed things up with Colin. She needed to think more like a woman with him and less like a psychologist. "Right. Sorry." And she was. Sorry that she'd pressured him, sorry that she'd tried to make him into a patient.

"Just don't try it again, Doc."

That she couldn't promise. "Look, Colin, it's kinda hard to turn off, you know?" He'd been on her couch, in her office, and when he'd started talking she'd slipped into counselor mode.

"Try."

Her eyes narrowed. "I'll see what I can do, and, hey, how about you try not to be such a jerk?"

He blinked, obviously caught off guard by the insult she'd just delivered in her soft, I'm-a-Professional voice.

Then he tossed back his head and laughed.

Emily fought the smile that curved her lips. Good. Looked like they were back on even ground.

"Agreed." Colin strolled around her office, eyeing her bookshelves and the framed Rorschach inkblot pictures on her walls.

After a few moments, he said, "I need to know about them. Need to know what I'm gonna be dealing with."

Yes, she understood that. Colin was ill prepared to deal with the world of the *Other,* especially considering his own rough introduction to the *Other* world. But before she could begin his lessons, there were a few other questions that she needed to ask.

"So you've come across other shifters?" All of the *Other* were born with an instinctive ability to recognize their own kind. Demons saw through the veil of glamour to other demons. Shifters could scent one another, thanks to their heightened sense of smell. Witches and wizards felt the power pull of their brethren.

Like to like. It was the way it had always been.

And for whatever reason, Emily had been born with the ability to sense them all. Even though she wasn't kindred to any of them.

Colin touched the spine of one of her books. "Yeah, I have. Once or twice."

"You could . . . smell them, right? Smell the difference between a shifter and a human?" As far as she knew, shifters didn't see the beasts they carried. They didn't know about the golden glow that cloaked their bodies. It was just something she saw.

"Yeah, I can smell 'em." He shook his head. "We all smell like animals."

Her nose wrinkled at that. She rather liked the way Colin smelled.

"Well, all the *Other* have a way of sensing their kind. Demons can look through the glamour and see the black eyes that mark them, witches feel a surge of power in the air when another is close, djinn can hear the thoughts of others like them, charmers can—"

He glanced back at her, a black brow raised. "What's a charmer?"

"You've heard of snake charmers, right?"

Colin nodded. "Big in India. Those guys who carry around cobras in baskets."

"Right." Well, partially right. "Charmers are beings who can communicate with certain animals. They can talk to them." Some charmers talked to snakes, some to birds, some to dogs or cats.

"Just how many types of *Other* exist?"

Oh, now that was a hard one. "Think of every legend of every magical being you've ever heard and then imagine all those stories are true. Then you've got the *Other*." Hundreds, thousands of types. Some kind and benevolent. Some downright evil and dangerous.

Just like humans.

"This city seems to have more than its share of supernaturals. When I lived in Grisam, Illinois, there weren't any others like me."

"Well, yes, but if you'd gone to Chicago, you would have found dozens of SBs." They liked the big cities. Loved them, in fact. "Think about it, Colin. Where is it easier to hide? In small-town America, where your neighbors know every move you make? Or would you want to go to a big city where—"

"You could disappear into a crowd and no one would give a shit what you were doing," Colin finished for her.

"Exactly." She waited a bit and then, because she really couldn't help herself, asked, "Isn't that why you came here?"

"Yeah, yeah, I guess it is." He ran a hand through his hair. "Let's talk about the demons first."

"What do you want to know?"

"They're fast healers, right?" At the slight inclination of her head, he continued, "What's the deal with the power-level thing you keep mentioning? Level one, level two—what does that mean?"

"Demons can work magic, just like witches can. A low-level demon, a one or a two, can do small things, like light a candle or make a breeze blow through a room. But a level nine or ten"—this was the bad part, the very bad part—"they can stir tornadoes, start five-alarm fires, and even steal the minds of others."

"*What?*" He paced toward her, brows furrowed. "You're telling me those bastards can control humans?"

"Sometimes." That was how the idea of demon possession had first come into being. "If a demon is strong enough, he can push his way into someone's mind, can control the person or, at the least, incapacitate him."

Colin walked around her desk, came to stand less than a foot away from her. "Is that what happened to you?"

"Wh-what do you mean?" There was a faint line of stubble on his jaw. And far too much knowledge in his eyes.

"You told me you were nearly put into a coma once by an *Other*. The guy who did it, he was a demon, wasn't he? One of those level nines or tens."

No sense denying it. "Yes."

She watched a muscle flex along his jaw. "Where is he now?" There was a banked rage in his voice, and for an instant, she saw the glow of the beast in his eyes.

"It doesn't matter. That was years ago." And Myles couldn't hurt anyone with his magic, not anymore. "I told you before, he burned out." *She'd* burned out the bastard.

"Would his powers have worked on me?" Before she could answer, he continued, "Niol tried something on me back at the bar. I could feel the hard shift in the air, but nothing happened."

"No." Shifters were the most powerful of the supernatural beings because they didn't have just one body and one soul. Shifters had two. And the strength that came from that double bond was too strong for demons to touch. "A powerful shifter is the only *Other* that can match a demon's strength."

"Well, that's something then." His jaw clenched, and for a moment his eyes seemed to glitter. "How the fuck did you meet a guy like that anyway?"

Emily swallowed. She'd wondered when he'd ask. And since she'd pushed her way into his private life earlier, well, she figured he deserved to know about her past too.

"Was he your lover?"

She shook her head. "No, he was—" Damn. What had he been? "All my life, I've never fit in with the humans. They don't understand me, and I doubt they ever will."

He watched her silently, and she knew that he understood.

"When I was eighteen, I stumbled into Niol's bar, pulled by the magic I could feel in the air. He knew I was human, of course, but he let me in. I think I amused him." And he'd watched her, always watched her with those fathomless black eyes of his.

"Niol was the one who introduced me to Myles." She'd felt the black waves of Niol's power right from the start, and she'd generally steered clear of him. After he'd arranged for her to meet Myles, well, then she'd known what a true bastard Niol was.

Colin stiffened. "Myles?"

"The charming demon who attacked me at Paradise."

His hands fisted.

"You know, sometimes I wonder about that. Sometimes I think . . ."

"What?"

"That Niol was testing me." Emily shook her head. "But that doesn't really make sense, does it?" Yet it was a suspicion she couldn't shake. Niol had casually introduced Myles to her one night as she'd stood, swaying to the music of the band. Every night she'd gone back to Paradise, Myles had been there, waiting for her. Always kind. Always the gentleman.

Until the night he'd attacked her.

And Niol had been watching from the shadows.

"I don't think a hell of a lot about that bastard Niol makes sense."

Yes, he was probably right.

The alarm on her wrist began to vibrate. Emily exhaled heavily. Time for her twelve o'clock with Margie.

Colin frowned and the faint lines around his eyes deepened. "What in the hell is that?"

Good old shifter hearing. Emily held up her arm. "My alarm. It's time for my next patient." And she was glad. It was a reprieve, of sorts, for her.

"In other words, you mean it's time for me to leave." Some of the tension faded from his expression, and his lips hitched into a half smile. "That's fine, Doc. I'll see you tonight."

"Tonight?"

"Sure." His hand lifted, cupped her cheek. "When I come over."

Her stomach tightened. In anticipation, not fear. "I don't remember inviting you over."

Colin's head lowered toward hers. "We've got to finish our lesson."

Other 101. "Umm, right."

One black brow rose. "Is that disappointment I hear?"

She flushed. Way to be transparent. "I—"

His lips brushed against hers. Warm. Wet. Open.

God, but she liked the way he kissed. Liked the slow thrust of his tongue into her mouth. And the man tasted good. Like rich chocolate, and she'd always been a serious sucker for chocolate.

He pulled away slowly. "You know, Doc, I'm glad as hell to know that you weren't Niol's lover."

So was she.

"And now that I've been in your office, I'm going to have fantasies."

She was already having a few of her own.

Colin spared a glance for her couch. "Mainly, I'll picture that couch. With you on it, naked, of course."

Of course. Damn. It was hot. She shouldn't have worn the black turtleneck.

Ah, hell, she couldn't even kid herself. She was just damn turned on. Because she could picture him on her couch too. And in her fantasies, he was most definitely naked.

Down, girl. You've got a patient waiting. It's not the right time for wild sex.

"I'll see you tonight." His hand fell away.

"O-Okay."

Colin strolled toward the door. Emily followed slowly behind him, trying to calm her racing heart.

"Good afternoon, Dr. Drake!" Margie's cheery voice greeted her the moment she stepped into the lobby.

Emily forced a friendly smile. She liked Margie, truly enjoyed their sessions, but at that moment she could have easily cursed the elderly woman's penchant for perfect punctuality.

A few minutes to get her body back under control . . . that's all she wanted.

"Hello, Margie."

In her late seventies, with a mane of salt and pepper hair, Margie was the epitome of elegance. She was dressed in immaculate, very high-end clothing, and a cloud of French perfume hung in the air around her.

A large wicker basket sat on the chair beside her. A basket that was currently hissing.

Colin halted, slanted a quick look at Margie and her basket.

Margie smiled innocently back at him.

"Hello, ma'am."

The basket hissed, a very loud, very disgruntled hiss that cut straight through Colin's words.

Emily cleared her throat. *Time to intervene before Colin gets too friendly with my patient.* "Thanks for stopping by, Detective. I'll look forward to our next meeting."

He tore his gaze away from the basket. "Me too, Doc. Me too."

Then he was gone.

"Hmmmph." The grumble came from Vanessa, who was currently on the exact opposite end of the room from Margie and her basket. In fact, Vanessa looked like she was trying to disappear into the wallpaper.

Vanessa didn't enjoy Margie's visits as much as Emily did. But in all honesty, her distaste had nothing to do with Margie personally.

Emily motioned for her client to follow her inside the main office.

She shut the door with a decisive click and watched as her client carefully sat the basket down onto the couch. Then Margie lifted the round lid.

The hisses were much, much louder now.

Emily crossed to her desk. Picked up her pen. "What seems to be the issue today?"

Margie pulled a large albino Burmese python from the basket, her fingers smoothing over its brightly colored body. The snake stretched beneath her touch, the orange and yellow marks across its long length immediately catching Emily's eye.

Then the snake hissed again.

"Oh, George, stop it." Margie frowned at the snake. "He's been like this for the last two days. Hissing, hissing, hissing. But he won't say a dang word to me."

Emily picked up her pad. *Silent treatment from George, again.*

"It started when I had a gentleman caller on Friday." Margie flushed a bit. "Well, George took one look at him and tried to constrict around his leg . . ."

"Heard you had a bit of excitement last night." Brooks leaned back in his chair and steepled his fingers beneath his chin. "Got jumped in an alley with your pretty psychologist, huh?" There was a touch of humor in his voice, but genuine concern shone in his eyes.

"Yeah, some punks"—*demons*—"caught us as we were leaving Paradise Found." He shook his head. "The uniforms sent out patrols, but"—Colin shrugged—"in that part of town, it's easy to disappear if you don't want to get caught."

Colin pulled out the Myers file. "Hey, tell me, did you interview the girlfriend?"

"Yeah." Brooks whistled softly as he leaned back in his chair. "One of those pretty, cover-girl types, a little too thin for my taste, but still—"

"Where was Gillian when Preston was killed?" Colin asked, cutting through his words. You had to do that when Brooks started talking about a pretty woman. Otherwise, the guy would just go on and on.

Brooks blinked. "Who the hell is Gillian?" He leaned forward, sitting straighter and motioning to the file. "The guy's girlfriend was a Hilary Bishop. You know her, she's the mayor's niece and—"

"I've got it on pretty good authority that the vic was involved with a Gillian Nemont." He paused a beat, waiting for the name to register. "Does the name ring a bell?"

His partner shook his head. "Never heard of her. And neither has the vic's family, friends, or neighbors." He smiled, his innocent-trust-me smile. "And believe me, if they knew about her, *I* would know by now."

"We need to find her," Colin said, tapping the file against the edge of his desk. *So Gillian had been the vic's dirty little secret . . .*

But had she been the secret that had led to his murder?

Only one way to find out.

Less than an hour later, Colin and Brooks stood in front of Gillian's apartment. When they saw that the lock was broken, that the door swayed drunkenly on its hinges, both men reached for their guns.

"I'll cover you." Brooks mouthed the words.

Colin nodded. He crouched near the wall, banged his fist against the wooden door. "Gillian Nemont! This is the police! We need to talk to you!"

No response, but then, based on the condition of the lock, he hadn't really expected one.

One more try. "Ms. Nemont! We're coming in!" He lifted his gun, took a deep breath, and shoved open her door.

He sprang inside, still crouching, searching the room in one fast glance.

The place had been trashed. Chairs were overturned, and the sofa was slashed to bits. Papers and books littered the floor.

Colin started inching around the right wall, heading toward what he thought was the bedroom. Brooks took the left wall.

Colin turned the corner. Found more chaos. A broken mirror, smashed dresser.

But no Gillian.

"Looks like someone beat us here," Brooks murmured as he lowered his gun. "Damn, the woman sure must have pissed someone off." He exhaled slowly.

Colin pushed his way to the small closet. "Her clothes are gone." Not tossed onto the floor. Not shredded. Just gone.

He crossed to the bathroom. Brooks was already in the small room, looking around at the broken shards that had once been a vanity mirror.

"I don't see a toothbrush, or toothpaste." Brooks looked up at him. "Looks like our girl got out before the trasher arrived."

"We need to get a crime scene unit in here." Colin reached for his cell phone. He'd only touched the door when he'd entered. Maybe they'd get lucky and find some prints in the apartment.

"What are the odds," Brooks began slowly as they made their way back to the front door, "that this woman's apartment—a woman you say was Preston's lover—just happened to be vandalized?"

"I'd say the odds are pretty high . . . that Gillian knows something." But if she was on the run, and it sure looked like she was, then they'd have a damn hard time finding her.

"You think he found what he was looking for?" Brooks scanned the living room, his eyes darting over the broken furniture, the smashed computer screen.

Colin shrugged as he punched in the number for the CSU. "Could be he wasn't looking for anything."

Brooks lifted a brow. "Think this was a message?"

They'd both seen situations like that before, of course. Homes trashed, cars vandalized, all to make witnesses too scared to talk to the cops.

"Yeah, I think it was."

His partner's brown eyes narrowed as he studied the floor. Crouching, he pulled out a pair of latex gloves from his back pocket.

"What've you got?"

Brooks shoved aside wood from the coffee table. "Looks like a day planner." He lifted a small, blue book. "Maybe we can track our girl's movements before she decided to skip out."

Decided to skip out. Nice phrasing. "Don't you mean before she ran as fast as she could from the psycho on her trail?"

"Yeah, that's what I meant." He flipped through the planner, skimming past the pages. "Let's just see what our lady had planned for the day of Preston's murder." He whistled. "Well, I'll be damned."

The CSU operator had picked up. He was asking for the scene's address. "Hold on." Colin's eyes narrowed. "What is it?"

Brooks lifted the planner. "Take a look at Gillian's one o'clock appointment."

His eyes tracked down the page. Saw the small, neat feminine scrawl. *2301 Mistro Tower. Dr. Drake.*

A hard tension swept through him. 2301 Mistro Tower. That was Doc's office. Gillian Nemont had been to see Emily.

"Did the good doctor happen to mention that she knew Ms. Nemont?" Brooks's voice was cool.

On the ride over, Colin had told him that it was he and Emily who had discovered the identity of Preston's lover. Of course, he hadn't mentioned the fact that a demon had tipped them off.

And now it looked like he might not be the only one withholding facts from a partner.

"Did she?" Brooks pressed, and there was suspicion in his eyes.

The CSU operator was muttering in his ear.

"No," Colin finally said, his voice very soft. "She didn't."

And he sure as hell planned to find out why the doc hadn't mentioned that important little fact.

Chapter 8

Colin arrived at her place just after eight, and the minute he walked into her house, Emily knew something was wrong.

Hell, it didn't take a psychic gift to figure out the man was angry.

Colin stalked past her without a word and jerked off his rather beaten-up jacket.

"Well, hello to you, too," she muttered, shutting the door. After the kiss in her office, she'd certainly been expecting a different greeting.

Correction, she'd been expecting a greeting, period. "Guess you had a bad day at the office, huh?" She trailed behind him. After just one visit, the guy sure seemed to be making himself at home.

Colin tossed his jacket onto the couch, then began to pace in front of the fireplace. "Bad day? You could say that." A muscle ticked along his jaw. "I need to ask you a few questions, Doc."

He sounded serious. Very serious. A nervous flutter tickled her stomach. "Uh, okay." She sat on the couch, pushed his jacket to the side, and tried not to dwell on the fact that the evening was not going according to plan.

"Why didn't you tell me that you knew Gillian Nemont?"

She blinked. "What?"

He stalked toward her. "You heard me."

Emily shook her head. "I didn't tell you because I don't know her." What, did the guy think she'd been holding out on him?

"She had an appointment to meet with you last Friday. At one."

"No," she told him, meeting that piercing blue stare head-on, "she didn't."

His head cocked to the side. "Your name was in her day planner. Your address."

"I'm telling you, I don't know the woman. Look, why don't you just ask her and—"

"Can't do that. Gillian Nemont is missing."

"Missing?" Oh, that didn't sound good.

"Neighbors said they saw her last Wednesday. She stuffed a suitcase in her car and left as fast as she could." He was watching her with expressionless eyes, waiting, gauging her response. "She hasn't been to work since then."

She felt his suspicion, heavy in the air. "Look, Colin, I don't know the woman and—"

"She's not a patient?"

"I just said I didn't know her!"

"But you'd protect your patients, wouldn't you, Doc?"

There was too much insinuation in that question for her to ignore. Emily shot to her feet. "I'd protect their confidentiality, yes, but I wouldn't protect someone who was involved in a murder, if that's what you're asking." Asking, implying, same damn thing in her book.

Her heart was racing now, her fists clenched. Colin thought she'd been lying to him, thought that she might even be protecting a killer.

Talk about a lack of trust.

But you don't trust him either, not completely. Or else you would have made love with him last night, a nagging inner voice reminded her.

It looked like they both had trust issues. Not a good sign. "If you don't believe me, why don't you just go ask Vanessa? She'll tell you that I didn't treat Gillian."

"My partner is interviewing her right now." He crossed his arms over his chest. "So if there is anything you need to come clean about, Doc, now's the time."

The bastard. "I'm working this investigation with you." In case he'd forgotten. "I'm not one of your suspects, and I sure as hell don't appreciate being treated like one."

A faint beeping sounded from her kitchen. *Dinner.*

Emily pushed past him. She felt like an idiot now. An absolute idiot. There was no way the two of them were going to sit down for a romantic dinner. The jerk thought she was— aw, hell, she didn't even know what he thought.

She opened the oven and took out the lasagna she'd so painstakingly prepared. A master chef she certainly was not. But over the years, she'd learned how to perfect a few dishes, and her lasagna was one of them.

She placed the dish on the stove top, turned—

And found Colin standing in the doorway, a bemused look in his eyes as he took in the tidily set table, the two plates, the two candles.

Heat rushed into her cheeks, and it wasn't due to the warmth of her oven.

"You cooked."

Well, wasn't he just Commander Obvious.

And wasn't she just the queen of stupid? He'd told her that he was coming over to talk about the *Other,* not for a date.

But she'd still wasted all that time on the meal. Wasted time showering and dressing. She'd even left her hair down, not that Colin had seemed to notice.

"Yeah, well, I have to eat," she muttered, crossing her arms over her chest. How was she going to get him out of her house?

His nostrils twitched. "Smells good."

"Umm." Her right foot began to tap. She decided to try the direct approach. "I want you to leave."

Colin blinked.

"Now, actually. I want you to leave now." Before she got even angrier.

He shook his head. "We need to talk more about the case—"

"You mean you want to question me more." From profiler to suspect in twenty-four hours. She bet that didn't happen often.

In fact, she bet it happened only to her.

The Monster Doctor strikes again.

His lips thinned. "I'm doing my job. I have to ask—"

The distinctive chime of a cell phone ring cut through his words.

Emily arched a brow. "Bet that's Brooks." Calling to report about his talk with Vanessa.

Colin growled and jerked out his phone.

Emily stared straight at him, eager to hear at least his part of the conversation.

"Yeah, Brooks, I'm here now." A pause. "So she confirmed an appointment?"

What? Not damn likely. There had been no appointment scheduled with a Gillian Nemont.

"Huh. Yeah, that is interesting."

Interesting that she had a client she didn't remember? Yes, she'd certainly say so.

Colin gave a short burst of surprised laughter.

Laughter? Oh, the man was starting to get on her nerves.

"I guess that'd be pretty interesting too." A brief pause, then, "I'll talk to you tomorrow. Eight o'clock, right." He punched a button to disconnect the call. His head cocked to the side as he studied her. "Seems you did have an appointment scheduled for last Friday."

Her eyes narrowed. "I. Did. Not. Have. An. Appointment. With. Gillian. Nemont." She spaced the words slowly, deliberately.

"No, you didn't."

His sudden, easy agreement threw her off.

"You had an appointment with a Michelle Tome. Something Vanessa called a *meeter.*" He slipped the cell phone back into his pocket. "Mind telling me just what a 'meeter' would be?"

She answered by rote. "I always have a sit-down meeting with anyone who is interested in my services. Before I do any evaluations, before I agree to work as counselor, I get the person to come in. We sit down, talk, and—"

"And you use your psychic gift to figure out if the would-be client is an ordinary human or one of the *Other*."

Emily nodded. She also partially lowered her shields at the meeter to get an idea of the person's power. If she felt the taint of darkness or power that was too uncontrolled, she gave a nice, polite speech about how she wasn't taking any new clients right then.

"Vanessa told Brooks that Michelle Tome never arrived for her appointment."

And he thought Michelle and Gillian were one and the same. "Why would she use an alias? I mean, I wouldn't know her either way."

"I don't know. There are quite a few things I don't know about Ms. Nemont."

"Do you think you'll be able to find her?" *Alive.*

"I'm gonna do my best." Not exactly the definitive answer she'd been hoping for.

She thought back to last Friday afternoon. She'd been mildly annoyed when Vanessa announced the appointment was a no-show. She felt a rush of shame now. She'd been annoyed, while Gillian had—what? Been in danger? Been running for her life?

Been killed?

Emily swallowed. And why had Gillian wanted to see her? She might never know.

"Doc, *Emily,* I had to ask you about her." Colin took a step toward her, his hands lifted.

Oh, now he wants to play nice. Now that he thinks I'm not in on a murder.

But the damn annoying thing was that she understood. He was a cop, working the most high-profile case in the city. He'd found her name in Gillian Nemont's appointment book. If he hadn't followed up on the link, well, she would have wondered about his detective skills.

And his ethics.

But he had followed up. He'd pissed her off, offended her, ruined her night, but he'd done his job.

"Next time, Gyth, don't come in with guns blazing." She ignored his raised hands and turned her back on him.

He exhaled heavily. "I screwed things up, didn't I?"

Hmmm. Commander Obvious had struck again. But maybe there'd be hope for him yet. Emily spun back around, a knife gripped in her fingers. "I don't like your methods, Gyth, but I understand why you had to question me." And why Brooks had to question Vanessa. Although she bet her assistant hadn't appreciated the interruption. Wednesday nights were her coven nights. And tonight, well, tonight the coven had a skyclad ritual on the agenda.

She had a pretty good idea what Brooks had said that elicited earlier appreciative male laughter.

"Ah, you do?" Colin barely glanced at the gleaming knife.

"Umm, next time"—she *really, really hoped* there wasn't a next time—"try playing good cop with me. It'll work much better."

Using the knife, she began cutting the lasagna. Colin stood there, a faint tension emanating from him. He didn't say anything, just watched her. She could feel his intense stare on her.

After a few minutes she broke, glanced at him from the corner of her eye. "Well, we have to eat, don't we?" She muttered. Waving toward the table, she ordered, "Sit down. There's no sense in wasting good food. Besides, we haven't gotten to finish our talk about the *Other*." She could play the professional card too.

They *did* need to finish the lesson.

And she wanted him to stay.

It looked like they both had some trust issues, but, hey, no one was perfect.

Not the Monster Doctor and not a shifter.

But perfect . . . perfect could be boring, she realized. And after living too much of her life on a regimented, by-the-minute schedule, she was ready for a bit of imperfection.

The shifter had better not screw up again. One free pass was all he was going to get from her.

So he'd royally fucked up. At least the doc had let him stay for dinner.

Dinner. The woman had actually cooked for him. Put out candles. Nice plates.

He couldn't remember anyone doing that for him before.

Sure, he'd had more than his share of women. But they'd usually gone out to restaurants. And the relationships hadn't lasted past a few sexual encounters and a couple of fancy meals.

He'd never had this cozy, relaxed kind of date before. And, yeah, despite the fact that he'd spent the first half hour of his time there grilling her, he still considered it a date.

Number two for them.

He wondered if the doc would let him get to second base.

A guy could hope.

"So, that's the main difference between wizards and warlocks. The warlocks have just as much power, but they use the darker magic, and if you ever make the mistake of calling a wizard by the term *warlock,* well"—Emily paused, downed a rather large swallow of her wine—"then you're in trouble, because you've just seriously insulted the guy."

"Right. I'll try to keep that in mind." Throughout their dinner, Emily had kept up a steady stream of conversation about the *Other.*

He now knew that charmers could talk with only one type of animal. Some charmers were born linked to snakes, some to birds, and so on.

There were two types of vampires, the born or the Blood as they were called, and the made or the Taken. To make a vampire, you didn't need the three blood exchanges like the books said. No, according to Emily, one was all it took. The victim had to be drained nearly dry by the vampire, then the would-be vamp had to drink from the sire—*that was what*

Emily had called the guy, a sire—and *boom,* you had yourself a brand, spanking new vampire.

He'd also grilled her about shifters. She'd been right when she mentioned earlier that he could smell others of his kind. He could. There was a wild, rich scent that clung to others like him. He'd first caught that scent when he'd been a nineteen-year-old rookie. He'd stumbled onto a bear shifter and been so surprised he'd nearly dropped his gun.

The bear had broken into a vacation home, ransacked the place. When he'd arrived, the shifter had changed in front of him, a quick, easy transformation from beast to man.

He'd apologized for the wreckage, saying, "Sorry, mate, the beast took over." He'd winked. "You know how it can get."

"So . . ." Emily said, her soft drawl pulling him from the past. "Anything else you want to know?"

"Yeah." He took a sip of his own wine. Normally, he wasn't much for wine. Give him a beer and he was a happy man. But the wine Emily had, it was pretty good. Sweet. A little tangy. *The taste reminded him of her.*

And he realized it'd been more than eight hours since he'd felt her lips beneath his. *Too damn long.*

He shifted in his chair. He'd had a hard-on from the moment he walked through her door. Her hair was down, looking all soft and silky around her shoulders. She was wearing a thin dress with delicate little spaghetti straps. One pull, just one quick tug, and he was sure he could snap those straps.

And he'd bet a month's pay that Emily wasn't wearing a bra. He could see the faint outline of her nipples. Those sweet, perfect nipples.

He could still feel them on his tongue, still see the flushed, pink-tipped areolas.

"Uh, Colin?"

He blinked, and realized that she'd just caught him staring at her chest.

Oh, nice. Definitely the way to charm a woman like her.
Playing the gentleman . . . not something he could do.

He managed to drag his eyes away from the too-tempting swell of her cleavage. He found her watching him, green eyes wide and mysterious behind the lenses of her glasses.

"You said you had something else to ask me."

"Right." He sat down his wineglass with a soft *chink*. "It's about the wolf shifters."

She tensed. "What about them?" Her fingers toyed with the rim of her glass.

"Are they really as bad as folks say? The other shifters I've met, they all said to steer clear of 'em, said they're dangerous." *Dangerous*. Yeah, that was one of the words he'd heard. A few others were psychotic, homicidal, and primitive.

Her fingers halted their stroking movements. Her eyes stared intently into his. "The wolf shifters are extremely dangerous, Colin. I can't stress that enough. In them, the animal they carry—it fights the men and women for control."

"Some say they're psychotic."

"That's because some of them are."

Some, not all.

Emily rubbed the bridge of her nose. "Shifters, in general, are very intense creatures. But, well, I suppose you know that, don't you?" She offered him a small, wan smile. "Wolf shifters, though, they can take that intensity to a whole new level.

"And when a wolf finds his mate, he will do anything, and I mean anything, to protect that mate. Attacking someone else, killing a person, it would be nothing to a wolf shifter if his mate were in jeopardy."

"But not all wolf shifters find their mates."

"No. They don't." Emily leaned forward, her expression suddenly intense. "And I think that's why the psychosis level is so high. These creatures want mates so badly, *need* them so desperately, and when they lose hope of finding their other halves, well, they lose control."

Now that was damn interesting. "You're saying the mated wolf shifters don't have this psychotic problem."

"No, I don't think they do, unless their mates are threatened." Emily shook her head, sitting back in her chair. "Of course, this is just my opinion based on, well, instinct, I guess. It's not like I've conducted a study on these guys."

"Right." Cause wolf shifters weren't exactly bountiful in the population.

"But my opinion is based on conversations I've had with other shifters," Emily continued, her voice serious and professional. "And I truly think it would explain a great deal about the wolf shifter psyche."

He realized there was another question he needed to ask her. "You said you were involved with a shifter once."

"Yes." A faint pink flush covered her cheeks.

"But the first time we met, I got the impression you didn't like my kind too much." He paused, long enough to make absolutely certain she kept looking in his eyes. "Or was it just me you didn't like?"

"I-I—" She stumbled to a stop, seemingly at a loss for words. Huh. Not the usual state for the Monster Doctor.

"Which is it, Doc? Do you have a thing against all shifters or just me?"

Her eyes hardened. "Neither." She shrugged. "It's true, the first time we met, I was a bit . . . hesitant. Shifters do have a certain reputation in the supernatural world, you know. Of all the *Other*, shifters are the best at subterfuge, the best at manipulation. I mean, come on, you guys live your lives hiding a damn huge part of yourselves from the rest of the population."

"And you don't?" He kept his voice soft. "Are you telling me that you don't trick people too? Don't lie? Don't hide?" They were more alike, much more than he thought she wanted to admit.

"I never said I was perfect." She blinked, as if startled, as she said the words.

"Neither am I."

"No." And there were secrets in her eyes. He could see them. "But I don't want you to be."

He realized then that while the doc still might not trust his kind too much, might not trust *him*, she wanted him. He could see the hunger she felt shining in her emerald gaze.

It was a stark, burning sexual hunger that matched his.

No, she didn't completely trust shifters. Maybe she never would. But he didn't really give a shit about her feelings for the rest of his kind. All that mattered was how she felt about him, and maybe, just maybe, she could come to trust him.

No more games. "I want you." Blunt. Hard.

She swallowed. "I-I know."

He reached for her hand. Reveled in the feel of her satiny smooth skin against his. "You want me."

Emily nodded. Her nipples were poking against the front of her dress, and he could smell the sweet scent of her woman's cream in the air.

Yeah, the doc wanted him.

Now, if he could just get her to trust him.

She rose from the table, carrying her glass to the sink. His gaze dropped to her legs, the long, bare expanse of skin that he itched to touch. She was wearing a pair of small, strappy shoes. Black.

"W-why don't we go into the den?"

He'd rather go into her bedroom, but beggars couldn't be choosers. Wasn't that the way the old saying went? And after his nice fuckup from earlier, he was definitely still feeling like a beggar.

Colin stood slowly and followed Emily from the room. He admired the nice sway of her ass. Oh, but the doc had a nice ass. Firm. Tight. Just perfect for his hands.

Emily paused in the hallway and glanced back at him. He didn't bother to hide the lust on his face. Hell, he'd just told her how he felt and she'd admitted to the same hungry desire.

No more games. The thought filled his mind once again as he snagged her wrist, pulling her back against him. And then took her mouth.

A faint moan rumbled in her throat and her lips parted for him. God, yes, but she tasted good. He couldn't tell the difference between the wine and the woman, but he knew he had to have more of that sweet taste.

His tongue stabbed deep into her mouth, and his hands cupped the curve of her ass. He pulled her against his arousal, rocking his erection against her.

Her scent was thick in the air around them. A heady, tempting scent that stirred the beast within him.

Her fingers tightened on his shoulders. She didn't try to push him away. *She pulled him closer.*

The time for play was definitely over.

He needed her, under him, naked, and ready.

Now.

He couldn't be a gentleman. Wasn't in his blood.

He swirled his tongue over hers. Lightly bit her lip. Then Colin forced his head to lift. "If you don't want this," *me*, "then you'd better say so now, Emily." While he could still stop.

Passion filled her eyes. A sort of dazed, wild lust. The controlled doctor was gone.

"I-I—" She shook her head.

His teeth clenched. His body stilled. His cock was swollen with hunger, thick and hard with need.

But she was saying no.

What did you expect? Mentally he berated himself. *Last night, she told you it was too soon. You're rushing her. You've got to take more time, more care with her.*

His hands lifted. He wondered if Emily would mind if he used her bathroom. Cause if he was gonna get through the night, he'd need a very cold shower.

And possibly a hand job.

"No." Emily grabbed his hands. "I don't want you to stop."

Dr. Drake wasn't alone.

He watched the house from his spot in the bushes. He'd been outside, watching, waiting for the last two hours.

He'd seen the guy arrive, the big, mean-looking bastard that had nearly caught him that first night. He'd held his breath when the guy jumped out of his Jeep.

He still wasn't sure how the man had figured out that he'd been hiding in the lot that night, and he'd been afraid the guy might pick up on his presence again.

But, no, the guy had stormed up the front steps, pounded on the door. Then disappeared inside.

What was the cop's angle? He'd have to find out. He couldn't take any risks with this situation.

The fellow could be a friend, a lover, a client. But he needed to know.

Had to know everything about Dr. Drake.

"You're safe another night," he whispered, knowing that he couldn't approach her with anyone else around. No, that wasn't the plan.

He had to catch her alone.

And he would. It was just a matter of time.

"Don't say yes if you don't mean it." Colin's body had stiffened against hers. "I'm trying as hard as I can to be the gentleman you wanted, but don't push me, Doc. There's only so much a man can take."

And there was only so much a woman could take. Only so many lonely, empty nights. Damn but she was tired of being afraid, tired of hiding herself away from life, from passion. "I don't want to play it safe anymore." And she didn't, Emily realized. She'd tried playing it safe before. Tried for the last ten years.

She'd done a hell of a lot of thinking since she'd met with Colin that morning. She'd realized she was treating him exactly as she'd treated Travis. She'd never let her guard down with him, never trusted him fully. She'd kept waiting, kept thinking there would be some perfect moment when she could reveal her secrets to him.

But that perfect moment had never come. Travis had left her, she'd kept playing it safe, and she'd finally come to the conclusion that safety, well, it was boring.

She wanted excitement. She wanted life. She wanted . . . Colin.

Besides, Colin already knew her secrets, most of them anyway. And he didn't think she was some kind of freak just because she had a little extra psychic sensitivity. No, he didn't
treat her like a freak.

He treated her like a woman. *His woman.*

And she liked that, liked it a lot.

So Ms. Six-Date-Rule took off her glasses, tossed them
onto a nearby table, and decided to take a risk. Staring up
into Colin's glittering eyes, she said softly, clearly, "I want to
be with you tonight."

"Emily . . ."

Her stomach clenched at the raw need in his voice. No one
had ever said her name with such hunger.

"Emily, I'm not like the men you've been with before."

Thank God. She stood directly in front of him, her body
trembling with anticipation. She knew he wasn't like the others. There was a wild, dominant sensuality about him that
none of her other lovers had ever possessed.

"I won't be able to take things slow. Not the first time."

The first time. Her sex clenched. Just how many times was
he planning for? "I don't want you to go slow." Slow wasn't
a word she associated with him. She wanted hard and fast.
She wanted screaming pleasure and mad passion.

She wanted everything.

A muscle ticked along his jaw. He glanced down the hallway. "Which one's the bedroom?"

Her fingers lifted, pointed to the second door.

A feral smile curved his lips, showing just the slightest hint
of fang.

The sight had scared her before. Given her pause.

Now, it just heightened her excitement.

I'm not like the men you've known before. Her panties
were already wet in eager anticipation.

Colin picked her up, carrying her easily into the bedroom.
She'd left a lamp on earlier, and a soft glow of light illuminated the room. He tossed her onto the bed and her dress
hiked up around her thighs.

His eyes narrowed at the sight of her sprawled legs, and before she could move, he was on her. Crawling onto the bed, onto her, shoving her legs even wider apart, and stroking his long, strong fingers up the length of her thighs.

She jumped at the touch of his warm hands.

"Easy, baby, I just want to feel you." He inhaled. "God, I love the smell of your cream." Then his fingers were on the crotch of her panties, stroking, rubbing.

Emily bit her lip, her body twisting against his. Oh, damn, but his fingers felt *good*. But she wanted more, needed—

He jerked her panties off, ripping the delicate silk. Then those fingers were on her sex, opening her, sliding between her wet folds and thrumming her clit.

Her head thrashed against the pillows. Her orgasm was building, her sex tightening, tightening—

Colin drove two fingers into her.

She came, shuddering, gasping his name.

"Ah, yes, Emily. Damn, you're so fucking sexy."

She was dazed, the drumming beat of her heart filling her ears. She'd never come that quickly, not with just a few touches.

"I want to taste you."

Her body was still trembling, her sex quivering with after-shocks of pleasure. His fingers were inside her, stroking, pulling out, thrusting deep in a maddening rhythm that made the need start to burn again.

It took a moment for his words to register, took a moment for her to realize what he—

Colin pulled his fingers out of her, brought them to his lips. Watching her, keeping his bright stare trained on her, he brought his hand to his mouth. And licked her cream from his fingers.

He smiled at her. "I want more."

So did she. *More of him.*

But he was still dressed. Still wearing far, far too many clothes. "Colin—"

His head lowered, and she felt his warm breath against her sex.

Every muscle in her body quivered in anticipation. *She wanted his mouth on her. Wanted to feel that clever, rough tongue.*

His tongue licked her labia. A slow, wet lick that had her arching off the bed, her high heels digging into the mattress.

He growled at her movement, and the rumble of vibration shot straight to her core.

Her thighs tightened around his shoulders. Her fingers were in his hair, urging him closer.

Another slow swipe of his tongue, then he licked her clit. Then again, harder.

"C-Colin . . ." A second orgasm was close. Her body was fighting, struggling to come again.

His tongue stabbed deep into her sex and his fingers pushed against her clit.

Her hips bucked against him.

The orgasm was coming, oh God, she was—

"Not yet, baby, not yet." He pulled back, and the hiss of his zipper filled the air. "Not without me this time."

Something ripped in the darkness. Plastic. *Condom wrapper.* The shifter had come prepared.

Then his hands were on her again. Opening the folds of her sex, and she felt the broad, hard tip of his cock against her.

Too late, a shiver of apprehension swept through her.

"Colin, I—"

His hands were on her shoulders. His fingers sliding under the straps of her dress.

"I fantasized about you all through dinner," he whispered. *And she'd been fantasizing about him since last night.*

"I thought about your nipples." He pulled on the straps, and the delicate material broke apart. "I wanted to see them." He pushed down the top of her dress. "Touch them." His fingers plucked her nipples, and she arched upward with a gasp. "Taste them." His head lowered and his mouth closed around her nipple, sucking strongly.

The faint edge of his teeth pressed against her, not pain . . . oh no, not pain. *Pleasure.*

No more fear. Only need.

While he tongued one breast, his hands tormented the other. Squeezing, rubbing, driving her mad with a hunger and voracious need that just built and built.

She squirmed against him, trying to impale herself on the thick cock that was lodged at the mouth of her sex. She wanted him inside. Deep inside. She was so close to climaxing again. So close. She needed him to fill her.

Her fingers curved over his hips, felt the rough touch of his jeans, and she shoved the heavy material down. She gripped his hips, feeling the hot skin against her. And she tightened her hold around him, urging him forward.

Colin lifted his head, his lips glistening with moisture, and laughed, but it was a tight, rough sound. "Impatient, are you?"

Hell, yes, she was impatient. Her body was yearning, needing, and sweet release was just one good thrust away.

Her eyes narrowed as she stared up at him. *Two could play this game.*

Her fingers trailed over his hip bones, skated down his abdomen, and found the dark nest of hair at his thighs.

He inhaled sharply at her touch, and she saw his nostrils flare even as he tensed against her.

Her fingers curled over the base of his erection, stroked slowly, squeezing him, moving from root to the tip that was pushing against her core.

His hands flashed out, grabbed her wrists, and pinned her hands to the bed. A growl sounded in his throat.

His eyes were burning with lust, and she knew she wouldn't have to wait any longer.

His mouth crashed onto hers, his tongue thrusting past her lips—

And he buried his cock balls deep in her body.

Emily came immediately, her body pulsing, shaking, squeezing tightly around his thick length as a wave of intense, God-yes pleasure rocked over her. And still he thrust into her—deep, hard thrusts that shook the bed, that shook her.

His fingers were clenched around her wrists, his hips hammering against hers. He was wild, completely out of control as he took her.

And she loved it.

Loved it.

His head lifted, and she caught the gleam of a fang, then his mouth was lowering toward her throat.

Her breath choked out. Her heart slammed against her breast, and her legs locked even tighter around his thrusting hips.

"I love the way you feel when you come," he whispered, "love the way you squeeze me. Love the tight, hot clasp of your sex."

His words wrapped around her, fed the orgasm that was still spinning through her.

His cock was rock hard, so big that she felt deliciously stretched. Long, warm, *perfect.*

She was riding an endless wave of release. It'd never been like this before, *never* and—

He bit her. Used those long canines in a bite on her neck that had her crying out in surprise and arching in shocked pleasure.

"Mine." His head lifted and his eyes glowed with a fierce blue fire. His cock drove into her, once, twice, then he was shuddering, stiffening, throwing back his head and gritting his teeth with the force of his release.

When it was over, when his hips stilled, when the tingling pleasure finally faded, Colin draped his body over hers. Freed her wrists, then took her hands and twined his fingers with hers.

Colin kissed her. A long, wet, open-mouthed kiss.

I'm not like the other men you've known.

Oh, but the man had certainly spoken the truth.

And, after having him, she was very much afraid that no other man would do for her again.

Chapter 9

Emily stood behind the podium, leaning forward slightly to pitch her voice into the microphone. A sea of cameras and bright lights stared back at her.

"After reviewing the case files, I've come to the conclusion that the perpetrator did, indeed, know the victim. This wasn't a random crime. Preston Myers was specifically targeted."

"Dr. Drake!" A thin Asian man raised his hand. "Lee Nguyen of the *Atlanta Metro Daily*." He paused, apparently letting her absorb that little nugget of information. "Will the Night Butcher strike again? Are there others who will be 'specifically targeted'?" He stared up at her, his head cocked, his photographer snapping shots right beside him.

Emily slanted a quick glance at Danny. She'd told the captain her belief that the killer would, indeed, strike again, but he and the district attorney had told her not to share that information with the reporters.

"Don't want folks to panic," Ben Mitchell, the DA, had muttered at her news.

Ben stepped forward, offering a vague smile to Nguyen and the rest of the reporters who'd gathered in the press room. "It's far too early to predict whether or not this disturbed individual will strike again." His old, Southern boy accent played on the words.

"So you think the guy's disturbed." This came from Darla Mitchell who was looking TV perfect as she leaned forward with a hungry glint in her eye. Jake was behind her, a tense, slightly haggard expression on his face.

"Well . . ."

"Disturbed isn't the right word for this man," Emily cut him off, trying to keep her voice calm, professional.

"Then what's the right word, Dr. Drake?" Darla was in the front row, easily seen as she stretched forward. "Psychotic? Deranged? Or maybe just plain crazy?"

It was quite possible all those terms applied. "It's difficult to say at this stage exactly what psychosis this individual has. I do know that this man is highly intelligent, organized, strong, and very, very dangerous."

"Dr. Drake, do you intend to work with the police until the Night Butcher is caught?" This came from Nguyen.

"I intend to work with the Atlanta PD until they no longer need my services." Time for her to step out of the limelight. "Thank you."

Ben motioned Smith forward. "Our ME has some findings she'd like to share."

Smith swallowed as she looked out at the sea of faces. She was looking even more gorgeous today. She'd ditched her white lab coat in favor of a simple black suit.

She pulled the microphone up, adjusting it slightly. "I'd like to clarify a few points that have previously been mentioned in the press."

There was a brief of buzz of excitement at her announcement.

Her lips tightened. "First, despite the rumors, the victim was not 'butchered.' His body was intact. Preston Myers died because of severed jugular and carotid veins."

"What weapon was used?" This question was fired from a middle-aged man in the back.

Dr. Smith shook her head. "I'm not at liberty to say at this point."

Yes, Emily really didn't think the DA wanted the press to know that the "weapon" used by the Night Butcher was his teeth.

"I would like the public to know that the suspect left several hairs behind."

Wolf shifter hairs. Pretty hard to do a DNA analysis on those, Emily thought.

"And I am confident that the evidence will soon lead us to the killer." Smith inclined her head like a queen dismissing servants. "Thank you."

Ben took over then, answering a few questions and ending the press conference with a promise to follow up as soon as more details became available.

Thank God.

Emily hurriedly exited the small stage area. She'd never liked talking in front of large groups. Always made her knees shake and caused a tight knot in her gut.

Classic anxiety disorder, of course. But knowing the clinical root of her condition didn't really make it any easier to bear.

"You did a good job, Doc." Colin stepped from the crowd, appearing at her side.

"I thought you'd be up there, too." She glanced at him, feeling a blush stain her cheeks. When she'd woken that morning, he'd been awake, gazing at her with his solemn stare.

He'd left just after seven, given her a hard but too brief kiss, and gone to the station.

They hadn't talked about last night. Hadn't said a word about the mind-blowing sex.

"Brooks is the one who handles the reporters." He jerked his thumb toward his partner who was just now leaving the staging area. "He's got the pretty-boy face that always looks good on camera."

Well, she thought Colin would look pretty good on camera too. Emily tensed. Damn. They really needed to talk, to clear the air.

But now was hardly the time and—

"Dr. Drake!"

Emily turned at Darla's call. Found the woman making a beeline straight for her. Jake tagged along in her wake.

Darla paused two feet away from her. A smug smile curved her lips. "I've got a few questions for you."

Colin stepped forward. "She's done talking about the case."

"Umm, well, it's not about the case. Not really."

At her Cheshire cat look, Emily got a very, very bad feeling in her gut. "What do you want to know?"

"Tell me, Doctor," Darla paused, arched one perfectly plucked brow, "what do you know about a place called Serenity Woods?"

Her heart stopped. Then raced in a double-time rhythm. "Serenity Woods?" Her voice was clear, calm. And her palms were sweating. "Once, it was a psychiatric facility for children and teens in northern Georgia." Emily shrugged. "I don't think the place is still in business anymore."

"No, it's not." Darla's eyes were narrowed. "There was a fire at the hospital a few years ago, and after that, the place closed down."

Emily stared back at the reporter, keeping her features carefully blank.

"Arson, according to the investigators."

Colin took her arm. "We need to go, Dr. Drake. I think Smith wants to talk with us about the case."

That was news to her. But Emily nodded, glad for an excuse to get away from Darla. *Serenity Woods.* She hadn't heard that name in years.

Darla's hand snaked out, snagging Emily's just as she was turning away. "One more question." The reporter's hand felt like ice against her skin. Darla leaned forward, pitched her voice whisper low, as she asked, "Do you still see demons?"

Emily tensed. Then forced a slightly confused expression onto her face. "See demons?" She shook her head. "Of course not." Emily strove to look concerned. "Why, my dear, do you?"

Darla's lips thinned as she snatched her hand back. Her pretty face twisted and she turned on her heel, shoving her way through the crowd.

Jake looked at Emily. Met her stare for just a moment. There was worry in his eyes. Worry for her and for himself.

He nodded to her, a slight inclination of his head, then disappeared into the throng of reporters.

Her breath left her in a hard *whoosh*.

Shit. Darla Mitchell was digging into her past.

And her past was *definitely* not pretty.

Emily looked pale. Scared.

Colin tightened his hold on her arm and steered her toward the stairwell. He shoved open the metal door and gently pushed her past the threshold. When the door swung shut behind them, he hesitated a moment, listening intently, then, satisfied that they were the only ones in the stairwell, he figured it was time for a question-and-answer session of their own.

"Doc, what's going on?"

Emily stared up at him, and her eyes looked very wide. "There are some things you don't know about me."

After last night, he'd started to think he knew the woman damn well. He knew just where to touch her to make that soft moan rumble in her throat. He knew what it felt like when she climaxed around him. Knew what she looked like first thing in the morning when the sunlight trickled through her blinds.

Yeah, he was starting to know the doc pretty well. But he knew she still had secrets.

So did he.

He figured he had the advantage though, considering he'd run a background check on her. After that first night, when he'd been sure someone was watching her, he'd started searching for information about the doc.

From what he'd gathered, the doc led a pretty quiet life. She dated occasionally but seemed to spend most of her time working with her patients.

He knew there was more to Emily though, knew secrets lay beneath her calm surface. And it looked like he was about to learn one of those secrets now . . .

"I think Darla's investigating me." Her lips tightened.

"Correction, I *know* she is." Anger hardened her voice. "I don't know how she got the file. It should have been destroyed. There is no way she should have—"

"Whoa. Slow down." He gripped her elbows. "I'm not the mind reader, baby. I don't know what in the hell you're talking about."

"Serenity Woods." She bit off the words. "She knows about the time I was at Serenity Woods."

He wasn't getting it. "So you worked at a psych ward." He'd heard Emily and Darla's conversation, and he'd thought the doc would be more rattled about the reporter's demon question than a vague mention of some old psychiatric hospital.

He remembered reading an old file about the fire a few years ago. No one had been hurt. The smoke alarms had alerted the staff and they'd gotten all the patients out safely. A sudden thought had him tensing. "Dammit, Emily, were you working there when—"

"I didn't *work* there!" Her voice was sharp. "Oh damn, I've got to go talk to Darla, find out what she knows."

"You mean *we've* got to talk to her." The doc should have gotten it by now. They were partners. Partners worked together. "But we can't question her with all those other reporters around. We'll wait, go to her later tonight."

Emily nodded, but she didn't look pleased with the delay. "Fine."

Tension had made her body stiffen against his. His gaze swept over her. She was wearing a black turtleneck again. He'd wondered if she'd worn that top to hide the faint mark he'd left on her throat.

He'd marked her deliberately, of course. It was the way of his kind.

And he'd do it again. As soon as he got her beneath him, or on top of him.

Hell, he'd take her any way he could get her. He'd gotten his first good taste of the doc, and he was hungry, starving, for more.

His gaze dropped to her waist. She was wearing a skirt. A slim black skirt.

Pity Smith was waiting on them. He'd sure love to lift up that skirt and find out if Emily was as soft as he remembered.

His cock swelled against his zipper.

Damn. Not the time.

Emily was angry, frightened, and sure as hell not in the mood for a horny shifter.

Later.

He forced his hands to release their grip on her. They needed to talk more. A hell of a lot more. He still didn't know what secret was burning her from the inside, but they were already running late. It would have to wait. He'd question her after they talked to Smith. "We need to get going. Smith wants us to meet her in the morgue."

A flash of distaste covered Emily's face.

"Yeah, Doc. I hate the smell down there, too." He sure as hell didn't know how Smith could stand it. "But she's got something to tell us." Maybe they'd gotten lucky and Smith had found a link to the killer.

Emily nodded jerkily and began hurrying down the stairs. He frowned as he watched her, remembering too late the words he'd all but ignored moments before.

I didn't work there.

But if Emily hadn't been working at Serenity Woods, then what *had* she been doing there?

Smith was waiting on them, already covered in her white lab coat. She had her radio turned on; she usually listened to it when she was doing paperwork, and soft, whispery jazz filled the air.

She frowned when she saw them. "Damn, Gyth. What'd you guys do, stop for coffee?"

"Sorry." Emily cleared her throat. "My fault. I was talking to a reporter."

"Hmmm. Freaking vultures." Smith shoved away from her desk. "Those idiots didn't care about the facts. They just want to hype the killer, sell more copies of their paper, and get folks so scared they stay glued to their TV sets."

"A little harsh, don't you think?" Colin asked. He knew Smith didn't love the media. She'd had a run-in a few years ago with a reporter for News Flash Five. The guy had tried to make it look like she'd contaminated evidence in a murder trial.

She hadn't, but the reporter had done a damn good job of insinuating that she and the department were corrupt.

Luckily, the jury had been sequestered and they'd missed the daily news reports and the murderer had gone to jail.

But Smith hadn't forgotten or forgiven.

One thing he'd learned about Smith in the six years they'd worked together, the woman could hold a serious grudge.

Smith grunted and looked at Emily. "You handled yourself pretty well. Glad you didn't let 'em push you in the corner about the killer being all crazy."

Emily blinked. "Uh, thanks." Her voice sounded a little absent, and Colin realized she wasn't looking at Smith. Or at him. Her focus was on the "cold chamber," the vaults near the back of the lab that were used to store the bodies.

She even started walking toward them, her eyes narrowed, her right lifted as if she'd touch the metal doors.

Smith snagged her hand. "Goin' somewhere, Dr. Drake?"

Colin knew Smith was very particular about her lab. Particular, or possessive as hell.

"Umm, sorry." But Emily was still gazing at the vaults. "I just . . . umm . . . what did you want to show us? And shouldn't McNeal be here?" Tension was back in her voice.

Now Smith was the one to stiffen. "*He* doesn't need to be here."

Oh, yeah. He'd forgotten about that, Colin realized. Word around the precinct was that Smith and McNeal had dated. Very briefly.

Emily finally looked back at him. "I think he should be here." There was a note in her voice, a glint in her eye that finally made him realize—

The doc is sensing something.

His own gaze drifted to the vaults that seemed to hold her so spellbound.

What had she said when she'd first examined Preston's body? The captain had wanted to know if she could tell whether the guy had been *Other,* and Emily had said, *"If the death is recent, some of the spirit will still be there."*

Anybody in the vaults, well, they wouldn't exactly be "recent," but Emily was sure acting odd. Acting like she knew something he didn't.

Yeah, big surprise there.

Colin jerked his thumb toward Smith's desk. "Maybe you should page the captain."

"What?" Smith dropped Emily's hand. "You guys don't even know what I want to show you." She spun on her heel, hurrying toward the vaults. "And it could be nothing, but, well, the other night, I was listening to the police radio when the APB was sent out on those guys who jumped you." She swung the lock on the middle vault, pulled open the door.

Colin urged Emily forward. Cold air hit him, followed closely by the thick stench of death.

Damn but he hated that smell.

Emily twisted her hands together and grimaced.

Smith hummed along to the music as she pulled out a slab. A sheet-covered body appeared, and when Smith's hip bumped the slab, a man's hand slipped from under the cover.

Colin's eyes immediately locked on the tattoo. A long, twisting black snake encircled the dead man's left wrist.

Sonofabitch. His gaze flew to Emily. She gave a nearly imperceptible nod. And the light of understanding finally dawned.

The dead man on the slab, he wasn't a man at all. He was one of the demons who'd attacked them last night. Emily had known, had sensed the truth when she'd come into the room.

Hell, no wonder she'd been trying to get them to call for McNeal.

"The tat's a match for the description you gave." Smith pulled back the sheet, revealing the white face of a young guy; he looked barely twenty, with a shaved head and a glinting nose ring. "Cops found his body downtown. He was in an alley."

Colin stared at the guy's still features. "We didn't see his face. He—they had masks on the whole time." But this was one of their attackers, he'd bet his life on it.

And the fact that Emily's psychic radar was going off just made him all the more certain.

You couldn't go wrong with a psychic.

Smith pulled the sheet down a few more inches, revealing a clear bullet hole right over the man's heart. "Close range," she murmured. "I found powder burns on his chest."

His hands clenched. He'd hoped to question the bastard. Hoped to find out who'd sent him.

A kid. The guy's just a kid. His gut tightened. *What a damn waste.*

"Three others were found with him." Smith stepped back and tapped the vault door near her. "Same MO. One shot, straight through the heart. The uniforms on scene thought it was a gang hit."

No, not a gang hit.

"W-were they all young? Like him?" Emily asked softly.

Smith nodded. Her eyes were narrowed as she appraised him. "Four attackers, right? That's what they said on the radio."

"Yeah." His mind was racing. If the men who'd attacked them were all dead . . . damn, that was no coincidence. The guy who'd hired them, the sonofabitch who'd sent those kids after them, had tied up his loose ends.

Probably afraid the kids would cave and reveal his identity if the cops caught them.

"Kind of a strange coincidence, isn't it?" Smith drawled. "You two getting attacked like that, and these poor guys getting killed? All within forty-eight hours."

"Very strange," Emily said, and she lifted her hand toward the dead man. Her fingers hovered in the air over his chest, not quite touching him. Her hand was a soft, light gold above the stark white body. "So much pain . . ." she whispered. "For so long . . ."

"What?" Smith shook her head. "No, Dr. Drake, didn't you hear me? The guy was shot in the heart. He died instantly. He didn't suffer, I guarantee you that."

Emily blinked and shook her head. "Uh, right. Sorry. I was"—a barely perceptible pause—"confused." Her hand balled into a fist. "You haven't done an autopsy yet."

"No, he was brought in just a few hours ago."

"McNeal needs to be notified before you cut into him." Colin made the words an order. "He should see the bodies first."

"See the bodies?" Smith's brows scrunched together. "Why would he need to see them?"

Because these guys are demons and he might not want you cutting inside them. Hmm. Better go with option B, instead. "Because there's a chance these guys are linked to the Night Butcher."

"This isn't his MO." Smith was definite. "A professional did these guys. Swift, clean."

The jazz music faded into silence.

Emily stared at him for a moment, then inclined her head slightly toward the door.

"Smith, just don't start cutting on them yet, okay? I'll send the captain down here."

He stalked across the gleaming floor, heading for the door. Emily was in front of him, moving quickly to the exit.

"Hey, wait! Don't you want to see the others?" Smith called after them.

Emily was at the door now. She paused a moment, glanced back over her shoulder, and whispered, "There's no need, Colin. I know it's them."

And you couldn't argue with a psychic. Since he'd never gotten a look at the guys, seeing their faces now wouldn't do him much good. He'd have to rely on Emily's sensitivity.

He spared a brief glance for Smith. She was watching them both, her brow furrowed. "I've got a suspect to question."

That was the truth. When four demon bodies turned up in the morgue, it looked damn suspicious.

Especially when those guys had attacked him right outside of Paradise Found.

Someone sure as hell had to be pulling the strings on the demons who'd attacked them. The odds were good that same person had been the one pulling the trigger and ending their lives.

And the guy at the top of his suspect list was a powerful demon, the kind strong enough to threaten others of his race.

Niol.

The door swung shut behind them. Emily hurried down the hallway, her high heels clicking on the tiles. Her shoulders were stiff, her back a tense, straight line.

"Em, wait up." He grabbed her arm, pulled her around to face them. She was still too pale for his taste, and secrets were burning in her eyes.

"I've got to go talk to McNeal."

"He can wait a minute." The cloth of her shirt was soft beneath his touch and her arm felt so delicate and small.

Sometimes he forgot just how delicate humans were. He'd have to remember. Have to make sure that he took every care with her.

He'd held onto his control last night. Managed to chain the beast. Yeah, he'd marked her neck, but he'd had to do it. Had to show that she was his.

It'd been too long since he'd had her. Too long since he'd felt her beneath him. He'd watched her during the press conference. Felt hunger coil tightly within him. Then afterward, when she'd talked to that blond reporter and he'd seen the fear flash in her eyes, anger had burned in him. He'd wanted to step in front of her, to protect her.

And where in the hell had that impulse come from? His kind, they weren't exactly a protective bunch. They were fighters. Hunters. They destroyed those who were weak. Devoured them.

They didn't protect them.

"Those men in there—I know they're the ones who attacked us." Her words jerked him out of his rambling thoughts and back to the present.

Yeah, he was pretty sure the tattooed kid had been the one he'd seen. He had an eye for the tats, and the details of the snake were extremely clear.

But Emily had known the guy was the perp even before they'd seen his wrist, he was sure of it. The doc had started acting weird the moment they'd gone inside. "How'd you know?" he asked, keeping his hand on her arm. He had the feeling that if he let her go, she'd run from him. And he didn't want her to run.

Jesus. What the hell is my deal? Did a little bit of good sex make me go crazy?

Course, it hadn't just been *good* sex. It'd been the *best damn sex* he'd had in, *hell,* he didn't even know how long.

"I felt the echo of their power when we went inside."

Yeah, he wasn't real sure what that meant. Emily must have read his expression, because she shrugged and muttered, "It was like shadows hanging in the room, okay? I could see them, *feel* them. And demon power is distinct."

"But they were dead." Pointing out the obvious there. "I thought the death had to be fresh in order for you to sense anything."

"They were fresh enough." She winced. "God, that sounds cold, doesn't it? But the kill—it was less than twenty-four hours ago, and I could still *feel* them in there." She shuddered. "Do you know how cold death feels?"

No, and he was pretty damn glad of that fact. Until then, he hadn't really thought about how hard the doc's gift might be on her. Seeing into people's minds, well, seemed it wasn't as exciting as most folks would think.

He opened his mouth to reply, but Emily pulled away from him, muttering, "Of course you don't know. No one else knows. Just me." She shook her head, the light glinted off her glasses, and he watched her pull into herself, watched her pull away from him. He could see her withdrawal, see it in the suddenly blank expression on her face, read it in the stiffness of her body.

The doc was trying to pull away from him.

Oh, hell, no. He grabbed her arms, jerked her back against him. Yeah, he liked that a whole lot better. "I might not know what it's like to *be* you, Doc. But I know you."

"You think you do." He had her pinned against his body, and she had to tilt her head back to meet his stare. "We had sex, and suddenly you think you know me."

He felt the flames of his temper stir. The doc should know better than to yank a shifter's tail.

"I've got news for you." Her voice was ice cold. "You *don't* know me. There's so much—" She exhaled slowly, then whispered, "You wouldn't understand."

His fingers tightened around her. "Try me."

"No." A shadow of pain appeared in her eyes. "Let me go."

Not an option. He'd just found her. Only started laying his claim. No fucking way was he going to let her slip through his fingers now.

Shit. He didn't like the way she was dismissing him. The doc was putting distance between them, erecting that ice-princess wall she'd worn the first day they'd met. He'd broken through that wall once before, and he'd be happy to smash it to bits again.

"You can't know me," she whispered, and there was a glint of pain in her eyes. "No one ever has."

"How many times do I have to tell you?" He growled the words as he lowered his mouth to hers. "I'm not like the men you've known before."

He kissed her, plunging his tongue deep in her mouth and drinking up her sweet essence. Her hands lifted, wrapped around his shoulders—and pulled him closer.

Yes. This was what he wanted. His woman, pressed breast to chest, sex to sex. His cock swelled against her as a heavy wave of arousal flooded his body.

Last night had been good. Fucking fantastic. And he wondered, just what would it be like if he let go of his control? Would the doc be able to handle him?

Her nipples were hard, stabbing into him, and he had to touch them. Keeping his mouth on hers, sweeping his tongue against hers, he lowered his right hand and cupped the warm weight of her breast.

Damn. He wanted that breast in his mouth. His fingers edged under her shirt, slid past the lacy bra, and found her nipple. When he squeezed her with the tip of his fingers, she gasped into his mouth, and the rich scent of her arousal perfumed the air.

They were alone in the hallway. Dimly, he could hear the slow beat of music coming from the ME's office. Smith had started the jazz CD again. She wasn't going to come out and find them. And no one else was down in the Crypt.

He walked Emily back a few steps, pushed her up against the wall and slowly lifted his head. She was watching him, her eyes wide behind her glasses, her bow shaped, fuck-me lips a dark red, glistening.

Oh, those lips. He wanted to feel them around his cock. He'd fantasized about the doc, imagined her taking him inside and licking him with that sweet, skillful tongue of hers.

But the Crypt wasn't the place for that. And they didn't have much time.

And he needed a better taste of her.

He jerked up her shirt, exposing her bra. Black, of course.

"Colin, no, someone might come—"

He pushed her bra aside. Gazed down at her breasts. The woman truly had the best breasts he'd ever seen. And he'd seen his fair share.

Not too big, not too small, just perfect for his hands. And so sweet . . .

He closed his lips over her nipple, pulling gently, then stroking her with his tongue.

"Oh, Jesus, *Colin* . . ." He could hear the need in her voice, and it filled him with fierce satisfaction.

I do know you, Emily. I know just how to touch you, know just what you want.

Emily might think she could dismiss their physical connection, but he'd show her just how wrong she was. Sex might not be the key to linking them, but he figured it was a damn good start.

He caught the fabric of her skirt in his hands, pulled up the material slowly, very slowly. He liked the way she felt against him. Warm. Soft.

He pulled her breast deeper into his mouth, sucking strongly. And he *fucking loved* the way she tasted.

Her hips bucked against him. Her nails cut through his shirt and dug into his skin.

The doc had claws. Oh yeah, he liked that.

Growling his pleasure, he pushed his hand between her spread thighs. Her panties were wet with cream, and when he eased his fingers beneath the small band of fabric, Emily's breath choked out. "Colin—"

"Easy." They both needed this. His fingers stroked her. His thumb pressed against the button of her desire. *Just a few more minutes . . .*

A slow, grinding rumble reached his ears. Then a soft, faint *ding* of sound.

Shit. The elevator. He jerked down her skirt, spun around, covering her with his body. "Someone's coming." Someone with extremely piss-poor timing.

He was so aroused that he hurt, and he'd been minutes, *seconds,* away from finding release with Emily.

He glanced over his shoulder. She was frantically rearranging her shirt. Her face was flushed, but he knew it wasn't due to passion.

Making out in the Crypt probably wasn't the doc's usual style.

Another strike against him? Or one in his favor?

Damn. He hadn't meant for things to go so far. He'd just wanted to touch her, wanted to remind her of what they had.

Sex like that—the heat, the fast combustion—it was damn rare. And worth fighting for.

"Emily . . ."

Her chin jerked up. Fire flashed in her eyes.

And the elevator doors swished open. Colin's head jerked back around just as Brooks stepped forward. Looked to the left, then the right—

"Gyth! Damn, man, I've been looking everywhere for you."

Pity the guy couldn't have kept looking for another two minutes.

Brooks noticed Emily. One brow rose, and the light seemed to dawn. "Uh, is this a bad time?"

A very bad time.

Emily pushed past him. Her clothes were perfect again, but her nipples were thrusting against the soft fabric of her shirt, her lips were plump and darkly pink, her eyes bright.

Brooks wasn't an idiot. He knew what those signs meant.

Wisely, his partner didn't say a word when Emily crossed in front of him.

"Where's McNeal?" she asked.

"His office." He also managed to keep his eyes on her face. Good man. He wouldn't get punched.

Emily nodded. Stepped into the elevator.

Well, damn. Not even a good-bye. Colin lunged forward, shot out his hand to stop the doors from closing. "I'll see you tonight."

Her jaw locked and she stared at the control panel. "I have to think, Colin. There's too much going on . . ."

He heard Brooks's soft footfalls. The guy was inching back, probably trying to give 'em some privacy.

"I'll see you tonight," he repeated. They had to talk. About Darla. About Serenity Woods. About the demons who'd attacked them.

Her gaze flashed to his. "This is the second time you've given yourself an invitation to my place."

"Yeah, but you want to finish what we started as much as

I do." He let his eyes drop to her breasts. His voice thickened as he said, "And we will finish, Doc, that's a promise."

Colin stepped back. The doors slid closed, and Emily disappeared.

Brooks whistled softly. "Tell me you weren't just making out with our profiler in the Crypt."

"Fine. I won't tell you." He actually didn't want to tell him a damn thing about Emily. She was his. His business. His woman.

"I don't think a place like this is, uh, quite what Dr. Drake is used to," Brooks said softly.

Yeah, no shit.

Damn. The doc—she was different. She made him feel different.

Wanting to fuck and wanting to protect—what in the hell was up with that?

"Listen, loverboy, I've got some pictures upstairs I want you to look at," Brooks said. "Maybe you can match the tat on that guy who jumped you."

"Forget it. He's not an issue now."

"What? You can't be serious, man, the guy tried to kill you—"

"And now he's lying on a slab in Smith's cold chamber." While the guy's spirit might be sending some kind of message to Emily, he sure as hell wasn't talking to them.

Brooks glanced toward the morgue. "What in the hell happened to him?"

"Oh, I've got an idea." *Niol.*

Time to go interrogate the master demon.

"You up for a little good cop, bad cop?"

"Always." A wolfish smile curved Brooks's lips.

Colin punched the button for the elevator. He figured Emily would be long gone by now. "Good. Cause I've got a bastard we need to press, hard." Niol wasn't going to cave easy. He was too cocky. But if they caught him unaware, he just might slip up.

That's what the bastards usually did. Got too confident. Thought they were too smart.

Then they screwed up.

Would Niol be the same?

Well, he'd just have to find out.

Yeah, time to go and question the master demon about the little matter of multiple murders.

Chapter 10

Emily sat in her car, her fingers gripping the steering wheel, and stared up at the tidy, two-story house.

After talking with McNeal, she'd fled the station, embarrassed, afraid that she'd see Colin or Brooks.

Lord, what the hell had she been thinking? She'd almost had sex *in a morgue for Christ's sake.*

When he'd touched her, lust had pumped through her, and she'd wanted to rip the man's clothes off his body.

Not her normal style.

Her emotions were high, she knew that. Knew she was running on a hard mixture of fear, worry, and adrenaline. And as a psychologist, she knew those emotions made her susceptible to certain things.

And she sure as hell was susceptible to Colin.

But a morgue? Her knuckles whitened. That wasn't just being susceptible. It was crossing the line into crazy.

If Brooks hadn't walked out of that elevator, she would have had sex with Colin. Right there in that smelly, dingy hallway. And she would have loved it.

Shit. Is this what good sex did to a woman? Made her take stupid risks?

Cause she had enough trouble right then without giving the cops at the 12th Precinct a peep show when they went to the morgue.

But, dammit, she'd been ten seconds away from coming. If Brooks had to interrupt, why couldn't the guy have waited just a bit?

A car horn sounded in the distance. A red-haired boy on a bike flew past her. Emily realized that she was sitting in her car, gazing blankly at the house and slowly rubbing the leather off her steering wheel.

Hell. She didn't want to be here, but when she'd run from the station, she hadn't even thought about going home or going to the office. No, she'd known exactly where she had to go. Exactly who she had to see.

Darla's words kept playing in her mind, rolling around and around like one of those songs you just couldn't get out of your head.

The reporter knew about her past. There was no denying that fact. No ignoring the smug look that had been on the blonde's face.

Emily had tried to hide her past. She thought she'd buried it in the ashes at Serenity Woods Psychiatric Hospital.

She'd planned the fire so carefully. Made absolutely certain that none of the patients were near the records room. Stayed close just in case someone had happened to wander by.

Yes, she'd been so careful, but her story had still leaked out.

Her gaze focused on the house. On the perfectly groomed lawn. The leaves that had been swept into a nice, neat pile.

What was she doing here? Talking to the woman would do no good, she knew that.

But the mention of Serenity Woods . . . oh damn, how long had it been since she'd even thought about that place? Years. Many blessedly forgetful years.

Now that the door to her past had swung open, she couldn't stop thinking about it.

She closed her eyes a moment and saw the girl she'd been.

"No!" Their hands were too tight around her. They were hurting her. "Let me go! Mommy! Mommy!"

Her mother was there. Watching from behind the thin sheet of glass. She was letting them do this to her, letting them hurt her.

They strapped her onto a bed. Put ties around her wrists, her ankles. Tears leaked from the corners of her eyes. They didn't understand. No one understood.

Monsters were everywhere. In the streets. In her school. Even at church. They were everywhere.

She'd told her mom, tried to point to one of the monsters with black eyes and show her mother what he was.

But her mother couldn't see them. Even though they were right there.

"Shh . . . sweetheart, relax, okay? Everything's going to be all right." It was one of the nurses talking. An older woman with bright red hair and lips and skin that looked too pale.

"I-I wanna go home." She'd never been away from home before, not once in her life. Her friends had sleepovers, but her mom had never let her go—

"You'll go home." The nurse stroked her cheek. "Once the doctors make you all better, you'll go home again."

She didn't need to be made better. Her hands balled into fists, jerked against the binds. "I'm not sick!" The words came out as a scream.

The nurse flinched, pulled her hand back.

"You need to calm down, honey." This came from one of the men in white who'd jerked her out of her mom's car.

She didn't like him. Didn't like the hard, sickly smell that clung to him. Didn't like his cold eyes.

"Mom!" Her mom couldn't leave her there. "I'm sorry! I won't talk about them again, I promise! Don't leave me, don't—"

Her mother was turning away, her shoulders hunched.

No, no, she couldn't leave her! She wanted to go back home, back to her room, back to—

Her mother was walking away. Not glancing back at her.

"Mom!" One of the straps snapped when she jerked up. "No!"

The men in white caught her shoulders, forced her back down with hands that stung.

"Get the doctor; get him in here, now!"

Emily fought the hands that held her. She didn't like this place. The people . . . something was wrong here. The air felt wrong. Too thick.

And it was so cold.

A white-haired man appeared at her side. He had a long, sharp needle in his hands. "This will calm her down."

She didn't want to be calm. She wanted to be up!

They held her tightly, and the needle pressed into her arm, burning with a hot flash of pain. She whimpered and finally met the gaze of the doctor.

His blue eyes stared into hers; then, for just an instant, they flashed black.

Her head thrashed against the table. "He's one of them!" *They had to see it!* "Look at his eyes! He's a monster!"

The men in white shifted and glanced at the doctor. The nurse didn't bother looking his way. "She's delusional. The mother says she's been seeing things for a while now, but it's getting worse."

The drug was kicking in and her body was starting to feel heavy.

"Hmmm." *The doctor was staring at her, his eyes once again a bright blue.* "And what does she see?"

"Monsters." *The nurse brushed a strand of hair back from Emily's face.* "The poor child always sees monsters."

And she saw one then. Staring down at her from behind the doctor's concerned face.

"Really . . . and she's been seeing them for years?"

The nurse nodded.

Her eyelids wanted to close, but she didn't want to sleep. Not with the monster so close.

The doctor motioned the others away. Leaned close to her. "What do you see, child, when you look at me?"

Her tongue was thick. Her mouth too dry. Emily wet her

*lips, swallowed. "M-monster. Y-your eyes . . ." Her voice was
a weak whisper.*

*He leaned even closer. So close she could feel his breath on
her cheek. "What about them?"*

"L-lying, t-trick. A-all black . . ."

*"Hmmm . . ." His lying eyes narrowed. "You see that, do
you?"*

*"F-feel y-you. In the a-air." Like a hard wind pressing on
her. He was all around. Why didn't the others feel it too?*

*Her fingers uncurled, fell back against the hard surface of
the bed. Her eyelids dropped, even though she tried to force
them open.*

Her breathing slowed and her mind began to drift.

*"It's all right, child." The doctor's voice sounded so far
away. He gripped her fingers, but the touch seemed feather
light. "I'll take care of you from now on."*

And he had, Emily realized, her thoughts sliding back to
the present. Dr. Marcus Catcherly, "Catch," had taken care
of her. He'd helped her to understand what she was seeing.
Taught her everything she knew about the *Other.*

And he'd taught her how to lie. How to pretend to be normal. To fit in at school, with her friends, and even with her
family.

He'd been her mentor, closer to her than anyone else in her
life.

After three months, Catch had convinced her mother that
Emily was well enough to return home. He'd visited her every
week, doing what he called follow-up care. She'd talked to him
about the different creatures she'd seen and he'd taught her
about them all.

And she'd never mentioned a word about monsters to her
mother again.

The fire had been his idea. He'd arranged for the patients
to go on a "therapy trip" that day. He'd helped her to time
the blaze, helped her to make certain every piece of evidence
about her stay was destroyed.

She'd been eleven years old when she entered Serenity Woods. At sixteen, she'd torched the place.

Catch had taken her secret to his grave. But one other person knew all of the details of her stay at the psychiatric hospital.

Emily opened her car door, stood, and felt the cool breeze of fall blow against her body.

The house was waiting for her.

Emily straightened her shoulders, walked slowly up the stone sidewalk. A cheerful welcome mat greeted her at the entranceway.

The house was so normal.

"Never trust anything normal. Cuz it's the normal stuff you've got to fear. Monsters, demons, witches . . . we're all more afraid of that normal world than you can ever imagine." Catch's words rang in her ears. He'd always thought humans were dangerous. Too unpredictable. *"They're more bloodthirsty than we are, remember that."*

Her hand curled into a fist. She rapped against the wooden door. Once, twice.

"Coming!" Muffled, feminine. Shuffling footsteps followed the call. The door opened with a faint squeak.

A small, dark-haired woman in her early fifties blinked. "Emily?"

"Hi, Mom." Deliberately, she kept her voice light, her body relaxed. "Mind if I come in?"

Her mother's knuckles whitened around the door frame, but after a moment, she stepped back, and Emily walked slowly into the home she hadn't seen in years.

"So, the doctor's your girlfriend now, huh?" Brooks asked as they approached Paradise Found. Two hulking guys were leaning against the outside of the building, their eyes scanning the streets.

"I'm not talking about her, Brooks." His partner was like a dog with a bone. A damn annoying dog.

"Well, it looked like she was your girlfriend. I mean, I hope you don't get that friendly in the Crypt with just every woman you meet."

The two men finally caught sight of them. They stiffened. One pulled out a radio and spoke quickly.

Good. Let the bastard know we're here.

"Damn. I think our boys are carrying." Finally, the guy was talking about something other than Emily. Brooks reached for his weapon. "You didn't tell me this Niol guy had muscle."

"Yeah, he's got muscle." Money. Muscle. And a serious attitude problem. Not the ideal candidate for an impromptu interrogation.

Colin flashed his badge to the guys at the door. Wondered if they were human or demon. For a moment, he wished he'd brought the doc with him. But he hadn't been able to find her at the precinct.

The woman had run from him. Not a good sign.

But he'd track her. Apologize for jumping on her like a starving asshole. He'd just been desperate for a taste of her, and he'd given in to the driving hunger.

A woman like her, a classy lady used to fancy restaurants and shows, she wouldn't like being pushed up against a dirty wall and stripped. Oh no, she wouldn't like that a damn bit.

He was prepared to apologize. And he was also prepared to get her naked beneath him. At the earliest opportunity.

The men grunted as they looked at his ID. "Whaddya want?" The bigger guy asked the question. The fellow had to be six foot seven, maybe eight, and his body was covered with brightly colored tattoos.

"We want to see Niol."

"Do you now?" The other guy stepped forward, the radio gripped in his hands. "You got a warrant?"

Ah, definitely not new to the game. Colin glanced toward Brooks, saw from his partner's lifted brow that he was thinking the same thing.

"We're not here to search the bar," Brooks told him, flashing his I'm-harmless-and-want-to-be-your-friend smile. "We just need to ask your boss a few questions."

"Well, maybe he don't wanna answer yer questions." Tattooed crossed his beefy arms over his chest and glowered at them.

The radio crackled to life. The smaller guy pushed a button. "Yeah?"

"Let 'em through."

Tattooed swore.

The smaller guy glared at them as he jerked his thumb toward the door. "Go on."

"Thanks," Colin muttered, and lifted his hand to his holster as he went inside. No telling what kind of reception Niol could have waiting for them . . .

The interior of Paradise Found was lit only by a few weak lights. Niol sat at a table near the bar, a pair of dark sunglasses over his eyes. He didn't rise when they approached, just inclined his head and said, "Detective, back so soon, eh?" A taunting smile curved his lips. "That's the way it is for most folks. They find my place a bit . . . addictive."

Yeah, he just bet they did.

"Drink?"

Colin shook his head.

"And what about you, Detective Brooks, can I get you a . . . whiskey, isn't it? That is your drink of choice, right?"

"I'm not thirsty." Brooks didn't appear the least bit surprised that Niol knew who he was or even his favorite drink. The guy had always been able to bluff his way through anything.

The chair squeaked as Niol leaned back. "I take it this isn't a social call?"

Colin reached into his jacket pocket. Pulled out the photos Smith had given him and tossed them onto the table. "Recognize these men?" They were head shots, but it was clear the guys were dead.

Niol touched one of the photos. "What happened to them?" Something that could have been anger hardened his words.

"Don't you know?" Colin stared back at him and kept his body loose, ready.

Very slowly, Niol took off his glasses. Colin heard a faint gasp of surprise come from Brooks.

"You think I did this?" Eyes as black as night stared back at him. A table to the left began to tremble.

Colin wasn't impressed. "Did you?"

"Not my style." Niol shoved the pictures away. "If I'd attacked them, there wouldn't have been enough left for a picture."

His words had the ring of truth.

"You know them, don't you?" Brooks asked as he stepped to the edge of the table.

Niol nodded. "I've seen them around Paradise." A vague admission, nothing more, but Colin had seen the tightening of the man's lips. The flaring of his nostrils. Hell, yeah, he knew the guys.

"You sent them to jump me and Dr. Drake the other night, didn't you?" Colin leaned over the table, getting right in Niol's face. He wasn't scared of the demon, didn't give a shit what level he was. If the guy had tried to have Emily killed, he was going to fucking rip him apart.

The demon didn't so much as blink. "I don't know what you're talking about."

"Bullshit!" Now Brooks was the one crowding him. He'd stalked around the table. Come right to Niol's side. "You know who these guys are and you hired them to rough up my partner and the doctor!"

Niol sighed softly and pushed away from the table. "I can see this isn't going to be a productive little talk." He began to stand, but Brooks caught him by the shoulder, holding him in place.

"We're not finished."

Colin felt the push of power then, felt the stir in the air—

Brooks was shoved across the room. Shoved a good ten feet. But Niol never touched him. His partner crashed into a table, fell to the floor.

Brooks jumped to his feet. "You sonofabitch!" He ran forward, arms outstretched.

Colin stepped in front of him. "Easy." The air seemed to be pushing against him, vibrating with malevolent force.

The doc would definitely have come in handy then.

"Keep your partner under control, Gyth." Niol lifted his chin, stared at him with those creepy-as-hell eyes. "Or I will."

"He assaulted me!" Brooks snapped, jerking his jacket back into place. "We can arrest the bastard."

Niol shrugged. "I never touched you. Ask your partner, he'll tell you."

Colin's jaw clenched. Brooks was no match for this guy. But Colin sure as hell would like to get two minutes alone with him. "Don't fuck with my partner again, Niol. You won't like the consequences."

A flash of amusement lightened his face. "You think you could actually take me on?"

A powerful shifter is the only Other *that can match a demon's strength.* Emily had told him that. And the doc knew her supernaturals. "No, I know I could."

The amusement vanished.

"Now cut the crap, Niol, and tell us what you know."

The demon's eyes narrowed. "The kids have been in the bar a few times. That's all I know."

"Were they working for you?" Brooks had regained some of his control, but anger still tinged his words.

"No." Niol picked up his glass, took a long swallow. "I told you, not my method."

"Look me in the eye," Colin demanded, "and tell me that you didn't send them to attack me and the doc."

Niol met his stare. "I wouldn't send someone to hurt Dr. Drake."

"But you'd send someone after my partner?" Brooks pounced on the words Niol hadn't spoken.

"No." Niol never looked away from him. "I'd do that myself."

He believed him. *Shit.* Colin finally lifted his right hand off his holster. "If you didn't send them, who did?"

"I don't know." Niol picked up his sunglasses, slid them back into place. "But I intend to find out." His face hardened. "No one uses my boys like this. *No one.*"

They were wasting their time. Niol wasn't going to tell them anything else, and Colin actually believed the demon might not know much else.

"We'll be in touch again, Niol," Colin told him.

"Oh, I don't doubt that."

"Come on," he muttered to Brooks. Time to get out of the devil's den. Bringing Brooks had been a mistake, but there hadn't seemed an easy way of ditching his partner. Not without raising too many questions.

Brooks shot a long, hard look at Niol. "I'm gonna be watching you from now on."

Niol didn't look particularly impressed.

"You fuck up, you do anything that suggests you were lying to us, I'll be back."

"Then I'll look forward to your visit. But until then, get out of my bar, Detective Brooks."

"Gladly."

Definitely a mistake bringing Brooks. He would never be able to handle a war with Niol. He didn't know who he was messing with.

Colin followed Brooks to the exit, trying to keep his body between Niol and his partner, just in case Niol was in the mood for any more of his little magical routines.

"Gyth . . ."

Niol's call stopped him just feet from the door. Colin glanced back.

"A word if you will." A pause. "Alone."

"Oh, hell, no, that's not gonna—"

"It's all right, Brooks. You can wait outside. We've got some . . . *Other* business to discuss." That would be the only reason Niol would ask him to stay.

"Fine." Brooks looked seriously pissed. "But if you need me, all you have to do is call out, and I'll be at your side."

He didn't doubt it for a minute. "Thanks, man." He waited until Brooks pushed open the door and stepped out into the light.

Then he crossed the room in two seconds. "What didn't you tell me, Niol?"

"You know the boys were demons."

No news there.

"When you and the doctor were attacked, I felt the stir of power in the air."

So he'd known about the attack. Renewed suspicion filled him.

"It wasn't me. You have my word on that."

But how much was the word of a demon worth? "You felt the attack, but you didn't try to stop it? I thought you said you wouldn't hurt Emily."

Niol stroked the top of his glass. Looked vaguely amused. "Who do you think called the cops? I mean, your brothers in blue have to be good for something, right?"

Colin wasn't amused. "If it wasn't you, then who the fuck was it?"

"Another level ten." He took a long swallow of the blood red drink. "And believe me, Gyth, we're pretty damn rare." He sat the glass down with a soft thud. "Just ask the pretty little monster doctor about that."

Another level ten. Shit. The day had not been good for him. And it had started so well, with Emily naked in bed with him.

"What do you know about hybrids?"

What? He'd heard the term *hybrid* before, but usually it'd been when he was watching TV and he'd flipped past the Discovery Channel. Hybrids were blends, mixes, like a flower produced from combining two different—

"Hmmm. Guess Emily didn't mention hybrids to you." Niol's lips curved. "Now I wonder why she wouldn't tell you about them."

Colin had the feeling he was missing a significant point in the conversation, and he didn't like that feeling. Not one damn bit.

He was around the table in a flash. He jerked the demon to his feet. "I'm not one of the humans you can screw around with." And he let the beast show in his eyes. His nails lengthened, his teeth sharpened.

"Shifter." Niol smiled. "Figured that's what you were."

"Tell me about the hybrids." Before he gave into the urges of the beast and threw the bastard across the room. It's what the demon had done to Brooks. It was what he deserved.

"Some *Other* don't mate with their own kind." He laughed, a grating, harsh sound. "But you've already figured that out, haven't you?"

His claws dug into Niol's shoulders. Not enough to tear, not yet. "Spit it out, demon."

"Rarely, very, very rarely, a child is born from those matings. A special child."

Colin lifted his claws. "And?"

"And he's a hybrid. A being of two magical lines, with the powers of both."

Why the hell were they even having this conversation? "I should care about these fucking hybrids, why?"

Niol laughed again. A long, dry laugh. "Oh, you should definitely care, shifter. You *and* Emily should care."

Ten more seconds. If the demon taunted him just a little longer, Niol would be flying across the room.

It'd be payback for his little trick on Brooks, and it'd make Colin feel damn good.

"My patience is running thin." His claws dug deeper. Niol flinched and finally stopped laughing.

"I've heard rumors . . ."

Now they were getting somewhere. Colin eased his grip. "What kind of rumors?"

"There's talk of a hybrid demon in town. A strong demon, a nine or ten."

Strong enough to cause the surge of power Emily had felt in the alley. "Half demon, huh? What else is the bastard?"

Niol pursed his lips. Glanced down at Colin's claws. "Shifter."

Oh, fuck.

"You gonna tell me what was going on back there?" Brooks demanded as they marched back to Colin's Jeep.

"We were interrogating a suspect." Colin glanced up at the sky. The sun was setting, throwing blood red streaks across the sky.

He needed to find Emily. Needed to ask her about hybrids. Damn. Could the guy they were looking for be some uber-combination of demon and shifter? If so, then the case had just taken a very dangerous turn.

Fighting and tracking another shifter was hard enough. But with a demon's magical powers . . .

The city could be screwed.

"Dammit, Colin! You know what I'm talking about!" Brooks grabbed him, shoved him against the back of the Jeep.

The beast howled, but Colin hung on to his control.

"You're holding out on me." Brooks glared at him. "You know more about the case than you've said."

Yeah, he did. And he'd have to keep holding out on his partner. Because Brooks wasn't ready for the truth.

"You didn't even have my back in there when that bastard threw me across the room!"

"He didn't throw you." Colin pushed away from the Jeep, crossed his arms over his chest, and met Brooks's angry stare.

"The hell he didn't, I—"

"I watched his hands. He never touched you." True. The demon had used his powers to push Brooks. But how did he explain that?

"I should have arrested him." Brooks rolled his left shoulder. "A night in the pen would have made him talk."

Doubtful. A night in the pen more likely would have resulted in Niol driving the guards insane. Literally.

"And what the hell was up with his eyes?" He shuddered. "Who'd want to wear contacts like that? *Everything* was pitch black."

He wanted to tell Brooks the truth.

But the last time he'd told his partner the truth about the *Other,* Colin had wound up with a bullet in him.

"I expect more from you, man." Brooks shook his head. "We've been teamed up for two years now. *I expect more.*"

He wanted to give more. Wished that he could tell Brooks everything.

But he couldn't guarantee his partner's reaction. And he didn't want to have to fight off another friend.

And the captain had said the case data he and the doc had collected was confidential. Too confidential for even Brooks.

At least for now.

Colin sighed. He had to offer Brooks something. The guy deserved that much. "You're right, there is more going on than I've told you."

A muscle flexed along his partner's jaw. "Why the hell are you keeping me out of the loop? *We're partners.*"

"I have to. What's going on has been deemed classified."

"What?"

Damn. This wasn't going well. "There's stuff going on here— it's too dangerous for you to know."

"Too dangerous for me?" His eyes narrowed to slits. "But let me guess. Dr. Drake knows, doesn't she? Why isn't it too dangerous for her?"

It was. But the doc was already in too deep to pull out.

"Shit! I don't like this." Brooks jabbed a finger in the air near Colin's chest. "Not a fucking bit."

Neither did he.

Brooks stalked around the Jeep. Jumped inside.

Colin sighed and rubbed the back of his neck. He'd have to tell the captain that Brooks was getting suspicious.

Maybe McNeal would say he should confide in him.

Or maybe not.

Colin climbed inside. Started the engine.

"I know he didn't touch me." Brooks wasn't looking at him. He was gazing straight through the windshield. "I saw his hands too. I *know* Niol didn't touch me."

"Brooks—"

"But I felt his hands on me, I *felt* him throw me across the room." He clenched his fingers into fists. "How is that possible?"

"Look, man, I—"

"Hell." Brooks sighed. "Maybe I'm the one who needs to be seeing the doctor. If I'm starting to imagine—"

"You didn't imagine it." He spun out of the lot. He couldn't risk telling Brooks much, but he'd be damned if he'd let his friend think he was going crazy. "I can't tell you what's happening, but believe me, you didn't imagine a damn thing."

No, his partner had just stepped into the world where monsters were real, and he didn't even realize it.

"We can't tell him the truth, Gyth. It's too risky."

"Yeah, I know that." But it didn't mean he had to like it. Colin paced around McNeal's office, tension tight in his body.

"The case is too big. I can't risk having one of my detectives losing his cool because he's suddenly aware that monsters are all around him."

"He might not," Colin muttered, gazing out the window into the darkness. Night had fallen over the city. It was a cloudy, starless night. The kind of night that hid secrets.

He had a bad feeling about the night. Niol's words about a hybrid had thrown him.

He wanted to talk to Emily. He'd tried to call her several times since he'd left Paradise Found, but he just kept getting her voice mail.

"Look at what happened the last time you told your partner the truth." McNeal was behind his desk. Hands resting easily on the scarred surface.

The last time you told your partner the truth. Colin stiffened. "What do you know about my old partner?"

"I know everything." McNeal arched a brow. "You think

I didn't do a full check on you before I brought you on down here? I know all about Mike Phillips."

Well, shit. "And you didn't say anything?"

McNeal shrugged. "What's to say? Your ex-partner found out that you aren't human. He tried to kill you, burn down your house."

Yeah, that about summed it up.

The captain leaned forward. "From what I learned, Phillips was unstable to begin with."

"He was a good man." He'd been a good friend, until that night. "He just couldn't handle what I—"

"Bullshit. The guy had a history of being on the edge. He'd attacked suspects, been warned by his superiors, and he'd been stalking his ex-wife."

Colin didn't speak. Mike Phillips had been his best friend for ten years. Until that one night.

"He was fleeing the scene of the fire when he hit that truck, wasn't he?" McNeal whistled softly. "Driving ninety in a twenty-five, running through the red light, driving straight into the side of that big rig."

Colin clenched his back teeth.

"He was running, wasn't he? He'd shot you, set the house on fire, then he left you to bleed out."

"Ancient history." History he sure as hell didn't feel like rehashing right then.

"But it showed you how some humans can react." His fingers drummed against the desk. "They're not all like that, but the fanatics, the ones who think monsters should be destroyed, they're the reason we still live in secret."

"You ever wonder what it would be like, Captain, if all the *Other* did reveal themselves? If we stopped pretending? Stopped hiding?" If they all came out of the shadows, what would the world be like then?

"Yeah, I wonder . . . and I think half of 'em probably wouldn't give a damn about us being different."

"And the other half?"

"They'd get the torches and try to burn us all out."

Colin nodded. "That's what I figured." And the world wasn't ready for a war between the humans and the *Other*. "So I tell Brooks nothing."

McNeal nodded. "If he gives you trouble, send him to me."

No, he could handle Brooks. But, "You know, there are only so many times a man can see magic and deny it." And if Brooks got tossed across a room by a demon a few more times, odds were good his partner would start to put the facts together.

"If he figures out what's going on, we'll deal with it. With him."

Easy words to say, but he knew Brooks wouldn't be that easy to handle. His gaze drifted to McNeal's desk. To the thin picture frame on the side.

A pretty, gray-haired lady smiled cheerfully. His eyes narrowed.

"Keep any information you find on the *Other* strictly confidential. Brief me, no one else."

"Right." He heard the captain's words, but his attention was caught by the woman in the photo. He inched closer to the frame. The woman was holding something—a basket!

He realized he was looking at a picture of the lady he'd seen in Emily's office. Margie something. The woman with the hissing wicker basket.

"My mother." McNeal tapped the picture. "Raised me by herself after my dad died in the war."

"Umm . . ." He had to ask. "What's in the basket?"

A half smile curved McNeal's lips. "Don't you know?"

"I—"

The phone beside McNeal rang. A loud, shrill cry. He picked it up, barking, "McNeal."

His eyes widened as he listened to the voice on the other end. "What? When?"

Colin tensed.

"Shit. My men are on their way." He slammed down the phone. Shot to his feet. "Get Brooks and get down to the

News Flash Five station. I'll call Emily, tell her to meet you there."

The News Flash Five station. "What's happened?"

"Some intern just found Darla Mitchell's body. Her throat's been ripped out."

Chapter 11

He smelled the blood the minute he climbed out of his Jeep. Caught the coppery scent on the wind.

A line of reporters from other stations had already gathered. Lights were flashing. Cameras rolling. "Shit. Guess who's gonna be on every station at six o'clock in the morning?"

He didn't have to guess. Dammit. The attention was just what the asshole wanted.

"Colin!" He turned at the feminine cry, found Emily hurrying toward him. Her hair was loose, her glasses slightly askew.

His insides seemed to tighten as he stared at her. He didn't want her going inside. Didn't want her seeing the carnage that waited.

But he needed her. And the needs of the cop had to outweigh the man's.

"I'm going to talk to Smith. See what she's saying about the victim." Brooks stepped away, disappearing into the swarm of blue uniforms.

"What's happening?" Emily's gaze darted to the line of police cruisers. "McNeal just told me to get down here, fast."

Shit. She didn't even know what she was walking into. He grabbed her arm, pulled her with him. "Another murder. Same MO as Myers." He bent, crouching under the yellow line of police tape at the entrance to the station.

Emily sucked in a sharp breath. "He struck again?"

"You said he probably would."

"Yes, but I'd hoped I was wrong." She licked her lips. "The victim . . . who is it?"

Colin flashed his badge to the cops blocking the crime scene. Emily pulled her ID out of her bag. "She's working the case as a profiler," he said.

The scent of blood was stronger now. Clogging his nostrils. Tickling the back of his throat.

If he'd been in his other form, he would have relished the smell. The beast loved the scent.

But the man hated it.

"Colin." Emily pulled against his hand. "Who's the victim?"

He dropped her fingers. Pulled out his latex gloves. Time to get to work. "Darla Mitchell." He shoved open the door and walked into hell.

It was the same as before. The exact same.

Darla's prone body lay on the floor, a pool of blood surrounding her body. Her throat had been ripped away, torn, clawed. Her eyes were wide open, frozen in horror, and her mouth was twisted in a silent scream.

She'd been pretty in life. But death hadn't been so kind.

Emily stared down at her still figure. The scents of blood and death filled her nostrils. Around her, she could vaguely hear a buzz of conversation. Brooks was whispering with Smith. Colin was talking to a uniformed officer, ordering the guy to get every piece of surveillance data the station had. A man in a white coat was walking around the body, snapping pictures.

And Darla stared up at her. Screaming.

Emily closed her eyes. Felt the rage simmering in the room. So strong . . .

She drew in a deep breath, exhaled slowly. The kill was fresh. And the dark power of the killer still hung in the air like a looming shadow.

There was no doubt in her mind that the killer who'd savaged Preston Myers and the killer who'd ripped out Darla's throat were one and the same. Even the blood spatters on the wall looked similar.

The taint of power surrounded her, and Emily realized there was something familiar about that remnant energy. About the hate and twisted fury.

Her eyes opened, scanned the room. Colin was a few steps away from her. Should she warn him about what she was going to do? But what if she did and the others overheard? Too many people were in the small room. No, she'd just be careful. Not pry too deeply into his mind.

But she had to see . . .

Emily looked back at the body and slowly, very slowly, lowered the mental shield in her mind.

Shit. I can't believe the bastard struck again so soon. We'd better find his face on the security camera. No way could he have gotten in and out of this place without someone knowing. The station's a freaking zoo.

Colin's mind. She pushed his thoughts away, tried to link with the flow of the killer.

I hope she didn't suffer.

Her brow furrowed. Not the killer. This guy felt . . . too sad, but he was definitely *Other.* Her head lifted and she looked toward the door. A young, uniformed cop stood in the entranceway, his hands clenched into fists. He hadn't been there when she'd arrived. Must have just come on duty.

A charmer.

She dismissed him, tried to search again. Damn. It'd been so long since she'd lowered her shields with a group of people. It was hard to narrow her focus. So hard to—

The bitch was too easy to kill.

Emily stiffened. That wasn't some kind of remnant energy.

Her blood tasted good. He could still feel it on his tongue.

Shit. Her body began to tremble. She moved her head carefully, inch by inch. Scanned the room.

Colin and the young cop were the only supernaturals she saw.

She was been better than that other bastard. Tasted sweeter. Maybe I'll go for a woman again the next time too.

Emily took one halting step toward the door, then another. Her body felt weighted, but at the same time it was as if she were being pulled. Pulled toward him.

The killer.

He was still in the building.

She had to find him.

Without a moment's hesitation, she dropped her shields all the way. Felt a flood of hot, dark power singe her, and she lunged for the door.

She'd find him now; she had his psychic trail. She'd get him and—

"Where the hell are you going?" Brooks stepped in front of her, frowning. "This is a crime scene, Dr. Drake, you can't go running—"

"Get out of my way."

The cops are right in front of me. The fucking idiots. Maybe I'll do one of them next. Yeah, that'd be good.

Brooks lifted a brow but stepped back.

Would cops taste different? Would they try to fight more?

Emily hurried out of Darla's office. Looked to the left. *That way.*

Cops were searching the hall, some crouching. Standing. Some were talking to reporters.

The dark trail of power was stronger now. Closer.

She shouldn't have fucked with me. Should have left the doctor alone.

Emily froze as she caught his thought. *The doctor.*

Darla had asked her questions at the press conference. Asked her about demons.

Had the killer known?

"Emily!" Colin's voice. A loud, demanding cry that turned every head in the hallway.

The voice in her mind shut off. The twisting power dissipated.

Shit.

Emily ran down the hallway, ignoring Colin's call. It was like the guy had just thrown up some kind of block. No, not a block. A shield. A shield just like hers.

That didn't make a damn bit of sense. She'd never met a shifter who had enough psychic power to put up a shield. A demon, yes, but not a shifter.

She pushed past two cops. Turned the corner. And ran straight into Jake.

"Dr. Drake!" His eyes widened and his arms automatically wrapped around her as she barreled into him.

She felt the weak flow of his magic surround her.

Not the guy she was looking for. "Excuse me." She pulled away from him, ran straight ahead.

But there was nothing. No telltale pull of power. No sign of any high-level supernaturals.

"Emily, what are you doing?" Colin grabbed her elbow, spun her around. "Why are you running?"

"He's here."

"What?"

"The killer. He's still in the building. Or he was . . . just a moment ago."

His fingers tightened around her. "How do you know? Did you see something?"

"I heard him."

Colin frowned, and Emily realized that her words probably weren't making much sense. But they were wasting time and she had to hurry.

"I lowered my shielding, okay?" Her voice was a whisper. "I wanted to see if I could sense anything about the killing and I-I sensed him. Heard his thoughts. Colin, *he was here,* just seconds ago."

He reached for his gun. "You still hear 'im?"

Emily bit her lip. "His voice stopped. When you called my name."

"Probably because the bastard realized you were here and that you could track him."

Yes, but how had a shifter known that?

Colin raised his voice, calling out to the cops. "I want a lockdown on this building. Round up every single employee. Put them all in one room."

"It might not be one of the employees," Emily said, leaning in close to him. "Colin, the killer could be a cop."

He swore.

"I-I need to go over every inch of this building, see if I can find him."

He clamped his hand around her wrist. "You're not goin' anywhere without me, Doc."

His gun was drawn, ready. "Now let's go find the bastard."

But they didn't find him. They searched the entire station, roof to basement. Emily saw every employee, studied every cop, but she couldn't find the killer.

The only *Other* she saw were Colin, the young charmer cop, and Jake Donnelley. And none of those men had the right magic trail to match the killer.

He'd gotten away. Somehow, he'd managed to slip past the police and escape.

Dammit.

They were back in Darla's office. Her body had been covered by a sheet, and two men pushing a gurney were entering the room.

Emily pulled off her glasses, rubbed the bridge of her nose. She'd been so close, and that bastard had gotten away.

"Crime scenes can be hard, can't they?"

She jerked at the soft voice, so close to her back. Emily turned around, found Smith staring at her with sympathy in her dark eyes. "Umm, yeah, they can be." Anything that involved a dead, bloody body automatically fell under "hard" in her book.

"I saw you run out earlier." Smith hesitated. "Are you all right?"

Emily realized what her sudden fast and furious departure must have looked like.

The profiler couldn't handle the crime scene.

But it wasn't like she could tell Smith the truth. So she forced a smile. "I'm fine now." Actually, she was furious. The murdering bastard had gotten away from her. If she'd had just a few more minutes to track him—

"My first few scenes made me sick. I mean, I'd been in medical school, and I'd seen dead bodies before." Smith shook her head. "But seeing a person like this, a person who fought to live just hours ago . . ." She sighed. "It's hard to get used to."

Emily wasn't sure she'd ever get used to seeing bodies that had been savaged like Darla's.

"Why don't you go on home?" Smith suggested. "It's late, and there can't be much else you can do here tonight."

No, there wasn't anything else she could do. The killer was gone, the reporter was dead, and she was left with the twisted flow of the Night Butcher's rage sliding through her mind.

"Good idea," she muttered. "Tell Colin I left, will you?" Cause she didn't want to face him again just then. After they'd finished searching, he'd looked at her with . . . damn, had that been doubt in his eyes?

Did the man think she'd made up the story about hearing the killer?

Hell, she really did need to get out of there. Needed to clear her head.

And try to stop hearing the killer's voice replaying in her mind.

Maybe next time I'll try a cop.

Her hands fisted. *Maybe next time I'll catch you first, you sonofabitch.*

"Hey, Gyth! There's a guy here who says he has to talk to you."

Colin glanced up from Darla's desk. Saw Jake Donnelley peering over a uniform's shoulder.

"Who's that?" Brooks asked, straightening to better study him.

"Darla's cameraman."

"Think he knows something?"

"One way to find out." He shoved to his feet, stalked over to meet the demon.

"W-we need to talk." Jake was sweating.

"Sure." Colin stepped into the hallway. The area had cleared out a lot in the last hour. Even as he spoke, Darla's body was wheeled out.

Jake looked at the body bag, gulped, then hurriedly glanced away.

"What do you know, Donnelley? Did you see something? The killer?" If only he could be that lucky.

Jake shook his head. "Didn't see anything. But you need to know—" He broke off as a female cop passed them. Lowering his voice, he continued, "You need to know what Darla was working on."

"Oh?" His interest was caught but he played it cool and easy. "And what story was she investigating?"

Jake met his gaze. "Dr. Drake."

Do you still see demons? Colin kept his face expressionless. "What about her?"

"Darla found out that Dr. Drake was sent to one of them psych wards when she was a kid."

I never said I worked there.

Shit. "She was going to run the story, wasn't she?"

Jake nodded.

"And is this the only story Darla was working on?" Please, let there be something else.

"Other than the robbery at Southern Bank, yeah."

Not good. "You told anybody else about this?"

Jake shook his head. "Not gonna either." His face tightened. "We both know why the doctor got sent to that place. And we know she wasn't seeing things."

He could all too easily imagine Emily as a child, seeing demons and monsters wherever she turned. Yeah, he knew why she'd wound up at Serenity Woods.

"All right, Donnelley. Thanks for the tip."

The cameraman shuffled off down the hallway.

Colin watched him for a moment, then turned back to the crime scene. He needed to find Emily. His gaze searched the room.

Where is she?

"Hey!" Brooks stepped forward. "What'd the guy have to say?"

Colin shrugged. "Nothing really." He met his partner's stare straight on. Lying wasn't hard for him. He'd been doing it his whole life. "Just that Darla was working on a bank robbery story before she was killed."

"Really?" Brooks's eyes narrowed. "That was all he said?"

"Yeah." Emily wasn't in the room. "Where's Dr. Drake?"

Smith brushed by him, paused. "She left about twenty minutes ago. Said she'd check in at the station tomorrow."

His stomach clenched. It was okay. The doc knew how to take care of herself. So she'd gone home alone. No big deal.

Except he was sure someone had been watching her house. Watching her.

And she'd just tapped into a killer's mind.

Probably no need to worry—*ah, bullshit.* "Can you finish things here?" he asked Brooks.

"Uh, yeah. There are just a few more interviews—"

"Good." The word had barely passed his lips before he marched out of the room, moving faster, faster with each step.

His gut was tight, and his instincts were screaming at him. Something was wrong. He had to get to Emily.

All of the lights were out. Emily sat in her car, staring up at her house. She'd left the light in the den on; she always did. But the house was dark. *Too dark.*

The bulb could have blown. She hadn't changed it in a few weeks—or, hell, she really couldn't remember the last time she'd changed it.

Emily climbed slowly out of the car. Just because the house

was dark, it didn't mean anything. She was jumpy because of the crime scene. Seeing a woman with her throat ripped out would make anyone a bit uncertain.

She pulled out her cell phone as she walked up the steps. Gripped her keys in her right hand. Her heart was racing, the drumming shaking her chest *all because her light was out.*

The porch light should have been on, too, Emily realized. It was night, so the light should have come on automatically.

Her shoes crunched against something hard. Sharp. Emily glanced down. It looked like . . . white glass. Her gaze darted up to the porch light. The bulb was broken.

Her breath caught. Two lights—that was too big of a coincidence for her. Her thumb pushed the call button on her phone. She'd programmed Colin's cell in yesterday. Emily started to back up.

"Gyth."

"I-I think someone's been in my house." Her voice was hushed as she retreated another slow step.

"Emily? Is that you?"

"Yes."

"What's wrong? I can barely hear you—"

Cause she didn't want to raise her voice and alert whoever might be inside. "Someone's been in my house," she repeated quietly.

"Shit." Good, he'd heard her. "I'm on my way, baby. Get in your car and stay there until—"

The wooden step behind her creaked. Her blood seemed to freeze.

He wasn't in the house. He was out there, *with her.*

Her fingers tightened around the keys. They were the only weapon she had. Drawing in a deep breath, Emily spun around, raising the keys and screaming.

He was ready for her. The guy punched out with his hand, catching her in the cheek and sending her sprawling back against the porch.

The cell phone fell from her fingers, crashed onto the wood.

And Emily realized that Colin wouldn't arrive soon enough.

She was on her own.

Just as she'd always been.

"Emily? *Emily! Fuck!*" The line was dead. He punched in a call to 911. "This is Detective Colin Gyth. Badge number 2517. I've got an assault in progress." Shit, he hoped he didn't. If anyone so much as touched Emily, the guy would find out just how much of an animal he could be. "Send patrols out *now* to 602 Lyons Lane."

He slammed the gas pedal down to the floor of the Jeep.

Hold on, baby, I'm coming.

The fight was short and brutal. Emily crouched on the porch, her cheek burning. The guy lunged for her, but she was ready. She couldn't see much in the dark, so she kicked out, aiming for what she sure as hell hoped was his groin.

He grunted, fell back. "Bitch!"

Yeah, she was. Emily leaped up, drove the keys down into his arm as hard as she could.

He grabbed her wrist, grinding bones together until she gasped and dropped the keys.

"Fucking demon. You're gonna pay." His voice was a high-pitched whisper, the whisper of . . . a boy?

And had he just called her a demon?

She twisted her hand, trying to break free. God, hadn't someone heard her scream? The Grantons had come back from Disney World two days ago—they should have heard her.

Emily opened her mouth, ready to scream so loud the dead would hear her, but her attacker slapped a thin, sweaty hand over her lips.

"Private party, demon. No one else is invited."

She bit him. As hard as she could. Until she tasted blood.

He howled and jerked his hand back. And she screamed. And screamed.

A light flashed on at the Grantons.

Finally.

Her attacker swore, stumbled back. "I'll be back for you, bitch."

Bitch or demon. Make up your mind, asshole.

Adrenaline pumped through her, and as he fled, for one mad moment, she actually thought about running after him.

Then she realized her hands were shaking. Her legs, hell, everything shook, and she didn't think that she could have made it four steps, much less all the way across the yard.

Her attacker ran to the wooded lot. For just an instant, the glow of a streetlight fell over him. He glanced back at her—

Just a kid. A kid with hair too long, a face too thin, and eyes too big.

Then he was gone. Disappearing into the night.

"Emily!" Mark pounded up the steps, grabbed her, and pulled her to her feet.

Damn. When had she fallen again?

"What happened?"

"Call the police . . ." She swallowed, realized her throat was desert dry. *Fear will do that to you.*

She'd been more scared of that kid than she had been tracking a killer through the News Flash Five station.

But Colin had been with her then. And she'd known he'd keep her safe.

She'd trusted him.

Her knees began to shake again.

"I thought I saw someone running—" Mark glanced toward the lot.

"Some kid. He hit me." *Called me a demon, said he'd be back for me.*

"Jesus." Mark wrapped his arm around her. "Let's get inside and we'll call the cops."

They stepped forward, and Emily saw that her door was ajar. *Oh, no, not a good sign.*

She pushed the door all the way open. Stepped inside the small foyer. Turned on the light.

"What in the hell . . ." Mark's voice trailed off.

Emily crept forward. Hit the light switch for the den.

Destroyed. Her furniture had been smashed, her couch and love seat ripped apart. The TV was on the floor, the screen in pieces. Papers, magazines, books littered the floor.

"Let's get out of here." Mark took her hand. "Go back to my place and call—"

"*Step away from the woman, now!*" Colin's voice snarled from directly behind them.

Emily whirled around and heard Mark gasp in surprise. Colin stood in the doorway, his gun drawn, his face tight with fury.

Mark made the mistake of tightening his hold. "You don't understand, I'm her neigh—"

"*Get your fucking hands off her or I'll shoot.*" His stare was intense. A turbulent blue that was, oh, shit, beginning to glow.

No, no, he couldn't shift. Not in front of Mark. She'd never be able to explain that.

Emily stepped forward, pulling away from Mark's suddenly sweaty touch. "It's all right, Colin. Mark's my neighbor and—"

His gaze flashed to her face. Narrowed. The gun never wavered. "What the hell happened to your cheek?"

Emily lifted her hand to her right cheek. She could only imagine how the mark must look in the harsh light. "Someone was here when I arrived." *A punk kid who thinks I'm a demon.* "He was waiting on the porch."

"Fuck."

Yeah, that pretty much summed it up.

"Umm . . . are you a policeman?" Mark sounded like he very much hoped that was the case.

Colin grunted. Dropped his gun and grabbed Emily. He pulled her against his chest, wrapped his arms tightly around her, and just held her.

Emily squeezed her eyes shut to stop the stupid tears she could feel welling. Aftereffects, she was sure. But, oh, it sure felt good to be in his arms.

The edge of his fingers dug into her skin. He pulled back slowly, stared down at her. Then he kissed her. A hard, hot, open-mouthed kiss that stole her breath.

"I guess you two know each other."

Sirens blared in the distance. Grew closer.

Emily wrapped her hands around Colin's shoulders, held him tighter.

God, but she loved the way the man kissed. Loved the smooth, sensual thrust of his tongue. Loved the faint bite of his teeth as he nibbled on her mouth.

His mouth lifted, just an inch. "Don't ever scare me like that again."

A choked laugh slipped past her lips. "I'll see what I can do."

Bright blue lights filled her yard, spilled through the open door.

The cavalry had arrived.

But too late to catch the bad guy.

Chapter 12

He took her back to his place. She'd argued at first, saying she should stay at her house, try to clean, but the crime scene guys had nixed that idea.

They'd left a team at her home, searching for fingerprints. Hairs. Anything that might give them a clue to the identity of the guy who'd broken in.

A kid. Emily had given him a description of the boy. Pegged him for being around sixteen.

Colin didn't give a damn how old the guy was. He just wanted to find him, make him pay.

The punk had hit Emily. The red stain on her cheek had already turned into a faint brown bruise.

And her house—*sonofabitch*. All her clothes had been destroyed. Her bed. The dresser. Her books. Even her food—the guy had dumped it all over the kitchen floor.

Emily's house had looked far too similar to Gillian Nemont's place, and Colin couldn't ignore the link. Hell, even the slash marks in the couch cushions had looked the same. Both were hard, long slashes from left to right.

Had the kid done both jobs? He'd find out, when he found the boy.

And the fact that Gillian Nemont still hadn't turned up worried him. A lot. People didn't just disappear. Not without a damn good reason. Or help.

Initially, he'd thought that Gillian had fled on her own.

But now, now he was very much afraid that she'd had help. The unfriendly kind.

"I-I could have stayed in a hotel, you know." Emily stood beside the couch, looking tired, disheveled, and so beautiful she made him ache.

"I wanted you to stay here." With him. Where he could keep an eye on her.

Colin stalked toward her. The woman had scared a good ten years off his life. He'd heard her scream, then the phone had disconnected.

He'd thought the Night Butcher had her.

He caught her chin in his hand. Forced her to look up, to meet his stare. "I meant what I said before, Em. Don't scare me like that again." Because the beast had come too close to the surface. It had taken every ounce of his control to fight the change.

And when he'd gone into her house, seen that guy with his hands on her—

The change had started. His bones had begun to snap. His claws to lengthen.

It had only been when he'd taken Emily into his arms that the beast had calmed. When he kissed her, held her, he'd regained his control.

Lucky for her neighbor. Otherwise, the guy would have found out what it was like to have an angry shifter attack.

"It's not like I did it deliberately, you know," Emily told him, and there was a faint bite to her tone. "I didn't go out looking for some junior asshole to jump me."

No, she hadn't. But she had gone searching for a killer at the station without telling him. Which was about, oh, ten times worse in his book.

If he hadn't glanced up as she ran from the room, Emily would have gone off alone.

And what would she have done if she'd actually managed to track the killer?

A cold fist seemed to squeeze his heart. Emily wasn't like him. She didn't have a shifter's strength or a demon's power.

She was human. Vulnerable. Weak. And right then, her vulnerability pissed him off.

"You have to be more careful." He dropped his hand but couldn't force himself to move back. Her scent was in the air, in his nostrils.

Emily arched a brow. "I'm not the cop. You're the one who likes to play with danger every day, not me." She sighed. "Damn. Look, I don't want to have this conversation right now, okay? I'm tired, my face hurts, and I just want to crawl into bed." Emily turned away from him. Started to walk down the hall.

"Tell me about Serenity Woods." He hadn't meant to ask, not then, but the words just slipped out.

Emily stiffened. "We already talked about that."

"Not enough we didn't. Darla Mitchell was planning to do a story on you. On Serenity Woods. An exposé."

She glanced back at him. "She wouldn't have had any real proof. The story never would've aired."

"What do you mean?"

"I mean she had an informer who fed her details about me, sure, but that person wouldn't have gone public."

"How do you know?"

"Because I visited my dear mother earlier today and warned her to stop talking to reporters." One shoulder lifted, fell. "My mom's a bit naive. She didn't understand what she was doing when she spoke with Darla."

She didn't understand she was selling out her daughter? He didn't press on that issue. Better save it for later. "So Darla didn't have any other evidence?"

Emily turned to fully face him. "I had my little stay at Serenity Woods more than twenty years ago. The records room burned down about five years after I was released."

"So no staff members could come forward and talk?" The cop in him just couldn't shut off.

"There is such a thing as patient confidentiality, you know."

"And I know that rule doesn't apply to orderlies or janitors or secretaries or—"

Her hand lifted. "No one would talk."

"You sure seem damn sure of that."

"I am." Her lips tightened. "The humans there were made to . . . forget my stay."

Alarm bells rang in his head. "And just how did that nice trick happen?"

"The psychiatrist in charge of the facility, Dr. Catcherly, he wasn't human. He was a level-six demon, strong enough to plant suggestions in people's minds."

"And he made the staff forget about you."

"Yes." Emily swallowed, balled her hands into fists. "I wasn't crazy, you know. I just didn't understand what was happening to me. I tried to tell my mother, but she didn't believe me. She thought I was having some kind of breakdown, like my dad."

"Your dad?"

Emily shook her head. "His obituary in the paper said that he'd died in a hunting accident." A short, bitter laugh tumbled past her lips. "But there was no accident. He picked up a gun, put it in his mouth, and pulled the trigger."

Jesus. That detail sure hadn't been in her background check.

"I was seven when I found him." She swallowed. "I'd already started seeing things by then. And when my dad killed himself, my mom just . . . she didn't want to hear that I was seeing things. She didn't want me to be . . . like he was."

Her husband had eaten his gun. Her kid was talking about seeing monsters. No wonder Emily had ended up in a psych ward.

"I just wanted her to believe me," Emily whispered, "but I guess I was asking too much."

He reached for her hand. Tightened his fingers around hers. "I understand."

Her gaze met his. "I know you do."

He pulled her closer. Lifted his left hand to stroke her lips. Such soft, sweet lips.

Her mouth parted on a gentle breath.

Keeping his eyes on hers, he lowered his head, brought his mouth to hers. Tasted her.

His tongue pushed into her mouth slowly. A long, deep thrust. Her tongue met his, sliding, stroking.

His cock tightened.

Hell, he'd been in a state of semiarousal ever since the kiss at her house. And having her in his arms again, feeling her mouth against his, her breasts against his chest, it was more temptation than he could handle.

His hand slid down the curve of her jaw, stroked her neck.

Emily pulled back, shaking her head. "Don't treat me like this."

What?

"I'm not some delicate flower."

No, but she was a delicate *human.*

"I don't want gentle and easy tonight." She jerked off her shirt, tossed it onto the floor. "I want you to take me, your way. Hard. Fast. And deep."

The beast snarled in agreement.

"I want you to make me forget that murdering bastard out there. That punk kid. Everything. I just want to feel you."

Colin jerked off his own shirt. "All you had to do was ask, baby."

Emily's green gaze swept down his body. She licked her lips, eyeing the erection that pressed against the front of his jeans.

Hunger pumped through him.

Emily pulled off her glasses, sat them near the TV. And slipped to her knees before him. "But before we get to the main event," she whispered, "I think it's my turn to touch you."

Her fingers were rock steady as she reached for his jeans. A quick flick of her hand and the button unsnapped. The slow hiss of his zipper filled the air.

His cock sprang forward, lunging for her eager hands. He hadn't bothered with underwear. Never did.

Her fingers skimmed over his cock. Stroked from base to

head. Her breath blew over him, slightly cool, and so arousing he shuddered.

A drop of pre-cum appeared on the head of his penis. Emily murmured softly and rubbed her index finger over the liquid. She glanced up at him and brought her finger to her lips. Tasted him.

"Umm, nice." She held his gaze a moment longer. "I like the way you taste." Her mouth hovered over his cock. Her tongue snaked out, licked the bulbous head of his arousal.

Oh, fuck, yes.

Then she took him inside, all the way inside the warm cavern of her mouth. Sucking. Licking. And stroking with her hand.

Damn, but the doc knows exactly how to touch me.

He reached down, found the soft weight of her breasts and fondled her.

She gasped against him. *Oh, that felt good.*

So he did it again. Stroked her. Slid his fingers beneath her lacy bra and found her nipples. He squeezed lightly, applying just enough pressure.

Her mouth trembled around him as she moaned.

His cock swelled even more. He began to thrust against her mouth. Shallow thrusts, then deeper, harder.

Her mouth was wet, warm, so fucking perfect that his orgasm was already building, building . . .

Her lips tightened around him as she sucked harder.

"No!" He jerked away from her, his cock standing straight up.

Emily blinked up at him, her face flushed. "Didn't you like—"

"Oh, hell, yeah, baby." The woman had given him the best blow job of his life. "You wanted it my way, right?"

She licked her lips, nodded.

Damn. Seeing her on the floor, on her knees before him, was making him so fucking hungry for her. He was fighting the beast. The animal in him wanted her just as badly as the man.

Maybe it was her vulnerability that drew the beast. He smelled prey.

And as for the man . . . He smelled her sweet cream. And he wanted her.

"Take off the rest of your clothes."

Emily pushed to her feet. Began to walk down the hall.

"No. In here."

No way would he make it to the bedroom. He wanted her naked, open, and ready *right then.*

He sure as hell hoped that Emily had meant what she'd said. Because they were definitely about to fuck *his* way.

Emily kicked off her shoes. Pushed down her skirt. And he almost climaxed right then.

She was wearing a thin scrap of black lace and a garter belt. *A garter belt.* He'd seen those only in his dreams.

Who would have thought his button-downed little doc would have his dream underwear?

"Get on your hands and knees." His voice was a guttural growl. More beast than man.

Emily tossed back her hair and damn if a come-hither smile didn't curve her lips as she slowly crouched on the floor. She placed her hands deliberately and pressed her knees against the wooden floor. Her hair trailed over her back, a silken mass that he wanted to touch.

But not as much as he wanted to touch her.

Her hips arched, her perfect ass tilted in the air. "Is this what you wanted?"

Hell, yes.

His teeth were lengthening. He'd have to take care with her, have to—

"Then come take me."

Fuck.

His control snapped.

Colin lunged for her, hitting the floor hard, but he didn't care. His hands curled around her hips, and his mouth pressed against her back. He tasted her skin. Licked her and lightly bit her flesh.

Emily tossed back her head and lifted her hips. "Colin . . ."
A demand.

He shoved his jeans all the way down. Forced her legs farther apart. Then trailed his fingers over the soft curve of her ass.

"What do you want, Emily? What do you want me to do?"

His hand slipped between the legs, found her warm, wet with arousal. He teased her, pushing his index finger just inside her small, tight opening, and rubbed his thumb against the center of her desire.

Her body stiffened. "Ah . . . God, yes!"

He pulled his finger back, drove it deep. "Tell me what you want."

"I want you inside me."

He growled. Grabbed his cock with one hand. Reached for the foil packet in his pocket.

"No!" Emily twisted, glaring back at him. "I want to feel *you*."

And he sure as hell wanted to feel her. But they had to be careful, they couldn't take any risks.

"Colin, I-I'm protected and I'm clean. And your kind—you don't get sick anyway. So we don't need to worry." Her hips rolled against him. "This time, I just want you."

His right hand clamped over her hips. Positioned her. He lodged the head of his erection against her opening, felt the warm, creamy welcome of her sex. "Then take me."

He plunged deep in one smooth, hard thrust.

Emily arched beneath him.

He pulled back, drove to the hilt. Again. Again.

Emily's hips were thrusting back against him, meeting him move for move. He was growling, she was moaning, the air was thick with the scent of their lovemaking.

Colin crouched over her, wrapping his body over hers as he thrust. *Ah, damn, but she feels good. Tight. Hot. Wet.*
So. Fucking. Perfect.

His hands covered hers. His nails sharpened.

Careful, careful—

His mouth found the curve of her throat. Licked. Sucked.

Her hips rolled against him, her sex squeezed. She was close to climaxing. He could feel the slight stiffening of her body that signaled her coming release.

His teeth pressed against her throat. He could feel her pulse beating. Faster. Faster. The blood was pounding just beneath the skin.

The edge of his canines raked against her.

Emily gasped, bucked beneath him. She came, her body shaking, squeezing his cock as she whispered his name.

He shifted, freeing her hands, pulling back just enough to grab her hips so that he could thrust, harder, *harder* . . .

His mouth stayed on her throat.

If she were his mate, he'd mark her again. *A true mark. A mark of shared blood. Of bonding.*

If she were his mate.

But she wasn't. She was human. *Human.*

His balls tightened. His spine stiffened. He clenched his teeth, forced his mouth to move away from the sweet flesh of her throat.

His hands were tight upon her. His hips pistoned. Oh, damn, it'd never been like this before, *never.*

Colin came, pumping into her, shuddering, and spilling his seed in the hot depths of her body.

Moonlight spilled through the open window, fell onto the bed. Emily stretched slowly beneath the covers and turned onto her side, staring at Colin.

His chest rose and fell slowly. But she knew he wasn't asleep. Not yet.

"I-I need to ask you something, Colin." When she'd gone into the bathroom, she'd found scratch marks on her hips. And when they'd been making love, she'd felt the sharpened edge of his teeth against her. Strangely, she hadn't been frightened when she thought he was going to bite her.

She'd been . . . aroused.

And she'd never been one of those girls with a vampire fetish.

But with Colin, none of her usual rules seemed to apply.

She lifted her hand, trailed her fingers over the broad expanse of his chest. She liked his chest. Liked the smooth muscles, the dark curling hair that arrowed down to his groin.

Her hand moved to his shoulder. Found the faint, raised scar.

"What do you want to know?" He caught her hand. Brought it to his lips and kissed her palm.

She drew in a quick breath. The signs were starting to mount up against Colin, and she really, *really* needed to know . . . "Colin, what animal do you carry?" The teeth, the claws, the shining eyes—had to be a panther, a leopard, or maybe a wolf.

He stiffened against her. "Does it matter?"

Once, she would have said that it did. But now, she wasn't so sure. "You don't have to hide from me."

"And you don't have to worry about the beast I carry." His fingers tightened around hers. "I'll never let him hurt you. I control him, he doesn't control me."

She'd heard that from others before. Heard them swear they could contain the beast inside. And she'd known they lied.

Because the beasts inside the shifters, they were strong. Deadly. And if the man was pushed too far, the animal would take over.

It was the nature of the beast.

Someone was pounding at the door. Emily grabbed a pillow, pulled it over her head. No, no, she didn't want to wake up yet.

"Shit!" A masculine growl that was way, way too close.

She shoved the pillow aside as her eyes snapped open. *Colin.* Her memory came flooding back.

Darla.
The killer.
The dumb-ass kid who'd busted into her house.
And the hottest sex she'd had in years.
"Stay here." She had only seconds to admire his tight ass before Colin jerked on a pair of jeans. His stare shot to the clock. "Whoever that is had better have a damn good reason for being here at 6 A.M."

Six o'clock. That meant they'd gotten a grand total of three hours' worth of sleep.

Emily pulled the sheet over her breasts. She wasn't sure where her clothes were. Maybe still in the den? And where were her glasses?

Colin stomped out of the room. She heard the click of the lock, then, "What the hell are you doing here, Brooks?"

Emily frowned and inched to the edge of the bed.

"Where's Dr. Drake?"

Her gaze scanned the room. *The closet.* She hurried across the floor, her toes tingling at the contact with the cold wood. She grabbed one of his shirts, pulling it quickly over her head. Luckily, the T-shirt fell to the middle of her thighs so she wouldn't be flashing Colin's partner.

"She's here, isn't she?" Brooks's voice rose. "Dr. Drake, I need to talk to you. *Now.*"

She blinked. He sounded pissed. *What's wrong with him?* Sure, she might have accidentally shoved him last night when she'd been locked on the killer, but that was hardly any reason for him to be an—

"Watch your tone, Brooks."

"You're the one who needs to watch what he's doing, *partner.* You're screwing this woman and you don't even know—"

Emily shot down the hallway, found Colin glaring nose to nose at Brooks. "What's going on here?"

Brooks glanced toward her, eyes narrowed. "You tell me."

Emily shook her head. "Look, it's too early for me to play some dumb-ass guessing game with you."

"Where were you last night between eight and ten P.M.?"

"What?" No, no way had that too-pretty, GQ wannabe just asked her for an alibi. "Why do you want to know?"

"I just spent the last three hours breaking apart Darla's hard drive." He cocked a brow. "Wanna know what I found?"

Serenity Woods.

"Back off, Brooks." Colin didn't raise his voice. The utter coldness of his tone cut through the room.

Comprehension widened Brooks's eyes. "You knew, didn't you? You knew and you didn't tell me."

"Cause there's nothing to tell. Darla had her facts wrong about Emily."

"Oh?" Brooks stepped away from Colin. Paced to her side. His gaze swept over her body. Returned to her face. "So she's not crazy? She wasn't admitted to a juvie psychiatric ward when she was eleven because she was seeing monsters?"

Emily lifted her chin. "*She* is right in front of you. And, no, I'm not crazy. I'm completely, perfectly sane."

"Umm, you just see monsters. But other than that little oddity, you're completely normal."

"Stop being a dick, Brooks." Colin positioned his body in front of her. "Emily, go get dressed."

"No." She'd be damned if she'd skulk away while the boy blunder called her a nutcase. "I think I need to clear up a few points with your partner here."

Colin looked over his shoulder, his jaw clenched. "Fine." He turned back to Brooks. Jabbed his finger into his chest. "But if your eyes drop one more time, I'm knocking you out. Partner or not."

Emily crossed her arms over her chest. Tapped her foot. "I don't know what you found on her computer, but Darla's facts were wrong. I'm not now nor have I ever been"—her back teeth ground together as she gritted—"crazy." No, she just saw monsters. But the monsters were real.

"A story like that, it would have ruined your practice."

Doubtful. Emily snorted. It probably would have just given her more business. It would have been as close to advertising for *Other* patients as she could get. "It wouldn't have effected me."

"Bullshit."

Colin rolled his shoulders, narrowed his eyes. "Watch it."

"Darla was going to ruin your career, tell the world about the little girl who'd hallucinated, whose mom sent her to a psych ward because she didn't want a crazy kid."

Emily stepped forward, punched her finger in his chest. "Listen up, Brooks. I told you already, I'm not crazy. Darla's story wouldn't have done a damn thing to my career because the story would never have run. She didn't have any facts to back up her wild ideas, okay?" Oh, the man was starting to royally piss her off.

She didn't want a crazy kid.

That hit just a little too close to home.

And it made her even angrier. "I don't have to listen to any more of this crap. I'm working this case with you, Detective. I didn't kill Darla Mitchell."

"Then tell me where you were between 8 and 10."

"At. My. Mother's. 2801 Terrace Lane. Check it out. Go ask her. Interview her neighbors. I'm sure someone saw me."

He pulled out a small notebook. Scribbled something down. The address, no doubt. Asshole.

"Now if you're done interrogating me, I'm going to shower." Before she gave into the impulse rushing through her and slugged him.

Being accused of ripping out a reporter's throat first thing in the morning had sure screwed up her mood.

Emily didn't wait for him to answer. She spun on her heel and stormed from the room.

The bathroom door slammed.

Colin stared at his partner, shook his head. "What the hell were you thinking?"

Very carefully, Brooks folded his notebook. Tucked it in

his jacket pocket. "I was thinking we have a murder to solve and that your girlfriend has a hell of a motive."

"Two murders," Colin corrected, trying hard to keep the anger out of his voice. "Two murders with the exact MO. What, you think Emily had a motive for offing Preston too?"

"I think she's linked to him. I haven't connected the pieces yet, but I will."

"What? The doc had nothing to do—"

"Her place was trashed last night, wasn't it? Just like Gillian Nemont's."

Exactly like Gillian's.

"What are the odds of that?" Brooks asked quietly. "What are the odds that both Dr. Drake's place and Gillian's would get trashed?"

Colin didn't reply. Cause he'd been wondering the same thing.

"I think she's holding out on us. She knows something, or else—"

"Or else what?"

"She's involved."

Shit. "You saw the bodies. There's no way Emily could have done that." No, she'd been horrified when she'd seen the victims and the blood.

"The facts aren't adding up. Not one damn bit." Brooks began pacing around the room. "The case smells to high heaven. And I know, *I know* I'm being kept in the dark." He rounded on Colin. "And I don't like it."

Colin glared right back at him. "And I don't like it when my partner comes here at dawn and starts harassing my lover."

"I don't trust her."

I do. "No one's asked you to."

"I'm checking out her alibi. You coming with me or not?"

"Right now, not." Hell, his eyes were still sandy from sleep. And Emily was pissed, and in the shower, naked.

But he had a fucking job to do, and on this case he couldn't afford to have anyone questioning his motives. Or his lover's.

"Give me an hour. I'll meet you at the station." He'd have to clear Emily so that Brooks would drop this lame-ass theory.

Brooks jerked his head in agreement, turned toward the door.

Colin caught his arm in a steely grip. He figured Emily should be proud of him; he'd held onto his cool a good fifteen minutes. "Not so fast, *partner*." He applied just enough pressure to grind bones.

"What the he—"

"Don't ever fucking come to my house and rip into my woman that way again, you understand me?" He didn't let up on the pressure, not for one minute.

Brooks tried to jerk away. Colin just tightened his grip. "I asked if you understood." He'd hate to break the guy's arm, but he had a point to make.

Don't mess with Emily.

"I'm doing my job. *Our* job." Moisture appeared above Brooks's upper lip. "I have to check her out."

Yeah, but it was more than that. He'd seen Brooks check out hundreds of suspects before, and he'd never had the tight rage in his voice that he'd had when he confronted Emily. Understanding dawned. "You don't like her, do you?"

"I don't trust her."

Colin eased his grip. He'd deliberately reached for his partner's left arm. No sense putting his shooting hand out of commission. "You don't have to trust her."

"You shouldn't either. There's something about her . . . it's just . . . off." When Colin's hold lightened, Brooks managed to jerk his arm free. "Don't let the fact that she's a good piece of ass screw up your head, Gyth. She's got secrets, and those secrets could be deadly."

He wrenched open the door, stalked into the bright morning light.

Colin watched him leave, watched as he revved his small sports car and spun out of the drive.

Brooks was getting drawn deeper and deeper into the Butcher case, and the guy was a good detective.

There was a chance he could find out the truth.

How would he handle it?

The guy seemed certain that Emily was a threat. How would he feel if he learned the true danger came from his own partner?

You fucking freak! I'll kill you! I'll kill you!

He rolled his right shoulder. Been there, done that. He hoped there wouldn't be a repeat performance this time around.

He shut the front door, heard the faint spray of water from the shower.

His head tilted at the sound, and an image of Emily, her pale body glistening with water, filled his mind.

Hmmm. He'd told Brooks he'd meet him in an hour.

More than enough time . . .

The warm water slid over her skin. Ah, God, it felt good. Emily tilted her head beneath the spray, letting the water soak her hair. Steam rose around her, light, foggy tendrils that drifted in the air. She turned back around—

And saw the outline of a man's body through the distorted glass of the shower door.

Her heart beat faster, faster—

Colin pulled open the door. He was naked. And aroused.

Emily swallowed. Forced her gaze to lift. "I-is your partner gone?"

"Umm." His own gaze swept down her body, lingering on her breasts, the dark hair at the juncture of her thighs.

He stepped into the shower, closed the door with a soft click behind him.

"H-he's wrong, you know. I didn't have anything to do with Darla's murder."

He pressed his fingertip against her lips. "I know."

The water poured over them in a warm, steady stream.

Emily opened her mouth. Her tongue snaked out, licked the tip of his finger.

His pupils flared in hungry response.

She drew his finger into her mouth, swirling her tongue around him and sucking softly.

"Don't tease me," he growled.

She released his finger. Heady power filled her. It was the kind of sensual power she'd never felt—until Colin. He made her feel beautiful, sexual.

Wanted.

She wasn't a freak with him. She didn't have to choose her words for fear he'd discover her secret. She didn't have to pretend with him. She could just . . . be.

Her fingers trailed over his chest. Found his nipples. Rubbed. "Who said I was teasing?" His cock pressed against her belly, fully aroused, easily thicker than her wrist.

She bent her head, let the water rush down her back, and took his nipple into her mouth.

His fingers tangled in her hair, held her closer. She heard him suck in a sharp breath.

Keeping her mouth on him, her fingers slipped down to his groin. Found the hard length of his arousal. Wrapped around him, squeezed.

Oh God, but she couldn't wait to feel that cock in her, driving deep, filling every inch of her sex.

Colin pulled lightly on her hair, forcing her head to lift. His mouth locked onto hers, his tongue sweeping inside, claiming her.

He spun around, pinned her against the smooth tile. His fingers dipped into the dark curls at her sex. Parted her folds and plunged inside.

Oh yes! Her hips ground against his hand. Her mouth jerked away from his and she hoarsely demanded, "Colin, more!" He knew just how to touch her. Knew where to press, where to stroke, where to—

He pushed three fingers inside of her. Emily squeezed her eyes shut. Her sex trembled around him.

"You're so damn sexy," he growled, licking his way down her neck. "Every time I see you, I want to take you."

Her hips twisted against him, jerked. He was holding his fingers still now. The pressure was maddening. She needed him to move, to—

He pulled his hand away and Emily moaned in protest.

Colin laughed, but the sound was strained. "It's all right, baby, I'll give you what you need."

His hands locked on her waist. Lifted her. "Wrap your legs around me."

Damn, but she'd forgotten just how strong he was. Shifter strength.

Her legs curled around his hips. The head of his cock nudged her entrance.

Then he drove deep inside, lodging his cock balls deep in her sheath.

Her sex clamped down on him, and she squeezed him, loving the feel of his flesh inside her.

He was moving then. Pulling back. Thrusting deep. Again and again.

Her hands rose to his shoulders, gripped the slick flesh.

His mouth captured her breast and his tongue swirled over her nipple.

His hips slammed into her. Withdrew, plunged.

And his mouth, oh, his mouth—

His fingers edged between their bodies. He found her clit, pressed with his thumb.

She came, her sex contracting as a powerful orgasm shot through her.

Colin lifted his head, watched her. "Damn, I love it when you come." Another thrust. "You. Feel. So. Fucking. Good." And then he was shuddering against her, his own climax claiming him.

When the waves of pleasure finally stopped, Emily didn't move. Her back felt bruised, sore from contact with the tile, but she didn't really care.

Her fingers stroked the back of Colin's neck.

He kissed her shoulder and held her.

* * *

Terrace Lane was one of those quiet, unassuming little streets that looked like it belonged on a greeting card. Perfectly groomed lawns. Large, brick houses. Neat little sidewalks. Cute kids playing in the yards.

The neighborhood made him tense. He didn't belong there. Wasn't part of that picture-perfect world.

And neither was the doc.

How had she felt, he wondered, growing up there? She'd been seeing demons and vampires, and the other kids had been playing basketball and hopscotch.

She'd never fit in. And neither had he.

"All right. Donna Tillman, the neighbor on the right"— Brooks lifted his notebook and pointed to a house with a large bay window—"said she saw Dr. Drake arrive a little after seven-thirty last night."

Colin grunted. It was the same story he'd gotten from Tom Henry, the neighbor on the left. "She sure about the time?"

"Yeah, said she was taking out her garbage when she saw her." Brooks turned his attention to 2801 Terrace Lane. "Mrs. Tillman thought it was real odd, too, because apparently, Dr. Drake never comes to visit, and when she did get here, she stayed in the car for about fifteen minutes before she went inside."

He was sure that the helpful Mrs. Tillman had been peering through her window that entire time, so she probably had an exact count on those minutes. "They've confirmed her alibi."

Brooks lifted a brow. "Neither of them remember when she left."

"Then let's go ask the mother." And Colin had to admit that he was curious about Emily's mom. The schoolteacher. The woman who'd sent her daughter to Serenity Woods.

They rang her doorbell, and the soft peal echoed back to them. A moment later, the door was opened and a small, delicate woman with short black hair and wide green eyes peered up at them. "Yes?"

Colin pulled out his badge. "Atlanta PD. I'm Detective Colin Gyth, and this is my partner, Todd Brooks."

Her fingers curled around the side of the door. Turned white. "Wh-what do you want?"

Brooks flashed her a smile. "We just have a few questions to ask you, ma'am."

Her eyes darted between them. "About what?"

"About your daughter, Emily Drake."

Colin saw her flinch.

Not the reaction he'd been expecting.

Brooks stepped forward, charming smile still in place. "Why don't we go inside and discuss this?"

As often happens, Mrs. Drake stumbled back, opening the door as she moved. "But I don't know what you want to discuss!"

Brooks walked into her foyer. "We told you. Emily."

Colin followed them inside, his glance sweeping over the spotlessly clean house. Emily's mother led them into a large den. There were no photos on the mantel, he noted. No photos anywhere.

"Wh-what do you want to know about Emily?" She'd crossed her arms over her chest and she lifted her chin, a gesture so like Emily's that Colin almost smiled.

"Was she here last night, Mrs. Drake—or actually, can we call you Karen?" Another of Brooks's tricks—make the witnesses feel comfortable, get 'em on a first-name basis and get 'em talking.

"What? Oh, yes, Karen's fine." She frowned. "And, ah, yes, Emily was here last night." Her eyes widened in sudden worry. "Nothing's happened, has it? Emily—"

"She's fine," Colin told her instantly. "We're just following up, asking some questions on a case we're working."

"Oh."

Did she sound disappointed? His stare sharpened. "How long was Emily here?"

"An hour, maybe two." Karen shrugged. "I don't know, I wasn't looking at a clock."

The grandfather clock behind them chimed.

Brooks and Colin stared at each other a moment. "It

would really help us if you could be more specific, Karen," Brooks murmured.

"Fine." She huffed out a breath. "Emeline arrived a little after seven and she stayed until around ten-thirty."

"And why did Emily come visit you?" Colin asked blandly. *Was it because you sold her out to a reporter and Emily told you to stop talking to the press?*

"She's my daughter. She doesn't need to have a reason to visit." Her words were a little too high.

"I see." Actually, he didn't. "So you and Em had a nice little mother–daughter visit last night?"

Her head tilted to the right. Her lips parted on a breath of surprise as she studied him. "You know my daughter?"

Ah, shit. Not the way he'd wanted the introductions to go. "Umm, yeah. She's actually working on a case with us. As a profiler."

All of the emotion vanished from her face. "Really." The temperature in the room seemed to drop about ten degrees. *What in the hell?*

"Why are you asking me these questions?" Her stare returned to Brooks. "It's almost as if you're trying to get an alibi for my daughter."

Well, yeah, that was exactly what they were trying to do.

Brooks kept his smile in place. "Karen, what can you tell me about Serenity Woods?"

She took a step back. "S-serenity Woods?"

He nodded.

And that chin shot into the air again. "I think I've answered enough questions. You should leave now."

His friendly smile faded. "There are records we can check, you know."

"No," she said very definitely, "there aren't."

She walked back to the foyer. Opened the front door. "Good-bye, Detectives."

Hmmm. She'd talked to them longer than he'd thought. Colin caught his partner's eye, shrugged. He'd known Karen Drake would back up her daughter's alibi, but he'd gone along with the investigation anyway. If he hadn't followed up on Emily's story, Brooks would have become even more suspicious and he might have started spreading some of his bullshit suspicions around the station.

And that was something Colin couldn't let happen.

Brooks left first, nodding politely to Karen Drake as he passed. Colin inclined his head as he walked by her.

"You're involved with my daughter, aren't you?" Her voice was hushed. Her gaze hooded.

"We work together, I told you that."

She shook her head. "You called her Em. And I could tell by your voice—"

Shit. He'd have to be a hell of a lot more careful in the future. But, wait, dammit, maybe she hadn't picked up on anything in his speech, maybe she sensed the truth. *Maybe she was just like her daughter.*

Colin was instantly on full alert. He'd underestimated Karen Drake. He needed to be on guard with her.

Brooks had walked down the sidewalk. He glanced back, frowning.

"Be careful, Detective," she said, her voice a harsh whisper. "You may think you know my daughter, but believe me, you don't."

He clenched his back teeth to hold back the not-so-polite response that sprang to his lips.

Karen shook her head sadly. "Emily is very . . . different."

Different was too tame a word for the doc. "I'll keep that in mind."

"You don't understand." She leaned forward, staring straight into his eyes. "Emily is—"

"Is there a problem?" Brooks called, moving back toward them.

Emily's mother straightened with a quick snap. Her lips firmed into a thin line.

"No," Colin told him, "I'll be right there." He was suddenly very eager to get away from the picturesque house on Terrace Lane.

"She's evil." Karen breathed the words, and Colin saw a tear track from the corner of her eye. "Remember that, and *don't trust her.*"

Then she turned and fled back into the house, slamming the door behind her.

Chapter 13

"We have a problem." Smith was waiting for them when they returned to the station. She'd made herself comfortable at Brooks's desk, and when they approached her, she swiveled around to face them, tapping a manila file against her desk.

"Yeah, and how is that new?" Brooks reached for the file. "This the report on those hairs you found on Myers?"

Colin glanced across the pen, saw McNeal making a beeline for them. "Has the captain read the file?"

Her lips turned down. "Not yet. I'll see him—"

"Now," McNeal finished, appearing at her side. "I told you, I wanted all data on this case given to me first." His shoulders were stiff as he loomed over her.

Smith didn't look particularly intimidated. She shrugged. "Procedure is for me to report to the lead detectives."

McNeal wrapped his hands around the arms of the chair. Leaned in close. "I gave you an order, Smith. It's not personal, but it sure as hell will be if you don't start doing exactly what I say on this case." He stared into her eyes a heartbeat of time, then softly said, "Are we clear now?"

"Oh yeah, Captain, we're clear." The Arctic had to be warmer than she was right then.

McNeal sighed and stepped back. "All of you, in my office, now."

Brooks and Smith looked surprised by the order as they

moved to obey, but Colin knew what McNeal was thinking. If there was anything abnormal—as in *Other* abnormal—he didn't want the rest of the station hearing about it then.

A few moments later, McNeal closed the door behind them with a soft click. "I'll take the file."

Brooks tossed it to him. McNeal flipped it open, read quickly, a furrow appearing between his eyes. "Unrecognizable? Not human? What the hell? Did the evidence get contaminated?"

Smith stiffened. Her entire body seemed to turn to stone before Colin's eyes. "My evidence is good."

Yeah, and he and McNeal both knew it.

McNeal scanned the file again. "*Canis lupus*—what is that, some kind of dog?"

"No," Smith told him, biting out the word. "It's a wolf, a gray wolf."

"You're saying a gray wolf attacked Myers?" Brooks asked, peering over McNeal's shoulder to get a better look at the file.

"No, I'm not saying that." She began to pace in front of them. "The analysis couldn't match up the hair that I found on Myers, not completely."

Not completely. Colin knew what was coming, but he knew he had to play it clueless. "Look, either the hair is a wolf's or it isn't, what are you—"

"It matches with part of a gray wolf's DNA, but—" She licked her lips, glanced at each of them quickly. "It also has unknown DNA."

"Ah, unknown?" Brooks shook his head. "Unknown as in—"

"Not human. Not animal. But some sort of really strange combination of both."

Shifter. Colin coughed delicately, caught McNeal's eye. "Umm, Smith, are you telling us that a werewolf attacked Myers?" Cause, yeah, that was pretty much what had happened.

She stopped pacing, stood in front of McNeal's desk, lifted her hands, and said, "Honestly, Gyth, I don't know what the hell I'm telling you. I've never seen anything like this before, and I just—I don't have an answer for you."

"Maybe the hair was planted," Brooks suggested, pursing his lips, "to throw us off."

"There were claw marks on the body. I called in an animal specialist. The marks match up with a wolf's."

McNeal snapped the file closed. Tossed it onto his desk. "I'm not going to the DA and telling him that a werewolf killed Myers."

Smith opened her mouth, then shook her head.

Uh-oh. "What is it, Smith?" She was holding back. He'd seen that expression on her face before.

"Not just Myers," she muttered. "The reporter too. I found more of the hairs on her."

"What in the hell is going on here?" Brooks demanded. "There is no way some rabid wolfman is going around the city killing people!"

Actually, that was exactly what was happening. And now they had proof. Definitive proof.

Unfortunately, it was proof that would never make it into a courtroom.

"The evidence has to be compromised," McNeal said flatly. "Either it was tampered with at the crime scene or it was exposed here—but it's no good to us."

"No, my evidence is—"

"*Compromised.* Now, we need to put a lid on this thing before word leaks to the press that our evidence in this case has been tainted."

Smith sucked in a sharp breath.

McNeal stabbed a finger in the air. "Now I want you three to get to work and *find me evidence that I can use.*" He glared at them, then snarled, "*Now! Go!*"

Smith threw him a look of disdain before she turned on her heel and marched out. Brooks followed her, and Colin trailed on their heels.

"Gyth, wait."

Colin stopped at the door. His hand reached out, pushed the

thin, wooden door shut. He glanced back. McNeal was feeding the file into his shredder. He arched a brow at the captain. "There are gonna be other copies of that, you know."

"I'll take care of them." He exhaled heavily and sank into his chair. "I need you to find this bastard, Detective. I can't have him terrifying my city and leaving a trail of dead humans in his wake."

"Yes, sir." But it was a hell of a lot easier said than done.

"Find him, Gyth," McNeal repeated, "and do whatever you have to do, *but stop the bastard.*"

Just after five that evening, Emily arrived at the station, her palms damp with sweat and her heart racing.

Gyth had called her twenty minutes ago. They had a suspect in custody for the break-in at her place. A kid who'd been busted for shoplifting and who just happened to have her address scribbled down in his wallet.

Talk about your lucky breaks.

Her gaze scanned the station. She didn't see Colin. Where was—

"Afternoon, Dr. Drake."

Brooks. Emily turned around, didn't bother forcing a smile. "Brooks." Her heart raced even faster. "Tell me, did you have a nice morning investigating me?"

He met her stare levelly. "I'm working on a murder."

Like she didn't know that.

"I have to follow every lead. Check out all suspects."

"And is that what I am now? A suspect?"

"Not anymore. Colin and I talked to your mother, her neighbors, they all backed up—"

"C-Colin talked to my mother?" She'd known, of course, that he'd have to go with Brooks to follow up on her alibi. She understood that he was doing his job. Hell, if their positions were reversed, she'd have done the same thing. And she even understood why Brooks had originally suspected her. She hated the guy's attitude, but she wasn't stupid. She understood.

But the sudden image of Colin talking to her mother. *Oh no. That couldn't have gone well.*

A faint smile curved his lips. "Don't worry. They just talked about the case."

Too late. She was already worried. "Where is Colin? He called me about a suspect in the break-in."

"He's getting the lineup ready. Come on." He took her arm, led her to the elevator. "He should be ready for you by now."

Within minutes, Emily found herself behind a large, tinted pane of glass. Colin stood behind her, Brooks at his side. A woman was there too, the DA, and another man—he'd identified himself as James Tyler, another lawyer, presumably for the guy she was hoping to identify.

There was a faint click behind her, then Colin ordered, "Bring 'em in."

A door opened on the other side of the glass. A line of men walked out, all holding white signs with black numbers on them.

"Face forward," Colin said into the intercom.

The men stared back at her. Emily swallowed. Lifted her hand to touch the cheek that still ached. She'd managed to cover the bruise with some makeup she'd bought at the drugstore that morning.

Her eyes scanned over the men. Not number one. Or two. Number three had the right hair, but—

"Number four." She met his stare through the mirror. Same wide eyes. A face that was pale, hair too long.

"Are you sure?" Brooks asked softly. "Take your time, you don't—"

"It's number four." She was absolutely certain.

"Well," Colin drawled as he fixed the public defender with a hard look. "Guess that means in addition to the shoplifting charges, your client is about to be booked with assault, breaking and entering, and vandalism. And just so we're clear, he's eighteen. No juvie charges."

James shook his head, his expression disgusted, as he reached for the door. "And here I was thinking I'd be home before seven."

With a polite "Thank you for your cooperation," the DA followed him out.

Emily rounded on Colin. "I want to talk to him." *I want to find out why the kid thinks I'm a demon.*

Brooks whistled softly. "Figured you'd ask for something like that. I'd be pissed as hell if the punk had broken into my place."

Colin shook his head. "Not gonna happen, Doc. That's not the way it works—"

"Don't make me go over your head." Lover or not, he wasn't going to keep her away from that boy. And if she had to go to McNeal, she would.

His blue eyes hardened. "You're a witness here. Nothing more."

Ouch. Emily lifted her chin. "I'm a victim here, and victims have rights." Screw it. Colin was in his overprotective mode and she didn't feel like wasting her time arguing with him. She'd talk to McNeal; she needed to update him and Colin on her profile anyway.

Emily marched to the door, yanked it open. She took three steps and came face-to-face with the boy who'd attacked her. His hands were cuffed and a uniformed officer stood on his right.

Her eyes widened in surprise. Perfect opportunity. She would—

"Demon! She's a fucking demon!" The kid started screaming at the top of his lungs, shaking.

He sounded so absolutely certain that he was seeing a demon that Emily actually turned and glanced behind her just to make sure one hadn't arrived. But no. It was just her.

"Look, kid, I'm not—"

"Kill the demon! Have to kill her!" He lunged forward in a blur of motion, his arms raised.

Emily heard a guttural shout from behind her. And then the boy barreled into her, sending her flying to the ground. He landed on top of her, and his fingers locked around her throat. *Hell, not again.*

"Have to destroy the demon. She's evil. Destroy—"

Colin grabbed the kid and jerked him off her, shoving him back up against the wall. "You just made a serious fucking mistake."

The kid raised his arms, tried to use his cuffs to hit Colin. Colin growled and hit him in the stomach, driving the air from the boy's lungs in a loud *whoosh*. Then he pulled back his fist and drove it into the boy's nose. Bones cracked. Blood shot down the perp's face.

Colin raised his fist back, bared his teeth.

The boy began to whimper. His body slid down to the floor and he wrapped his arms around his stomach, rocking back and forth.

Colin grabbed him by the collar and—

"Stop!" Emily ordered, pushing to her knees. Something about that kid—something was very, very wrong. "He's not going to attack again."

"Damn right he's not." Colin turned his furious stare onto the uniform. "What the fuck were you doing? Don't you know how to secure a perp?"

The cop gulped, muttering apologies as he reached for the boy.

"Get him out of here, *now!*"

Emily stared down at the boy. "What's your name?"

He shook his head, whispered, "Demon."

The uniform pulled him to his feet. "Come on, Trace. Fun's over."

The boy went forward obediently, but he kept looking back at Emily, a frightened, lost look on his face.

"Well . . ." Brooks murmured, eyeing Emily with a hint of wariness. "Guess you aren't the only one preoccupied with demons, huh?"

*   *   *

"The killer wants the world to know what he is." Emily sat in the chair across from McNeal's desk. Colin sat beside her, and she could feel his intent stare on her.

He hadn't spoken with her since the attack. *But if looks could kill . . .*

Damn. She'd been the one to get choked. She would have thought the guy could have shown more sympathy.

Colin wasn't feeling particularly sympathetic. She knew that. Could feel that. His rage practically filled the room.

She'd taken a few minutes to regain her composure after the attack. She'd retreated to the restroom. Discovered that she had red fingerprints on her neck. Her voice was scratchy, and the new suit jacket she'd purchased that morning had been ripped.

Actually, she'd had to buy a whole new wardrobe that morning. Thanks to the boy, Trace, all of her old clothes had been slashed. And so far, things weren't looking up for her new items.

"Are you saying the Night Bastard wants to get caught?" McNeal asked, leaning forward.

His question jerked Emily back to the matter at hand. *The Night Butcher,* or, as McNeal liked to call him, the Night Bastard. She'd been working on his profile, updating it with information she'd garnered at the crime scene last night. "No, I didn't say he wants to get caught. I said he wants people to find out what he is. He wants the humans to know about him, and to fear him."

"He wants them to know he's a shifter," Colin muttered. "And that's why he's killing in his animal form?"

She nodded. "I think so. I also think he's choosing human victims who are high profile to get more attention. Preston Myers was rich, high society. His murder was bound to go straight to the front page. Darla—"

"Was a hotshot reporter," Colin finished. "Course her killing would make every broadcast and paper in the state."

"This guy—he's tired of hiding what he is. He wants the world to know about him. About all the *Other*. And I think he'll kill as many humans as it takes to get his message out there."

"Shit." McNeal's gaze darted to his shredder. "He's deliberately leaving evidence for us, isn't he? Evidence that proves he's not human."

"Yeah, I think he is."

"Why?" McNeal's fist hit the desk. "Coming out like this will just make humans terrified. They'll fear him, hate him, hate all of us."

"He doesn't care," she told him softly. "This guy—he thinks he's all powerful. He's gotten a taste for the killing." *Her blood tasted good.* "There's something else you should both know." She took a deep breath. "I think the next victim—it's going to be a cop."

"Fuck." From Gyth.

"How the hell do you know that?"

"Because he told me." *Maybe I'll do one of them next. Oh yeah, that'd be good.* "He was at the television station last night. I-I felt him. Managed to get close enough to touch his thoughts." But the killer had gotten away.

So close.

"A cop." McNeal squeezed his eyes shut. "Christ. Yeah, that would definitely get the asshole more attention. He'd make the national news then. A fucking werewolf killing cops. Shit."

Would cops taste different? Would they try to fight more?

"It's going to be a woman," Emily said, wanting to give them all the information she had. "He . . . ah . . . likes the way women taste better."

Colin tensed.

"*Shit!*" McNeal lunged to his feet. "I want this bastard off the streets. I don't want to play any more of his fucking games."

But there wasn't much of a choice.

McNeal frowned at Colin. "Put everyone on alert. Let 'em know this crazy SOB is out there, gunning for one of our own."

Colin nodded, rose from his seat.

"I don't want a bloodbath in my city," McNeal snarled. "And I sure as hell don't want to see a cop with her throat ripped out on the six o'clock news."

But if the Night Butcher wasn't caught, Emily knew that was exactly what would happen.

A hard knock sounded at the door. Brooks popped his head inside, not waiting for an invitation. "I've got some news you've all got to hear." He stepped forward, gripping a white piece of paper in his hands. "Guess whose prints just matched up with the unknowns we found at Gillian Nemont's?"

Emily's stomach knotted. Gillian was a demon. *Have to destroy the demon. She's evil.*

"Sonofabitch." Colin shook his head slowly. "The kid."

Brooks handed him the printout. "Bryan Trace. Runaway. High school dropout. Demon hunter." His lips twisted at the last. "That's what he told me he was, by the way. When the doctor was patching up his nose, he told me he was used to pain. Demon hunters have to be, of course."

Emily rubbed her temple. "I don't understand what's going on! Why would this guy target me? It makes no sense!" Unless . . . Emily straightened her shoulders. Unless the guy knew that some of her patients were *Other* and he'd thought that she was too.

"It gets better," Brooks murmured. "I've got a security tape of the guy going into the News Flash Five station yesterday afternoon."

The kid was connected to all the murders. But . . . "He's not the Butcher," Emily said very definitely. Yes, the evidence was starting to mount, but it wasn't Trace.

The boy was human. She hadn't sensed anything supernatural about him.

Just an angry, confused, *dangerous* human.

Brooks shook his head. "It could be him," he argued. "He

trashed Nemont's place. That links him to Myers. If we canvas the neighborhood, we might even find someone who remembers seeing him at Preston's place before the murder."

"You might," Emily said, "but I'm telling you, *this kid isn't the Night Butcher.*"

"Umm . . ." McNeal shot her a searching glance. "Doc, you sure about this?"

She nodded.

"If the kid didn't do it," Colin said, glancing up from the printout, "I think he knows who did."

Now that she couldn't argue with.

"There are too many coincidences here," he continued. "And they make me damn suspicious."

"Me too." McNeal studied them in silence for a moment, then said, "Get him into Interrogation. Find out what the hell he knows."

Colin and Brooks strode toward the door.

"Ah, Captain?" She wasn't about to let this chance pass. "I think I can help here."

Colin swung around, eyes narrowed.

McNeal arched a brow. "You want in with him, don't you?"

She nodded.

McNeal rubbed a hand over his bare scalp. "It's risky, sending you in. His lawyer will have a field day with it since you're one of his victims."

"She shouldn't go in," Colin snapped. "The guy just attacked her. Emily doesn't need to be anywhere near him!"

"I won't get too close," she promised, not looking at Colin. Dammit, this was her case too. If he'd been attacked, she knew Colin would have gone right back in with the perp. "Look, McNeal, the guy needs help. His mind—" Was twisted, confused. She bit her lip, muttered, "I don't think they're going to be able to get to him. But I can." She knew it. If she could just get the chance.

"Observe first. And then—"

"Captain, no!"

McNeal glared at Colin. "My rules here, Gyth. Not yours. We may need the doctor on this one. She'll observe the interrogation with me, and if I think we need her, I'll send her in."

Emily finally glanced toward Colin. Found him watching her with a burning stare.

"Do we have a problem, Gyth?" McNeal asked.

"No, not yet." A muscle flexed along his jaw. "But if that bastard tries to touch her again, you might have a dead man on your hands."

"Bryan Trace . . ." Brooks drawled out his name and flashed a friendly smile. "Did the doctor get you all patched up?"

The boy nodded jerkily.

His lawyer leaned forward, cast a menacing glance toward Colin. "We will be filing assault charges."

"Umm, you try doing that." Colin didn't seem particularly concerned as he reached for a stack of photos. "I've got a station full of officers who saw the guy attack Dr. Drake. I was doing my job and subduing him."

"Your 'subduing' technique broke his nose and bruised his ribs."

"Umm." Again, little concern. Colin stared down at the photos. "He was out of control. I did what I had to do."

Yes, and Emily knew he'd do it again, in a heartbeat. Her hands curled in front of her as she stared through the two-way mirror.

"But if you wanna try to press charges . . ." He shrugged. "It'll be your wasted hours."

Emily looked back at McNeal. "Could the assault charges stick?"

"Nah. Too many cops for witnesses."

Brooks straddled the chair closest to the boy. "Bryan, I need to ask you a few questions." Light, easy tone.

"O-okay."

"Were you acquainted with a Preston Myers?"

Bryan flinched.

"Umm, Bryan, did you hear my question?"

The boy stared down at his cuffed hands. "Didn't know him."

"But you'd been to his house before, right, Bryan?" Colin asked, his voice snapping like a whip. "The neighbors saw you, said that you'd been hanging around, hiding in bushes like some kind of Peeping Tom."

Another flinch.

Emily knew Colin was making up the story about the neighbors' testimony, but judging by Bryan's response, he was definitely on the right track.

"My client doesn't have to—"

Bryan lifted his head. His cheeks were flushed. A wide, white bandage covered his nose. "I was there."

"Why?" Brooks asked softly.

"He was a demon. I watch the demons, make sure they don't hurt anyone."

"Ah . . . my client is obviously suffering from delusions. His mental capacity isn't strong enough for these questions—"

"*Shut up!*" Bryan screamed, lunging to his feet. "I'm not crazy! I'm not crazy!"

Colin locked one hand on his shoulder, shoved him back down.

James pulled his chair back a few feet. "Uh, I think we should stop—"

"*Shut the fuck up!* You don't know what's going on here. It's a war, man. *A war.*" Bryan curled his lip at the attorney, spat, "I don't need you. I'll say what I want. These guys can't do anything to me. I'm a Hunter." He jerked his thumb toward his chest. "*I'm the law.*"

McNeal stepped beside her, whistling softly. "The kid really was stalking Myers."

And Gillian Nemont. And her.

"I take it you're waiving your right to your attorney's advice?" Brooks murmured, glancing down at his nails.

"Hell, yes!" Bryan suddenly seemed energized, eyes glowing, head tilted proudly, body humming with excitement. "I don't need a dumb suit trying to tell me what to say."

"Your funeral, kid," James murmured, and sat back.

"So . . ." Colin tapped the photos against the tabletop. "You admit to stalking Preston Myers."

"I was *demon hunting.*"

"And were you also hunting Gillian Nemont?"

Bryan smiled. "Saw what I did to her place, didn't you?"

I'll take that as a yes, Emily thought.

"And Dr. Drake? You been hunting her too?" Colin's voice was razor sharp.

Bryan just smirked. "Almost caught her."

Colin's left hand balled into a fist. "Did you now?"

"Bitch got away from me." His lips thinned. "Kicked me in the balls. Fought like a hellcat." He laughed then, a high-pitched, almost girlish sound. "Course that's what she is, right?"

"Umm . . ." Colin glanced down at the photos. His jaw was clenched tight. "And Darla Mitchell? Were you hunting her?"

"The bitch thought she could go on TV, could hide what she was and laugh at us stupid humans." He shook his head. "But I knew what she was. *I knew!*"

"So you admit to hunting her." Colin slid a photograph across the table. "Did you kill her too?"

Bryan stared down at the photo. The color drained from his face. "*What the fuck!*"

"Look at it," Colin snarled. "You see the blood? You see her face? Her throat was ripped out, clawed out—and she died in a pool of her own blood."

Bryan's eyes had doubled in size. His Adam's apple bobbed as he stared at the photo.

"He had no idea what the body looked like," Emily whispered. *Because he hadn't been there for the kill.*

"She wasn't a demon," Brooks told him, tapping his fingers against the photo. "She was human, just like you and me. And she screamed and she bled, and she died."

The boy was shaking his head. "No, no, I didn't do that! I didn't—"

"But you were hunting her, right?" Colin pushed. "Just like you were hunting Preston." He pushed another photo in front of Bryan.

The boy gagged.

"You were hunting them, planning to kill them—"

Bryan shoved the pictures away. "I-I wasn't—I was just w-watching them—"

"Stalking them," Brooks corrected, the warmth gone from his voice. "You were stalking the victims because you thought they were demons and you wanted to kill them."

"No! No!" Bryan's head shook frantically. "I-I was just— just supposed to watch!"

Supposed to watch. Emily's breath caught. This was it.

"Supposed to, huh?" Brooks leaned back in his chair. "And just who told you that you were supposed to watch them?"

Horror filled the kid's face. His lips clamped together.

Don't stop now. Emily touched the cold mirror pane.

"Who told you to watch the demons?" Colin snarled.

"No." Bryan fisted his hands. Lifted his chin. "I ain't say-ing another word."

"You should've stopped talking fifteen minutes ago, kid," his lawyer muttered.

"Shit." McNeal touched Emily's shoulder. "All right, Doc. It's showtime. Get in there and find out everything that punk knows about the Night Butcher."

Chapter 14

The door squeaked softly when she entered the small interrogation room. Bryan Trace looked up at her approach, his eyes flaring. "What the hell is she doing here?" He started to rise, but Colin clamped his hand down on the boy's shoulder again and held him in his seat.

Her stomach was in knots. Her knees shaking. But Emily calmly walked across the small room. A chair was waiting for her. A chair right across from the would-be demon hunter.

Emily sat down. Stared at him. And waited.

She didn't have to wait long.

"Keep her away from me," he muttered, rocking back and forth in his seat as he stared at her. A trickle of sweat slid down his temple. "She's a fucking demon! Can't you see that?"

Emily pushed her glasses higher onto the bridge of her nose. "When you look at me, Bryan, what do you see?"

He opened his mouth, blinked, shook his head. "It's a trick, it's a—"

"Do I have horns?" Course, only the really, really old demons had those. "A pointed tail? Glowing eyes?"

"You're mocking me," he gritted.

"No, I'm trying to understand you." And she was. "What makes you think I'm a demon? That Preston was a demon? Gillian? Darla?"

"You're tricking me," he said again, glancing nervously

around the room. "It's not gonna work. I know what you are!"

"A demon."

A quick, jerky nod.

"How do you know?" She pitched her voice low, tried to soothe. "How do you know who is a demon and who isn't?"

"I-I just do."

Emily leaned across the table. Tapped the crime scene photo of Darla. "You sure she was a demon? Cause she just looks like a dead woman to me."

His gaze dropped to the photo. His lips trembled. "I didn't do that."

"But I thought you were a hunter." She kept her voice calm. "And hunters kill, don't they?"

"I-I was watching."

"Watching? You weren't just watching with me." Her hand rose to her cheek. Lightly touched the bruise. His bright stare shot to her cheek.

"I-I was warning—"

Time to push him over the edge. "Warning me? Or trying to kill me . . . the way you did the others?"

"*I didn't kill them! I was watching, learning—*"

Learning. Her heart was thumping like crazy. "Learning what?" Emily asked softly. Brooks and Colin were silent, watchful. And Colin still had his hand clamped on Bryan's shoulder. "Learning our routines? Learning when we were alone, when we weren't?" It was the only thing that made sense.

Bryan didn't reply.

"Someone told you to watch us, right, Bryan?"

He turned to his lawyer. "I don't want to talk to this demon bitch anymore."

James raised his brows. "You heard my client."

Dammit. Emily sucked in a sharp breath. The boy was stubborn. Scared to death. And not talking.

She wet her lips. There was one other method she could try.

Her psychic gift had never worked with humans. She couldn't read them like she did the *Other*, and she'd only been able to pick up the barest of impressions in the past, but she didn't have anything to lose by trying.

She inhaled deeply, exhaled. Kept her eyes locked on Bryan. And slowly lowered her mental shields.

She shouldn't be here. Bastard marked her. Can see his fingers on her neck. She shouldn't—

Colin's thoughts hit her like a train, slamming into her mind with the force of his fury behind them.

Emily drew in another deep breath, tried to shift her focus away from him.

Kid's lying. We've got to break him. I don't want a dead cop on tomorrow's news.

McNeal.

Another breath. Her eyes narrowed as she stared at Bryan. Colin and McNeal's thoughts became a distant buzz in her mind.

She couldn't hear any thoughts from the boy. Couldn't feel any emotions. She could see his fear and anger, see it on his face, but she couldn't *feel* anything.

Catch had tried to teach her to hone her gift. During her "therapy" sessions, they'd spent hours trying to strengthen her abilities. But the lessons had never seemed to take.

She stared into Bryan's eyes, stared straight into his black pupils and tried to put every ounce of her power into forming a link with him. The air seemed to thicken around her. To tighten and—

Emily jerked back, gasping. "*He* told you we were demons."

Bryan shook his head. "You don't know—"

Emily stood. She'd gotten only a vague impression from the boy. But it was all she'd need. She glanced at James. "Your client needs serious counseling. He's not competent for trial." No, he wasn't competent. And it would take years to get him back to some semblance of normalcy.

Because a demon had been playing with his head. Twisting his thoughts. Using him.

She hadn't been able to touch Bryan's mind. The human mind was closed to her. But she'd touched the remnants of a demon's power.

A very powerful demon.

She needed to talk with Colin and McNeal. Because either they were looking for two monsters who were working together or the killer was one damn strong hybrid.

A demon/shifter hybrid.

It was the deadliest combination she could think of, and the one guaranteed to bring a wake of murder and destruction to the city.

Something is wrong with Emily. Colin waited until another detective tagged out with him before he followed her out of the interrogation room.

She was standing next to McNeal, whispering furiously.

His insides tightened at the strained expression on her face. *Oh yeah, something is definitely up.*

He stalked toward and fought the urge to pull Emily against him. Now wasn't the time.

When Trace had attacked her, the beast had snarled within him, and he'd thought, for one terrible, timeless moment, that he was going to shift. Right there, in front of a dozen cops.

But his control had held. He'd told Emily that the man controlled the beast. So far, that statement had been true in his life. He was realizing, though, that if anyone could make him lose control, it would be Emily.

"What the hell do you mean, two killers?"

"I don't—" She broke off, glancing up at Colin's approach. "Good. I wanted to talk to you."

And he wanted to do a hell of a lot more than talk to her. "What's happening?"

"During interrogation, umm, I—" She flushed, looking vaguely guilty and admitted, "I dropped my mental shields and tried to touch Bryan's mind."

"But he's human." A pause. "Isn't he?" The kid didn't

smell like a shifter. He just smelled like prey. The way most humans did.

Except Emily.

She smelled like . . . roses. Cream. Woman.

"Yeah, he's human. And I couldn't read a thing from him." She licked her lips. "But I felt the trace of power."

"Whose power?" McNeal asked sharply.

"A demon's. High level." She glanced around quickly to make certain they weren't being overheard. "Some demons can control humans, if they're strong enough. Make them into puppets."

"The possessed." McNeal nodded, apparently familiar with the term.

"Right. I-I think that's what happened with Bryan. He honestly doesn't know why he thinks I'm a demon. He doesn't know why he's supposed to follow me. He just does."

"Because some all-powerful demon put the idea in his head?" Colin frowned. "Look, that sounds crazy as—"

"It's happened before. Many, many times. Demons kill this way—they keep their hands clean and let their puppets do the dirty work." Emily met his gaze. "It even happened to me once."

When she'd nearly been put into a coma.

"I was able to fight the guy off, but someone without my psychic gift, he'd be helpless."

Possessed.

"So this punk's been stalking, sorry, *hunting,* because some demon put it in his head that was his duty?" Sounded like bullshit. Damn. Why couldn't the cases be easy anymore?

"Yes, that's exactly what I think happened."

"So are we looking for two killers?" McNeal demanded. "Is the demon making the shifter take his kills? What in the hell is going on?"

"Actually, I think I know." Colin spoke slowly. A powerful demon. A deadly shifter. He met Emily's gaze and realized the doc was thinking the same thing.

Fuck.

There's talk of a hybrid demon in town. A strong demon, a nine or ten. Niol's words echoed in his mind. The sonofabitch had known, Colin realized. He'd known exactly what the killer was.

But did he know *who* he was?

"Doc, why don't you give the captain a science lesson on hybrids." He turned on his heel, heading for the door.

"Gyth! Where are you going?" McNeal called out.

He glanced back over his shoulder, eyes narrowed. "To Paradise. I'm going to find a demon and make the bastard tell me everything he knows about the Butcher." And if he had to use claws and teeth to get the information, all the better.

"Wait! I'll come, too! You'll need me—"

Colin turned around, caught Emily by her wrists, and jerked her against him. "The fucking last place I want you to be is Paradise Found." The killer could be there, waiting.

Her eyes seemed so wide behind her glasses, so green.

"I can help you, Gyth, just let me—"

He kissed her. A hard, fast kiss with his mouth open, his tongue stabbing deep. Yeah, it was unprofessional. Yeah, the captain saw him.

But he didn't really care.

He pulled away from her. "I need to do this alone, Doc." No Monster Doctor. No police partner. He inclined his head toward McNeal. "And it needs to be off the record." Because he'd do whatever he had to do to catch the killer.

No more humans were going to die on his watch.

He didn't wait for a reply. Just turned and marched away, his mind already on the coming confrontation.

It was time to find out once and for all just who was stronger—the beast or the demon.

Colin had been gone for four hours. Emily paced the lobby of the station. *Shit.* She should have forced Colin to take her with him. Colin didn't know the *Other* world like she did. He wouldn't understand the demons, the vampires, the—

Her cell phone beeped. *Colin.* She grabbed the phone, frowning at the caller ID. She didn't recognize the number.

"Emily Drake."

"Dr. Drake!" The voice was male. Highly agitated. Voices rumbled in the background. Music blared.

"Thomas? Is that you?" It sounded like her newest patient. She'd given him her number because of the serious nature of his situation, but—

"I-I c-can't control it! I-I'm c-changing—"

Ice seemed to freeze her veins. "Where are you, Thomas? Thomas!"

"P-paradise Fou . . ." His words ended in a snarl of pain. The line went dead.

Niol had gone to ground. Colin sat at the bar, a cold beer bottle in his hand, and turned to slowly survey the bar.

He'd searched for the demon. Gone to his house. Gone to the human girlfriend's. But the demon was nowhere to be found. Dammit.

He gulped down some of his brew, the slightly bitter taste burning the back of his throat. He turned back to face the bartender. He figured the guy for a demon. If the guy worked for Niol, he probably had to be. Something in the employment contract . . .

"So how much longer is he goin' to keep me waitin'?"

The bartender—a big, tall, black guy—smiled. "As long as he wants."

Colin sat his beer down very carefully. "You know, the game's old now. You go tell your boss," 'cause he had a feeling he was close by, "that if he doesn't bring his pointy-tailed ass out here, I'm gonna get a warrant and bust into every room in this damn hellhole you call a bar." He smiled, too, a smile that showed a lot of teeth. "And I bet I'll find a few interesting surprises while the boys in blue and I search."

The bartender stopped smiling. Glanced slightly over Colin's shoulder.

Niol.

Colin spun around, claws ready, fangs bared, and caught the demon around the throat. He slammed him against the bar, holding him down with one hand.

The demon's black eyes stared up at him. "Hello, shif . . . ter." He choked a bit on the last word.

Emily had choked like that, when that bastard had wrapped his fingers around her.

With an effort, Colin loosened his hold. "You've been holdin' out on me, Niol." And he didn't have time to pussyfoot around with him anymore. "I want the hybrid's name."

The bartender was standing stock still, staring at them.

Niol lifted his hand, waved him away, but his black stare never left Colin. "Let me go."

"Tell me the name." He wasn't in the mood for this shit.

A fist plowed into his back. A strong, hard punch that drove straight into his spine.

Colin snarled and spun around. A demon stood behind him, fists raised. Colin kicked out at him, catching the guy in the ribs and sending him flying into a nearby table. People moved out of the way when the table and the demon crashed to the floor. But the music and dancing never stopped.

"Enough!" Niol ordered. He pointed at the fallen demon. "Mentaur, give us a minute."

Mentaur rose to his feet, spit at Colin, then stomped away.

Colin stepped forward, that demon ass—

"You can't expect to attack me and not get retaliation," Niol informed him softly. "My men, they don't like to see me bothered."

Bothered. "Yeah, well, if you don't tell me what I want to know in the next ten seconds, they're going to see you bloody." He lifted his claws. "And we don't want that, do we?" The band began yelling a hard, fast tune. Guitars squealed.

Niol cocked his head to the side. "You're convinced the hybrid's behind the killings."

"Aren't you?"

Niol didn't answer.

"*His name.*"

"I don't know it."

"Bullshit, you know—"

"I know he's in town because I felt the rush of his power the night you and the good doctor were attacked. But then, I'm sure she felt it too. Being as how she's the professional at sensing our kind, I'm sure she got a better lock on him than I did."

Niol sighed and shook his head. "*I don't know who he is. I only know that he's out there. He's not one of mine, shifter.*"

"You'd better not be lying to me." But wasn't that what demons did? Lie? Twist the truth?

Damn. He should have brought Emily with him. She'd be able to sense the truth or the deception.

But he hadn't wanted to risk her.

Hadn't wanted to put her in any more danger.

"You think I don't want this guy stopped?" Niol sounded mildly curious as he stared back at him.

"I think you don't give a damn what happens to the humans."

"But I do care about what happens to my kind."

Gillian Nemont. "Where is she?"

Niol didn't pretend to misunderstand. "She's already been taken care of, shifter. She was his first victim."

Sonofa— "Taken care of? What the hell does that mean?"

Niol's black eyes hardened and the air vibrated with the force of his rage. "It means I didn't want her dissected by one of the human doctors. Cut open. Studied. She deserved better than that."

"So what? You took her body? Hid her? Took her clothes to make it look like she'd skipped town? Destroyed evidence—"

"I gave her a burial in the way of our kind. I showed her the respect in death that bastard didn't give her in life."

A third victim. "You can't do that, Niol. You can't have your own laws, your own—"

"She was my sister." His knuckles whitened as he fisted his

hands. "He . . . broke her. Left her in an alley, with the garbage and the rats. Left terror in her eyes and left her in a bed of blood." He shook his head. "Don't tell me what I can and can't do. She was mine to protect, and I did for her the only thing that I could."

The band stopped playing. A swirl of voices filled the brief silence.

"If I knew who he was, he wouldn't still be out there, hunting," Niol muttered. "The bastard would be dead."

Colin believed him, and he also believed that Niol would have made the killer suffer, for a very long time, before he got the release of death.

A grim, humorless smile curved Niol's lips. "Wonder which of us will find him first?" He leaned closer. "And wonder which of us will make the bastard scream the loudest for mercy?"

The animal within howled at the challenge. The man spoke through gritted teeth, "This isn't just an *Other* matter. Humans have died. The law will punish him. The law will—"

"Then the law had better get to him before I do." Niol inclined his head. "Enjoy your beer, Detective. And good hunting."

Colin growled a response as Niol was swallowed by the crowd.

Good hunting.

If only it were that easy. If he could just catch the bastard's scent . . .

Broodingly, his gaze once again scanned the crowd. Searched the nameless faces, saw—

Emily. His heart began to race in a hard, fast rhythm. She shouldn't be there. He'd told her to stay away from Paradise Found. And here she was, walking beside some blond guy, her hand on his arm, stroking him.

What the fuck?

A musky, familiar scent flooded his nostrils. Colin surged to his feet.

Emily and her mystery guy walked through the back door of the bar.

Without a second thought, he followed them, claws bared.

"Thomas! No, don't!"

Colin ran forward at Emily's shout, took in the scene before him in one horror-filled glance.

The man was gone. In his place stood a huge, black panther. A panther with fangs open, glistening, with a body tensed to spring.

A *shifter*. He'd known the instant he caught the bastard's stench in the air.

Emily stood before the beast, her right hand raised, fear on her face. She stumbled back, whispering something he couldn't hear.

The panther growled, stepped toward her, mouth ready to rip and tear—

No! Not Emily. Not his mate.

Colin snarled, and the panther's head whipped toward him. The animal's back legs bunched as it prepared to leap through the air.

Shit.

There was no time to move. To draw his weapon. The panther lunged and knocked him to the ground. The animal's hot breath blew against his throat and its saliva dripped onto him as the beast lowered its mouth for the kill.

He hadn't wanted it to be this way. Hadn't wanted her to know . . .

Emily was screaming, running toward them.

The panther paused, its nostrils flaring, its head turning slowly, slowly toward her.

Human. Weak. Prey. It was the way of the beast. To hunt, to destroy the weak.

Not. Emily.

Razor-sharp claws dug into his chest, burned a path of fire over his skin.

And he knew there was no choice.

His teeth clenched as he opened the door of the cage inside . . . and let his own beast out.

Time to hunt. Time to kill.

Kill.

OhGodohGodohGod . . . "Thomas! No! Stop!" The panther was on top of Colin. Even in the dim light, she could see the blood streaming down Colin's chest.

Thomas was going to kill him. She had to do something. Emily ran forward.

A long, angry howl filled the night. The hair on her nape rose. That howl . . .

The crunch and snapping of bones reached her ears. Colin's hands lengthened, fur sprang from his flesh.

Shifting, he was shifting . . .

One powerful forearm caught the panther, sent it hurtling through the air.

Colin pushed to his knees, crouched. Went to all fours. His eyes were glowing. Bright, bright blue that shone in the night.

His face was changing. The cheeks becoming sharper, the jaw longer.

The teeth much, much sharper.

"Don't . . . fear . . . me." Not Colin's voice. A rumble, a grating demand.

The panther growled, surged to its feet, glanced at her.

Danger. Run. Kill.

Thomas's thoughts blasted her, and she could only shake her head. Who was more dangerous to her? The panther, her lover . . . or—

Colin tossed back his head and howled.

A wolf's howl.

"No," she whispered.

His clothes ripped, the fabric split apart. His body shifted, changing before her eyes from man to beast.

In seconds, Colin was gone. In his place stood a large, muscled, fangs wide-open wolf.

A fucking wolf. Colin wasn't just any shifter. *He was a wolf.* The black wolf's bright stare centered on the panther. He growled.

And she knew that both she and Thomas were in serious danger. *The wolf shifters are the strongest, the deadliest. By far, the most dangerous of their kind.* She tried to touch Colin's mind. Found only a tangle of animal rage and primitive instincts demanding a kill.

Oh God. She had to try and reach him. Emily lifted her hand, palm out. "Colin. Colin, no."

The wolf's head turned toward her. Stared at her with eyes bright with blood hunger.

The wolf padded toward her, head low to the ground. The panther didn't move from the corner, the creature sensing the deadly threat before it.

Emily found she couldn't move either. Fear held her immobile. If she fled, he'd just chase her. Wolves were notorious in their lust for the hunt.

The wolf stopped less than a foot away from her. Watched her with his fangs glinting. Then he leaped forward, driving his head into her thighs.

Emily cried out, stumbling back.

This can't be happening. Not Colin. I never thought he'd hurt me. Never thought—

Her back was against the wall of the alley. The wolf was in front of her.

Thomas snarled, advancing.

"No! Stay back!"

The wolf spun around, hackles rising. His claws dug into the ground as he faced the panther.

As he faced the panther.

He wasn't attacking, not yet. He'd pushed her into the corner, put himself before her and—

He was protecting her.

Emily shook her head. If he'd wanted to kill her, she'd have been dead already, she realized. But he wasn't hurting her, he was placing his body between her and the panther.

I control the beast. He doesn't control me.

The panther swiped out with his claws, trying to catch the wolf in the throat. But the wolf was ready. He jerked to the side and snapped his teeth down on the panther's front leg.

The panther cried out in pain. Jerked back, limping slightly. The panther was bigger than the wolf, but only by a slim margin. Both were heavily muscled with powerful claws and razor-sharp teeth.

But the wolf—there was no creature on earth stronger than a wolf shifter, and while the panther might be able to fight him for a time, in the end he would lose.

He would die.

"No," she whispered. Dammit, she couldn't reach Colin's mind. The red haze of bloodlust was too strong. But maybe she could stop Thomas, send him away. "Thomas . . ." The panther's head jerked toward her. "Go, Thomas, go. I'll be all right."

The panther's eyes slit and his body pressed tightly to the ground as he prepared for another attack.

The wolf growled, raking the ground with his claws, leaving deep grooves in the pavement.

"*Thomas, go!*" She screamed the command with her voice and her mind. Used every bit of her psychic strength to push the order at the panther.

The beast whimpered, then sprang toward the street, disappearing easily into the blackness of the night.

Thank God. One beast down. One to go.

Thomas would be okay. The panther shifter had been unable to transform since the death of his mate, and he'd feared an uncontrolled change in public, before human eyes.

But he'd managed to hold onto his human form until she'd arrived and then he'd shifted easily under her watchful eye in the alley. Yes, Thomas would be fine now. But, well, *she* might not be.

All alone with a wolf shifter. What, was she insane? Emily gulped as the wolf swung to face her, blood dripping from his mouth.

Damn. *Wolves are the most dangerous breed. They can kill without remorse.* Catch had told her that, when he'd started her *Other* training. *Beware of the wolves. They have loyalty only to their mates . . . everyone else is just prey to them.*

You don't want to be a wolf shifter's prey. She'd believed him then, and everything else she'd learned about the wolves had only reinforced her fear of the unpredictable breed.

But she didn't have much choice now. Running wasn't an option. The wolf would just love the hunt too much. And he would catch her, she knew that. No way could she outrun a wolf shifter in his prime.

No, running wasn't an option. Only one choice left.

Emily fell to her knees. Stared into the monster's eyes.

Her hands lifted.

The wolf tensed.

The thick scent of blood filled her nostrils. The wild musk of animal wrapped around her.

Old, half-forgotten phrases from her childhood danced through her mind.

What big teeth you have.

The better to eat you, my dear.

He could kill her in a heartbeat. Could rip her throat out in one bite.

Emily licked her lips. Pushed her trembling fingers against the beast's fur.

She wasn't Little Red Riding Hood.

Time to stop being afraid of the big, bad wolf.

Chapter 15

Blood was on his tongue. The warm, wet blood of his enemy. Colin threw back his head, howling in victory. He wanted to chase after the panther, to finish the kill, but—

But Emily knelt in front of him. Her glasses gone. Her eyes wide and her face too pale. He could smell her fear in the air, and as always, that heady smell roused the beast.

He crept closer to her, wondering if he'd be able to taste her fear on her skin, in her blood.

Her hands were on him, trembling as they stroked his fur. She was fucking terrified, but she didn't run.

And that fact made him angry. He'd wanted her to run, then he could have hunted her, claimed her.

The man fought to leash the beast once again. Grappled to harness the strength for the shift.

Claim her. Have to claim her. The words were burning in his mind. His blood. There was no choice any longer.

Claim. Mate. Take.

The animal's instincts blended with the man's, became one.

Mate. Take.

Mine.

He'd fought for her, drawn blood for her, earned her.

Mine.

His muscles burned as the fiery pain of the shift swept through him. Bones stretched, snapped, reshaped. Fur melted from his body. Hands, legs reappeared. He shuddered as his body transformed. Anger filled him, furious rage. Emily was watching him, seeing what he was.

The monster.

Not a man, never a man.

He opened his mouth, howling, screaming into the night . . . and as the shift ended, the howl changed into a man's bellow of fury.

He was crouched in front of her. Emily's hands had fallen away from him. She stared into his eyes, her breath too fast, her pulse thundering at the base of her neck.

"Colin, are you all—"

He grabbed her, surging to his feet. He was naked, but he didn't feel the bite of the cold night air on his flesh. He only felt . . . her.

Claim. Mate. Take.

Was it the beast or the man? He didn't know. Didn't care.

He jerked open her shirt, sending buttons flying. Shoved aside her bra. His mouth locked on her nipple, sucking hard, pulling her ripe flesh deep into his mouth.

"Colin!" Her hips twisted against his. "Not here, we can't—"

"Here." Guttural. "Now." His cock was fully erect, thick with lust. He wanted inside her. Needed to feel the tight clamp of her sex around him.

Mate.

He took her other breast into his mouth. Sucking. Licking. Biting.

She shuddered and moaned, a hungry, desperate sound.

Emily wanted him. Euphoria ripped through him. She knew what he was and she still wanted him.

She wasn't turning away. Her fingers were gripping his shoulders, her hips thrusting against his.

Fuck, yes.

She was wearing a skirt. A loose, black skirt that fell to her ankles.

He grabbed the material, jerking it up to her waist. His left hand found her through her panties, stroked the plump folds through the cotton. The rich scent of her arousal flooded his nostrils.

Take.

He spun her around. Her hands flew up, steadied against the wall.

Colin was shaking with the pulsing hunger thundering through him. He knew he was being too rough, but he couldn't stop.

He had to claim her. *Take.*

Her panties tore beneath his fingers. The lush curves of her ass beckoned him. So tempting.

He grabbed his cock, stroked the length. A drop of moisture was already on the tip.

Inside her.

Colin parted her delicate folds, lodged the tip of his cock against her opening.

"Not . . . gonna . . . be . . . gentle." He couldn't be. Not with the lust riding him so hard. Sweat coated his body. His muscles quivered with the effort of holding back.

"I . . . ah . . . don't care!" She squirmed against him, her creamy core sliding around his flesh. "T-take me!"

His control snapped. The man, the beast, growled in pleasure. Colin thrust into Emily's sex, shoving as deep and as hard as he could.

"*Colin!*" She rammed back against him. Her hands were flat against the wall as she braced her body.

He grabbed her hair, pulled it back, baring her neck. His cock slammed into her, again, and again . . .

She was moaning, panting, squirming against him. Every move, every sound she made just built the furious hunger within him.

His mouth pressed against her neck, tasted her skin. His canines were long and sharp in his mouth and he raked them across her flesh.

Bite. Mark. Claim.

"Ah . . . God . . . Colin." Her hips slammed back against him and her neck arched even more. "I'm coming!"

Her sex squeezed him, tightly clenching his cock. *Fuck, yes!* His teeth clamped down on her, pierced the delicate skin and drove into her vein.

As her hot, rich blood flowed over his tongue, he exploded inside of her, shoving deep one final time and burying his cock to the hilt inside of her.

His heart was drumming frantically. Sweat coated his body. And his teeth were still embedded in her throat.

Emily moaned softly. The sound not one of pain, but pleasure. Her sex shivered around him in a little aftershock caress.

He'd been right, Colin realized. He could taste her fear. And it was heady. But so was her passion.

A vampire drank from his victims to survive. To grow stronger.

A wolf shifter drank to kill or to claim.

To kill, well, you just ripped out the throat, let the hot blood pour into your mouth or you pierced the jugular and sucked the victim slowly dry.

Emily's body sagged lightly against him.

But to claim . . . a wolf shifter claimed a mate only once in his life. He marked her, bit her, tasted her blood so that he took her essence inside himself.

Take. Mate.

Until death.

And sometimes beyond.

Emily's heart was slowing. Her breath becoming shallow. Colin forced his head to lift.

Emily wasn't prey.

She was something far, far more valuable.

He lifted her into his arms. Her head rolled back against him.

Now how in the hell was he going to tell her that he'd just performed the equivalent of a wolf shifter marriage with her?

A wolf shifter. The detective was a wolf. Too fucking perfect.

How long had it been since he'd been able to pit his strength against another of his kind?

Too long.

Too many years of killing weaker species. But now, now there was finally someone worthy of his attack.

He watched from the shadows as Gyth cradled the woman against his body.

He'd marked her. Taken her as a mate. Did the good doctor know?

She was such an *Other* expert . . . she had to suspect.

Who would have thought? The doctor, a fitting mate for a wolf shifter.

Apparently, there was more to Emily Drake than met the eye.

Not just anyone could mate with the wolves.

But Emily could.

How very interesting.

Colin held her close for another moment, then eased Emily to her feet. He grabbed his torn jeans, tried to cover his body. Shouldered into what was left of his shirt and reached for her again.

His posture was possessive, protective as he led her from the alley.

It was a pity that the detective had just given away his weakness.

A woman.

A weak, human woman.

The humans . . . they died so easily. And screamed so well.

Time for another kill.

The doctor had already been on his list. Had been from the moment he'd learned of Gillian's appointment with her.

No loose ends.

But now, the game had changed.

He'd have to use care. The detective guarded his little doctor so well. He'd have to draw her away from him, make them both vulnerable.

A smile curved his lips, pressed against his fangs.

And he knew just how to bait his trap.

* * *

Emily awoke with a start the next morning. Her heart was racing as memories of a twisted nightmare drifted from her mind. She'd been hunted, bitten . . .

Not a dream, she realized, her hand lifting to touch her neck. The flesh was sore, slightly raised.

Last night, Colin had bitten her. Taken her blood.

Oh shit.

She swallowed, glancing around the room. *His room.* She didn't remember much about the ride back to Colin's place. She'd been groggy from pleasure and . . . *freaking blood loss.*

She'd heard of shifters biting their prey before, of course. Panthers, lions, bears . . . they all did it—often in human form just with their sharpened teeth. Supposedly, the blood gave them a sexual boost.

But she'd also heard of shifters taking the blood of their mates. And last night, with Colin, she hadn't felt like prey.

She'd felt like a mate.

Shit.

She'd always thought she'd wind up with some nice, easy-going, *normal* guy. A banker or an accountant or something equally boring and nondangerous.

Not a wolf shifter.

What had she done?

And why was the house so silent? "Colin?" No response. Emily raised her voice, tried again, "Colin!"

Nothing. She glanced at the bedside clock. Eight-thirty. He'd probably already gone to the station.

There was a bag near the foot of the bed. Emily saw the bright logo on the side. *Her new clothes.*

How had they gotten there? She'd thought she left them in her car at the station—

A faint beeping filled the room, and Emily recognized her ring tone. She stumbled from the bed, finding her purse on the floor. She grabbed the phone. "Drake."

"Dr. Drake . . . it's Smith."

The ME's voice sounded slightly distorted. Emily hurried across the room in an attempt to get better reception. "Smith? What is it?"

"Need . . . see . . . you."

Her voice was too high, Emily thought, and the fear she heard had nothing to do with bad reception. Had Smith found out something about the case? About the *Other*? "A-all right. Are you at the lab?"

"Yes. Hurry." The call ended with a click.

Emily frowned down at the phone.

Colin had been busy, Emily realized. When she went outside, she found her car waiting for her. *That explains the clothes.* She'd left the new bag of clothing on her backseat.

Twenty minutes later, she was walking into the station. She deliberately avoided Colin's floor, not wanting to see him then. She'd left her hair loose in an effort to hide the bruise on her throat.

She didn't know what she'd do if she saw him. Kiss him . . . or hit the bastard as hard as she could. Damn but she felt so confused. She wanted him, there was no denying that. But more, she'd started to trust Colin, and she hadn't trusted a man in years.

She was in trouble. Serious trouble. Because she wasn't exactly sure where the physical need for Colin ended and where something much more serious began.

The elevator chimed and the doors opened on the bottom floor. Emily stepped into the hallway, hearing the faint beat of Smith's jazz music. Her high heels clicked on the floor as she stepped forward. She pushed open the door to the lab. "Smith, I'm here—"

Her words ended on a rush of breath as she saw the puddle of blood near Smith's desk.

Maybe I'll go for a woman again the next time too.

No, oh God, no.

"*Smith!*" Emily ran forward, screaming the ME's name. Her shoes slipped in the blood.

Oh shit. The lab was trashed. Desks overturned. Files littering the floor. Equipment smashed.

More blood. Pooling on the floor.

But no body. No sign of Smith.

Without a hesitation, Emily lowered her mental shields. She had to know if the Butcher had been there.

The rage hit her, driving her to her knees. The same black taint of power that she'd felt before lingered in the air.

The Night Butcher. But it looked like the bastard had changed his MO. He'd struck during the day. When no one would suspect.

And he'd taken Smith.

Why? Emily stood slowly, knees shaking. Her gaze swept over the lab. He left his kills. Left them to taunt the police. There was no reason for him to take Smith.

Unless . . .

Emily turned on her heel and ran down the hall.

Unless the bastard had kept her alive.

Twelve hours had passed. Emily sat at Colin's desk, a mug of coffee cradled in her hands.

McNeal paced in front of her, his face blood red. "Not one fucking cop saw him! The asshole came into my station, took Smith, and not one fucking cop saw him!"

It was the same thing he'd been saying for hours. His hands were shaking, and his eyes were wild with worry and rage.

There was something there, Emily thought. The way McNeal was acting, he and Smith were more than just—

Colin's phone rang. They all seemed to freeze, then Colin's hand flashed out, jerked up the black receiver.

"Gyth."

His eyes widened and he motioned to Brooks. His partner instantly turned on the small, black tracking device that was attached to the phone.

The station fell silent as Colin's call echoed on the nearby speaker.

"Were you waiting for my call, Detective?" The voice was distorted, robotic.

"Who is this?" Colin demanded, his knuckles whitening around the phone.

"You know who I am."

"No, I don't. So why don't you just—"

"The press calls me the Night Butcher, but as you've seen, I don't just hunt at night." He laughed, a grating sound that sent a shiver down Emily's back.

"Ask the bastard about Smith," McNeal ordered.

"I want to talk to Smith," Colin snapped.

"Ah, yes, I figured you would. Good thing I haven't ripped her throat out, yet. It would make talking so hard."

A woman's scream echoed across the line.

Smith.

"M-McNeal, h-help—" A pain-filled moan broke her words.

More laughter. And dead silence from Smith.

Emily swallowed.

The officers gathered around her were pale, their faces tight with concentration.

But Colin . . . he had rage in his eyes. So much rage. *The beast wants out.*

"What the fuck do you want, Butcher?"

Silence. Too long. Too thick.

Colin gritted his teeth. "Dammit—"

"I have the wrong doctor."

Emily's blood froze.

Colin's gaze shot to hers.

"I want the other one."

His stare never left her. "I don't know what you're talking about, you crazy bastard, but—"

"She's in front of you, isn't she? Pretty little Doctor Drake. She's rather extraordinary. Knows so much about . . . our kind."

McNeal swore.

"I'll offer you a deal, Detective. Smith for Dr. Drake. An even trade."

And she saw Colin's control snap. "Fuck, no, you sonofa—"

Emily shot to her feet. Punched the button for the phone's intercom so she could speak. "Tell me where and when." No way was she going to sit back and let Smith die. Not if there was a chance they could save her.

A beat of silence, then, "Dr. Drake." He purred the words. As much as a robot could purr. "I had a feeling you were there."

So the asshole got bonus points for being right. "Don't hurt Smith," she ordered, her voice flat and cold. "Tell me where to be, and I'll make the trade."

Colin was shaking his head. His hand flashed out, locked around her wrist. "No damn way."

Emily lifted her chin. "Tell me where," she repeated.

"Warehouse district. Building 13. You come alone, Doctor. All alone. If I so much as smell a cop, you'll be swimming in Smith's blood."

She believed him.

"Midnight, Dr. Drake. I'll see you then." The hum of a dial tone resonated from the phone.

Emily exhaled the breath she'd been holding. Colin stared down at her, his face an iron mask. "You're not going." An order. One that he fully expected to be obeyed.

"If I don't, she's dead." And she couldn't have Smith's death on her conscience.

"*In my office, now.*" McNeal stormed ahead of them, not glancing back to see if he was obeyed.

Colin dragged Emily with him, keeping his tight grip on her wrist. He jerked her inside, slamming the door behind them.

"What the fuck were you thinking?" he snarled. "You do not, *do not*, ever interfere in my investigation like that again, do you—"

"I did what I had to do." Smith's life was on the line. There'd been no choice. "Tell me, Colin, if he'd offered to trade her for you, what would you have done?"

His clenched jaw was her answer.

"I've got to help her. If I don't, he'll kill her." *Rip out her throat, just as he'd done to the others.*

"When you walk into that warehouse, he'll kill you," he gritted. He yanked her closer to him, pressing his body against hers, flesh to flesh. His heat wrapped around her, his fury hovered in the air surrounding them. "You think I'm just gonna stand by and let that happen?" He kissed her hard, his lips bruising and hot. "No fucking way. I just found you. I'm not about to lose you now."

Her breath caught. "Colin . . ."

"If you two are done, we need to figure out just what the hell our next move is gonna be," McNeal growled, slamming his fist against the desk.

Emily jerked. She'd almost forgotten about him.

"This guy's a shifter, so when he said he could smell a cop, I know the bastard meant it." His lips thinned. "So how are we supposed to get backup in there without him going crazy and killing Smith?"

Emily glanced up at Colin. There might be a way . . .

"I'll shift," Colin muttered. "He'll smell animal, not man."

McNeal's eyes narrowed. "Shift." He whistled. "So you're one of them." A pause. "I knew you were *Other*, but I didn't realize—"

McNeal broke off, shaking his head. "A shifter."

If he only knew the full story, Emily thought.

"I'll follow Emily, track her into the warehouse." His hand tightened around her wrist. "And I'll catch the bastard."

McNeal cast a brief glance toward Emily. "Give us a minute, would you, Emily?"

She nodded, aware of a new tension in the room. She stepped forward, but Colin's hold didn't budge.

"Colin . . ."

He swallowed. Slowly, his fingers uncurled. Lifted. His eyes were burning with emotion and the faintest hint of fang gleamed behind his lips.

Emily lifted her hand, stroked his cheek. "It's going to be

all right." She said the words, not certain if she meant them, just wanting to ease the fear she could see lurking in his gaze.

He turned his face. Pressed his lips against her palm.

The mark on her neck seemed to throb.

"I-I'll be right outside." Getting ready to face a killer. Trying to stop her knees from knocking together.

Pretending that she was brave when really she was so scared she thought she'd vomit.

Oh God. What if she couldn't stop him from killing Smith? Or from killing her?

Emily pulled away from Colin and hurried out of the office, fighting the fear that pummeled her.

He wanted to take his mate away. Wanted to toss her over his shoulder and carry her far away. To someplace safe.

A place without psychotic killers. A place quiet, peaceful. A place where he could put her in a big, nice bed and make love to her for hours.

He wanted to take her anyplace but to that godforsaken warehouse.

"I can't send any other men in with you." McNeal was watching him with eyes that saw too much. "I can't risk the humans finding out what we're fighting."

He understood that. When they got to the warehouse, the Butcher might not be in human form. And if the other cops saw him shift . . .

"And I don't want you to 'catch' this guy, Gyth." McNeal stared him straight in the eye. "He can't see the inside of a courtroom."

Colin nodded. He'd already figured that out.

"Do what you have to do. Just get the women back safe." A pause. "And make certain that bastard doesn't have the chance to ever hurt anyone else."

"Don't worry." His voice had turned guttural. The wolf was close.

The Night Butcher had claimed his last victim.

Colin held his captain's stare, let the other man see the intent in his eyes. "The bastard was a dead man the minute he asked for the trade." No one would threaten his mate and live.

No one.

Time to hunt his prey . . .

And protect his mate.

Chapter 16

The night air was cold. Emily's breath formed a small cloud before her as she walked through the darkened warehouse district. There were rustles all around her. The scurry of rats and cockroaches. The howl of wind. The distant hum of a train.

Building 13 stood in front of her. Windows boarded up. Completely black.

The holster of her gun dug into Emily's back. McNeal had given her the weapon and the bullets before she'd left the station.

"Aim and shoot," he'd said.

And she would. She knew how to shoot, and she wouldn't hesitate to fire when she saw the Butcher.

She didn't hear Colin behind her, but she knew he was there. Tracking her, as the wolf.

His scent was already on her, so that had to work to their advantage. The Butcher wouldn't be able to distinguish between them. He'd think it was just one person.

The doors were in front of her. Emily lifted her hands and shoved against the old wood. With a loud groan, it gave way beneath her fingers.

A dark cavern waited for her. She stared into the darkness, knowing that the killer was waiting for her.

A faint moan reached her ears. Broken. Full of pain.

She licked her lips. Reached for the small flashlight she'd

tucked into her jacket pocket. The light flashed on, cut a thin swath of light through the blackness. She wasn't worried about the light giving away her position. If the killer was a hybrid like she suspected, he'd be able to see just as easily in the darkness.

The building smelled of mold and rotted wood. Cobwebs brushed her face and something ran across her left foot.

"Smith?" Emily raised her voice, tried again. "Smith?"

A whimper came from the darkness.

Emily crept forward. Swung her light to the left, the right—

There. Crumpled against the back wall. Head sagging to the side. *A broken doll.*

Smith.

Emily ran to her. The light hit Smith's body, showing the cuts and bites that covered her skin. Blood matted her hair, trickled down her bare arms and legs.

"I'm afraid I got a little bored while I was waiting for you." The voice came from the darkness, echoed all around her. No longer distorted. Male. Strong. Hard.

She stiffened. She knew that voice. Emily passed the flashlight to her left hand. Slowly inched her right toward her gun.

It can't be, it doesn't make any sense. How can it be him? I've felt his power before. He isn't strong enough to—

There was a rush of wind against her body and then his hands were on her, jerking her around, spinning her to face him. "Tell me, Doctor," Jake Donnelley murmured, his fangs bared and his eyes eerily black in the glow of her flashlight, "are you going to scream for me?"

Then his claws raked across her stomach, and she screamed as her flesh ripped open.

Emily! Her scream cut through him. Colin lunged through the open doors of the factory, his body springing through the air and landing in a deadly crouch. A snarl twisted the wolf's lips as he searched for his mate.

The scent of blood filled the air.

Emily's blood.

A red haze swam before his eyes. *Kill. Destroy—*

A man laughed. A sinister, cold laugh. "I thought you'd be joining us, Gyth."

Emily appeared before him, and Colin could easily see the blood running down the front of her shirt. Her eyes were huge. Her lips shaking.

Behind her, Jake Donnelley stood smiling at him. He had a hand wrapped around Emily's throat. His claws pressed against her flesh and a drop of blood trailed down her neck.

Colin scraped his claws across the cement floor, preparing to attack.

"Not so fast, wolf." The claws dug deeper and a soft moan slipped past Emily's lips. "If you move another inch, I'll slice her open in front of you."

Colin snarled at him, but he didn't move, not yet.

"So now the question becomes, who to kill first?" Jake lowered his head to Emily's throat, slowly licked away the drop of blood. "Oh, I do like the way you taste . . ."

Emily steeled herself against the feel of his tongue on her neck. She wanted to scream, to howl in pain and fear, but she vowed not to cry out again.

Because he wanted it too much.

Colin snarled in front of her, snapping his teeth, his glowing eyes locked on Jake.

Jake. God, she'd been so wrong about him. She'd thought he was weak, harmless. How the hell could she have made such a mistake?

She'd never even sensed that he was a hybrid. Never seen the glow of the beast he carried. She'd thought he was just a low-level demon.

Wrong. So wrong. And her mistake just might cost them all their lives.

She'd kept her shields in place too long, Emily realized. She'd been so afraid of finding a being like the one who'd attacked her years before, and she'd guarded herself too well.

Yes, she'd been safe, but she'd unknowingly let a killer run free when she could have stopped him.

Her stomach felt as if it were on fire. She didn't know how bad her injury was, and she was afraid to look down. So she kept her gaze on Colin, knowing that they had to find a way to defeat Jake.

One unguarded moment. That's all Colin would need. If he could just get one moment, she knew he'd attack.

"You don't understand our kind nearly as well as you thought, Doctor." Jake whispered the words into her ear, blowing his breath lightly against her. "You thought you were so superior, so damn smart, judging us all. Reading us. But you were wrong . . ."

"Y-yes . . . I was." *Lull him. Make him think I'm not a threat.*

"You saw what I wanted you to see," he muttered, and his claws scraped against her throat. "You thought you were immune to a demon's power . . . but I fooled you . . . made you see, feel, what I wanted."

And she'd "seen" a low-level demon. Emily swallowed, feeling the prick of his claws. She should have looked harder, searched his mind.

Too late for regrets. Focus, dammit! I have to give Colin a chance to attack.

Or they were dead.

Colin's gaze bored into her.

Just how much power did Jake have? There was really only one way to find out.

The last time she'd gone against a high-level demon, she'd wound up unconscious on the floor.

But she'd almost managed to burn out the bastard's power.

Maybe she could do it again.

Her jaw clenched and she lowered her shields.

The rage hit her first. Blinding. Pulsing. Hate. Fury. The emotions seethed within the demon hybrid behind her.

Then she felt his power. A dark, coiling black force that

shot from his body, filled the very air itself and twined around her and Colin.

Level ten. Maybe even stronger. Shit.

"Doctor . . ." Hot breath on her cheek. "Is that you I feel, tiptoeing in my head?"

A psychic blast of power hit her, shooting pain through every inch of her body. Emily bit her lip, swaying under the impact.

Too strong. I'll never be able to—

"You have no idea what I can do," he muttered. "But maybe I should show you." His head lifted. "Time to play with the wolf."

The waves of his power shifted for a moment, pulsed darker, then swept completely around Colin.

Shifters are immune to a demon's power. Colin hadn't even flinched under the whip of Niol's dark gifts.

He'd be able to withstand Jake's magical assault.

Wouldn't he?

There was so much power.

The wolf inched back a step, tail lowering.

"I can control anyone," Jake snarled. "*Anything.*"

He'd controlled the boy, Bryan Trace. Gotten him to stalk Jake's victims.

But not Colin, please, not Colin.

Emily frantically tried to pull away from Jake's mind, tried to reach Colin's thoughts—

But she couldn't feel him, couldn't touch his mind.

"Why?" The word burst from her lips. "Why the hell are you doing this?"

His laughter rumbled against her back. "Because I can."

Started with that whore Gillian. Bitch thought she could leave me for a human.

Showed her. Showed them both.

Emily tensed as his thoughts slipped through her mind. She couldn't reach Colin, but she was tuned in as hell to Jake.

Forgotten how good the blood tasted.

Want more.

An image of Darla's ravaged body flashed through her mind.

More. Tired of hiding, pretending. Fucking humans will fear me now. Show 'em. Show 'em all.

Once the beast got a taste, he couldn't be stopped.

Suddenly, Jake shoved her forward, right into Colin's path. "Here's the fun part. I'm not gonna kill you, Doctor."

Why wasn't Colin attacking him? His claws were down. It'd be the perfect time. Emily glanced frantically between the two of them.

"No, I'm not gonna be the one to rip that pretty throat open. I'm gonna let your lover do it."

I can control anyone. Anything. Even a shifter. Blood to blood.

Shit. Jake could control his kind—not just demons, but also shifters. The power was always in the blood.

The wolf's jaws were open, glistening. His eyes bright with blood hunger.

"No." Not Colin. She had to reach him. Had to help him. "You control the beast," she whispered, lifting her hand slowly toward him. "He doesn't control you . . ."

"No, *I* control him."

She reached for her gun, but the holster was empty. Jake must have disarmed her when he'd first grabbed her. *Dammit!* Colin growled and stalked toward her.

No. Not like this. She wasn't going to die like this. Not in some dank building, not by her lover's hand.

Her shields were down, completely gone. And with all of her energy, with every bit of psychic power that she had, Emily focused on reaching Colin's mind. On getting past the killing fury and touching the man.

No, don't let him do this to you. To us. Fight him, dammit! You have to be stronger, I need you—

"Ahhh!" Blinding pain exploded in her head, and Emily fell to her knees. Jake's dark power poured through her, ripping apart her mind, taking her memories, stealing her power—

"Not gonna happen, bitch," he snarled. "Tonight you die." Just like before. The pain was the same. He was forcing his way into her mind, using his magic against her, hurting her.

"Stop!" She pushed the flow of her psychic energy back on him, digging just as hard into his mind as he was hers. She'd burn the bastard out, *just like before.*

Or she'd fucking die trying.

The images began rolling in front of her mind's eye. Faster, faster . . .

"It's over, Jake . . ."

A dark alley. A woman in a red dress.

A scream.

The woman dropped to the ground. Throat slashed. Blood all around.

Oh God. The pain was ripping her apart.

A circle of men, all in black, stood glaring next to an abandoned building. "You didn't tell us he was a shifter," one snarled, lifting his hand and pointing his finger straight ahead. A snake tattoo bared its fangs on his wrist. "We ain't fuckin' with no shifter again—"

A shot rang out. A circle of blood appeared on his chest. Three more shots.

Down, down go the demons.

Emily bit her lip, tasted blood as she fought to force the psychic power back on him.

"What the fuck do you want?" Darla frowned, her brows drawn low. "You know I'm working on the story about—"

Her blood sprayed on the wall behind her.

So much blood.

Emily grabbed her head, screaming. The pain was too much. She couldn't fight him much longer.

Break, you sonofabitch!

Before she did . . .

A young boy, with the claws of a wolf and the eyes of a demon. He walked up to an old man, shuffling through the park and pushing a buggy of cans . . .

The blood sprayed onto the snow-covered ground.

The taste . . . so good . . . more

More . . .

More . . .

Emily fell onto the floor, her body shaking, twitching. Too much. She couldn't fight anymore.

Colin snarled. She forced her heavy eyelids open, saw him above her, jaws open.

No, not Colin.

She'd . . . loved him . . . as much as she could love anyone.

Maybe this *was* the way she would die . . . she hoped he made it quick. She stared into his glowing eyes, her body and mind shuddering with agony and she waited.

Her lips parted, "Love . . ." It was all she could manage. But she needed to say it, even though he wouldn't understand. She had to say it once in her life, dammit, and actually mean it.

Colin sprang forward, jaws open, claws outstretched.

He flew right over her and barreled into Jake. The demon screamed in fury—but the sound ended in a sudden gurgle of pain.

The agonizing torture in her mind ended. Vanished in an instant. Emily pushed up on her knees. Jake's body was twitching. She squinted in the darkness, trying to see more.

The wolf was over him, teeth lodged in the hybrid's throat.

Looked like Jake hadn't been able to control her wolf after all.

He shifted back into a man with the taste of Donnelley's blood still in his mouth. The shift came easier because the beast was satiated.

His hands clenched and the claws slowly receded. For a time there, he knew Donnelley had tried to get him to attack Emily.

He'd seen the fear in her eyes, and there hadn't been a damn thing he could do about it.

Then she'd started fighting, and he'd sensed her energy in the air around them. He'd realized that Emily and Donnelley were locked in a psychic battle, and when his mate had fallen to her knees, he'd understood that she was fighting for him, struggling to give him the time he needed to attack.

He wiped the back of his hand over his mouth. Blood coated his fingers, still dripped down his chin.

Part of him wished he'd made the bastard suffer more. *You died too easily. You should have screamed for death.*

Donnelley stared sightlessly up at him, blood pooling beneath him. His throat was ripped wide open, his head barely hanging on.

Not even a full-blooded shifter could heal from a wound like that.

A soft footfall sounded behind him. He didn't glance back. Emily shouldn't see him this way. He didn't *want* her to see him this way. Not with the blood of the kill on him.

For one terrible moment, he'd wanted to feel *her* neck beneath his claws and teeth.

For that, he wanted to kill the bastard all over again.

"Colin . . ." Soft, husky. "A-are you all right?"

I nearly killed you. No, he wasn't fucking all right. A growl rumbled in his throat.

A quick inhalation of breath. "H-he's dead."

Unless Donnelley could somehow breathe without a windpipe, yeah, he was dead.

Colin stared down at Donnelley's face. His eyes were wide open, his mouth twisted in a snarl. *Didn't think you'd die, did you, asshole?*

His hands clenched into fists and he forced himself to look at Emily. He could still smell her blood. The blood that had tempted him.

"We need to get you to a hospital."

She was squinting down at the body, trying to see clearer with her human eyes in the darkness.

"No, I'm okay, I just—" Her hand lifted, brushed against her stomach, and a hiss of pain slipped past her lips. "It's bloody as hell, but I-I don't think it's too deep. I-I'll be all right."

He reached for her, pulling her against him and cradling her carefully. He'd come too close to losing her. *Too close.*

A sudden scream shattered the silence.

Smith.

Colin looked up, found her standing in front of him, clad in her underwear, blood smearing her body. She had a gun in her hand, Emily's gun, and she was shaking and pointing it straight at him.

"*Monster!*" The cock of the hammer was too loud. "*I saw you change! You're like him, just like—*"

The shock and the horror had gotten to her. She was going to fire, Colin realized. She was going to—

Emily shoved him to the ground. Her soft body fell onto his, and he heard the *whoosh* of the bullet fly past them.

Sonofabitch. Why did every human try to shoot him when they found out what he was?

He carefully pushed Emily to the side. Scanned her body to make damn sure the bullet hadn't touched her. Then, satisfied but seriously pissed, Colin sprang to his feet. "Dammit, I saved your life!" Didn't that count for anything? Or was he just another monster to her?

She stared up at him, mouth agape, gun still trembling in her fingers. Then her lips began to quiver. The gun fell to the floor and great, gulping sobs burst from within her.

Smith threw herself into his arms, pressing her wet face against his neck.

Humans.

Colin awkwardly stroked her back.

"Smith." Emily's soft voice. "How badly are you hurt?"

The ME lifted her face. Blinked. "I-I—"

"What did he do to you?" Colin asked, pitching his voice low. He didn't want to set her off again.

"B-bit. Cl-clawed." A shudder of revulsion swept over her.

Emily pulled out her cell phone. Quickly dialed and then asked to speak with McNeal. Colin heard her tell the captain the killer had been contained and that they needed an ambulance, ASAP.

She disconnected the call and then looked back at Colin.

Smith was still pressed against him, still crying, but softly now. Almost whimpering.

"Smith, before the others arrive, we need to talk." Emily's voice was calm, soothing. The professional psychologist was back in place.

If he hadn't been there, he never would have known the lady had just come moments away from death.

That was his doc. Core of steel.

Being as gentle as possible, Colin pushed Smith back until he could look into her eyes. "You know what I am." And she'd tried to kill him. *So what is new?*

She nodded. "W-werewolf."

Not exactly, but close enough for the time being.

"There are many . . . beings out there like Colin," Emily told her. "They're the *Other* and they walk right beside humans in this world."

Smith shook her head, but Colin didn't think she was denying Emily's words.

"You can't tell anyone about them, Smith. You can't say what you saw . . . what Colin is . . . what Jake was." Sirens echoed in the distance. The cops had been stationed close by. Not too close to alert the killer, but close enough for backup. "I'll explain everything to you later, but please, promise me you won't say anything to the other officers. Th-they wouldn't understand." Emily cast a quick, desperate look in Colin's direction, but she kept her voice calm and easy.

A flash of blue lights lit up the warehouse.

"Smith, I need you to give me your word," Colin said. "Don't tell anyone what you saw here."

Brakes squealed. Doors slammed. Voices rumbled.

Smith's shoulders straightened and she looked at him with a touch of her old confidence. "D-don't worry, Gyth . . . n-no one would b-believe me anyway . . ."

McNeal burst into the building. "Smith!"

She didn't take her eyes off Colin. "B-but now I know . . . m-monsters—"

"Smith, thank God!" McNeal grabbed her, pulled her tight against his chest. "Woman, I thought I'd lost you." His face was tormented.

Colin glanced over at Emily. She was staring at Donnelley's body. He pushed to her side, needing to touch her.

His fingers found hers. Locked.

Jesus. He felt like he'd just lost a good ten years of his life. Emily had come so close to death . . . by his hand.

"You aren't anything like him, you know," she whispered, her words barely a breath of sound. "People think all wolf shifters are the same."

Psychotic. Homicidal. Uncontrollable.

"But you're different."

He wasn't so sure. Donnelley lay before him, throat almost completely gone. He'd killed him, just as easily as Donnelley had killed his victims. And given the same set of circumstances, he wouldn't hesitate to do it again.

"You're not like him," she repeated softly, glancing up at him. "You could never be."

If something happened to her, he could be. The knowledge was there. Uncomfortable. Painful. But true. If anything ever happened to the doc, his beast would break his cage.

She is mine. Every instinct in his body screamed of the possession. He didn't understand how it had happened, but the doc . . . she was his mate.

A human, mated to a wolf shifter.

The Monster Doctor bound to a monster.

Fate could be a twisted bitch.

Emily stared up at him. Blood trickled down her throat.

Mine.

A circle of uniformed cops gaped down at Donnelley's body. "Another one?" a young female officer exclaimed. "But I thought the Night Butcher was taken down—"

"He was." Colin took Emily's arm. Led her away from the body. He wanted to get her home. Naked. Under him. Not necessarily in that order. "That's him." McNeal could bullshit his way through an explanation of the killer's torn throat. He was getting out of there and taking his mate with him.

She awoke to the feel of a man's hand slowly stroking her thigh. It was a soft touch. Light.

Colin.

Emily stretched slowly and opened her eyes. It was still dark in the bedroom, but the faint light from the hallway trickled into the room. Colin was crouched between her thighs, naked.

And aroused.

The paramedics had grabbed her when they'd left the crime scene. They'd patched her up, bandaged her stomach— luckily, the cuts hadn't been deep enough to require stitches.

They'd finally escaped from the EMTs, and Colin had taken her home.

They made love as soon as the front door closed behind them. Fast. Hard. He'd had her naked in less than a minute, and she'd been coming thirty seconds later.

For all of his strength, he'd taken care not to jar her injuries. He'd held her immobile against the wall, and thrust into her, deep, so deep.

They'd fallen asleep in his bed. His arms had been around her. His right hand lying on her heart.

And now . . .

His finger trailed up her thigh, eased between the folds of her legs.

"I want to taste you." His voice was a growl in the darkness.

Oh yes. Sounded like a fabulous plan to her. Emily arched her hips.

Then felt the warm stroke of his tongue on the center of her desire. She closed her eyes, sighing with pleasure. *Oh, that is good. So—*

His tongue swirled over her clitoris, sucked lightly.

Her heels dug into the mattress.

His breath blew across her flesh, and one finger slid into her hungry sex. Another slow swirl of his tongue.

Her entire body tightened. "C-Colin!"

He kept licking her, moving that tongue over every inch of her sex in long, maddening swipes that had her twisting, moaning, then—

Colin drove his tongue deep inside of her.

Her fingers locked in his hair. Not to push him away, but to hold him closer. Tighter.

"*More!*" She was close, so close.

His thumb pushed the button of her need and his tongue drove deep again, licking inside her core with just the perfect touch.

Her hips bucked and her orgasm rolled over her in a tide of red-hot pleasure. And as her sex clenched, he kept lapping her, licking and sucking on her tender flesh until the waves of her release finally ended.

Emily sagged against the bed. *Wow.*

Colin stretched out beside her. Curled his body around hers. She could feel his aroused flesh pressing into her buttocks, but he made no move to take her. "Colin, aren't you—"

"It was for you. Just you." He pressed a kiss to her neck, to the faint bruise on her skin. The mark not made by Jake's claws, but by Colin's mouth.

"But why don't—"

"I don't want to take this time. I just wanted to give."

And he'd sure as hell done that. Given her so much pleasure that her body still tingled. Emily rolled to face him. Found his expression tense, guarded. "I'm not sure I understand you, shifter." Just when she thought she'd figured him out, he managed to surprise her.

"You don't have to understand me." A pause. "But . . ." He stopped, jaw tightening.

Emily pushed out of his arms, sat up, uncaring of her nudity and the bandages that covered her stomach. "What?" Something was happening here. Something important. She could feel his tension. His . . . fear?

Why would Colin be afraid? Donnelley was dead. No more homicidal monsters were wandering the streets. The city was safe . . . for the moment. "What is it?"

"Do you think . . . you could ever love me?" Stark words. And she saw the fear then. In his eyes, in the unguarded expression on his face.

She touched his cheek. Smoothed her fingers down the side of his face.

Not a human. Not the simple, easygoing partner she would have chosen.

He carried a beast with him. A creature of enormous power. Man and beast. Strength and danger.

Do you think . . . you could ever love me?

Being moments from death had made her realize a damn important fact. Her hand lifted, stroked his cheek. "I already do, Colin. I already do." She kissed him, brushing her lips lightly across his. His hands curled around her and he pulled her close, holding her right against his pounding heart.

Just where she wanted to be.

Safe . . . with her monster.

Epilogue

"Jake Donnelley, the perpetrator known as the Night Butcher, was killed last night when the woman he'd kidnapped, Chief Medical Examiner Natalhia Smith, shot him in the throat."

A chorus of questions erupted at this news.

But McNeal just kept talking. "Evidence links Jake Donnelley to the murders of Gillian Nemont, Preston Myers, and Darla Mitchell. We also have reason to suspect that he was behind the recent killing of four John Does . . ."

The watch on Emily's arm vibrated. Glancing down, she saw that it was nearly time for her to meet up with her last appointment of the day. Marvin was scheduled to come in, and she was eager to see how the vampire fared.

She'd snuck away from the office to catch the news conference. She'd been curious about how McNeal would spin Jake's death.

Shot in the throat. Nice touch.

Colin stood just behind McNeal. Brooks was at his side. Both were looking straight ahead, their attention on the crowd.

Time to go.

Emily stepped back, turned—

And nearly walked into Smith.

The ME looked tired. Her eyes were bloodshot. Scratches covered her face and arms. But her chin was lifted high, and there was a determined expression on her face.

"How many of them . . ." she muttered, her attention on the crowd of reporters, "are even human?"

Emily glanced back at the group. "At least two-thirds." *Once you know the truth, you can never stop suspecting.*

Smith sucked in a sharp breath of surprise. "You see them, don't you?"

It would be too hard to explain how she could really recognize them all, so she just nodded.

"Do . . . they scare you?"

Niol's image flashed through her mind. "Some of them do." She met Smith's stare. "But then, some humans scare the hell out of me too."

The ME nodded, understanding. "It's just . . . what am I supposed to do now? Now that I—"

Know.

"Keep doing exactly what you've been doing." Only now, maybe McNeal wouldn't have to come up with so many stories to explain certain anomalies Smith found with the bodies. "Everything is just like it was before, you know."

Smith's dark gaze swept over the crowd. "No, it isn't."

"The monsters were there before, you just didn't see them." But now she would—she'd notice every difference. Always wonder.

The blinders were off for Smith.

But still on for the rest of the world.

One day they'd all realize. They'd wake up, and they'd all finally understand.

Monsters weren't just stories to frighten small children. Weren't just myths to whisper in the dark.

They were real.

And they were everywhere.

Emily reached into her purse, pulled out a small, white business card. She offered it to Smith. "If you ever want to talk about what happened, call me." Being nearly murdered by a creature straight out of a nightmare wouldn't be an easy thing to deal with, and if she could help Smith, she would. Even if the ME wasn't her usual type of client.

Smith's fingers curled around the card. "Thanks." She swallowed, then stepped away.

Emily watched her slow stride across the room. Smith had a long road to go, but the woman was a survivor. She'd make it.

And she'd learn to live with the monsters around her.

Emily's attention turned back to the swarm of reporters. The humans were leaning forward, a sort of greedy interest on their faces, but the *Other*, they hung back, as if realizing there were more details to this particular case that were best left uncovered.

Yes, one day the humans would turn around and realize they were surrounded by the *Other*.

But today, well, today wasn't going to be that day of dawning realization. *Not today . . .*

Her wrist alarm vibrated again.

Time to get back to work. She needed to chat with her vampire. See how his blood diet was going.

And after that . . . she turned her head slightly, met Colin's bright stare. Saw the hunger in his eyes.

After meeting the vampire, she had a date with a wolf.

Another busy night for the Monster Doctor.

Meet the BADDEST BAD BOYS in
three wickedly irresistible stories from
Shannon McKenna, E.C. Sheedy, and Cate Noble.
Available now from Brava.
Here's an excerpt from Shannon's story,
"Anytime, Anywhere."

He forced his leaden body into action. Shoved open the truck door, grabbed his grip and the bag of groceries. He made his way with heavy feet up the switchback path to the hillside cabin—and froze.

Footsteps around the corner of the cabin. Someone was passing through the foliage. The *shush-shush* of jeans legs rubbing each other. The *swish-slap* of bushes. He heard every sound like it was miked.

He let the duffel, the groceries drop. His gun materialized in his hand, though he had no memory of drawing it, or flattening his back to the weather-beaten shingles, creeping towards the corner . . . waiting—

Grab, twist, and he had the fucker bent over in a hammerlock, wrist torqued at an agonizing angle, gun to the nape. It squawked.

Female. Long hair, swishing and tickling over his bare arm. A delicate wrist that felt like it might break in his grip. What the *hell* . . . ?

"Jon! Stop this! Let go! It's me!"

Huh? The chick knew him? His body had ascertained that she was no physical threat, so he shoved her away to take a better look.

His jaw dropped when she straightened up, rubbing her twisted wrist. He tried to drag in oxygen, but his lungs were locked. Holy shit. No way had he met this girl before. He would have remembered. *Wow.*

Long hair swung to her waist. Big dark eyes, exotically tilted, flashing with anger. High cheekbones, perfect skin, pointy chin. That full pink mouth, glossed up with lip goo, calculated to make a guy think of one thing only, and suffer the immediate physiological consequences.

And her body, Jesus. Feline grace; long legs, slim waist, round hips. High, suckable, braless tits, the nipples of which poked through a thin cotton blouse. Low-rise jeans that clung desperately to the undercurve of that perfect ass. Who the hell . . . ? This was private property, in the middle of nowhere. His dick twitched, swelled.

She did not look armed. He slipped the Glock back into the shoulder holster. "You scared me," he said. "Who the hell are you?"

Her eyes widened in outrage. "What do you mean, who the hell am I? It's me! Robin!"

Robin? His brain spun its wheels to reconcile the irreconcilable.

Danny's baby sister? He'd practically pissed himself laughing the night she'd juggled flaming torches in Danny's kitchen, although Danny hadn't been amused when the rib-eye he'd grilled got unexpectedly flambéd. The steak had tasted faintly of petroleum fuel, but what the hell. She hadn't burned down the building.

Robin . . . ? Robin of the dorky glasses, the mouthful of metal? Robin who was as cute and funny as a bouncing Labrador puppy?

The irreconcilable images slammed together, like a truck hitting his mind. Those big brown eyes, magnified behind Coke bottle lenses.

It *was* Robin. Holy shit. In his mind he'd already been nailing this girl, right and left and center. Danny would kill him if he knew Jon had entertained pornographic thoughts about his baby sister. "Ah, sorry," he muttered lamely. "I didn't recognize you. You look . . . different than I remembered. Do your brothers know you're out dressed like that?"

Her back straightened, and her eyes narrowed to gleaming brown slits. "Mac and Danny have nothing to say about my wardrobe."

"Maybe they should." He jerked his chin in the general direction of her taut brown nipples, all too evident in the chill, and averted his eyes.

"Why should they?" Her slender arms folded over her chest, propping the tits up higher for his tormented perusal. "I'm twenty-five, Jon. That's a two, and then a five."

He blinked at her. "No shit."

"Absolutely, shit. Want to see my driver's license? I wear what I please. I answer to no one."

This was surreal. He dragged his eyes away from her gleaming pink lips, and pulled himself together. "Uh, I don't mean to be rude, but what the fuck does your age have to do with anything? And what are you doing up here, anyhow?"

The gleaming lips pursed. "I could ask you the same question."

"You could," he conceded. "But it would be none of your goddamn business. Your brother gave me the keys. I'm crashing up here for a couple of weeks to do some fishing and stare at the wall with my mouth hanging open. And now, your turn. What did you come up here for?"

Her gaze fell. She started to speak. Pressed her hand to her belly.

"Um . . . you," she said.

You've got to try
THE ONE I WANT
by Nancy Warren,
new this month from Brava . . .

Matthew wandered past his front door, yawning, fantasizing about the first strong, black cup of coffee of the day when he noticed a fat envelope on the mat inside his front door.

He stood there for a moment regarding it, eyes unconsciously narrowing. It wasn't part of the regular mail delivery. He'd locked up just after midnight and the envelope hadn't been there then. He glanced at his watch and wondered who had dropped off a fat piece of mail in the last seven hours and whether he should be alarmed.

As usual, curiosity was stronger than caution. He picked up the envelope. *Chloe* was handwritten on the front. The envelope was soft, the flap tucked in but not sealed. A man with strong moral fiber and a healthy conscience would walk right next door and push the envelope through the correct mail slot.

He pulled out the tucked flap and peeked inside, where he found a wad of cash. And a note.

> *"Chloe, thanks so much. Didn't want this on my credit card for obvious reasons. Everything worked out great. I'd use you again. Allan."*

He counted the money. Stood there chewing his upper lip with an unpleasant feeling that both he and his London acquaintance Gerald had been snowed. Then he shoved the money back and walked outside into the cool of the morning. Lights were on in a few of his neighbors' windows and Horace Black across the street and two down, was backing his new truck down the driveway.

Up and down the street signs of life, but in his new neighbor's house nothing. She'd been here for two weeks and while she seemed like a good tenant, she came and went at strange hours. He had a bad feeling he now knew why.

He strode next door and knocked on her front door, perhaps a little more aggressively than necessary.

He'd been conned and he didn't like being conned.

Probably he should go back to his house and drink some coffee, give himself a chance to cool down and little miss 'I'll use your services again,' time to wake up. But he didn't feel like doing the sensible thing.

He gave it a minute, then banged again, holding the bell with his finger at the same time.

After an age and a half, the front door opened. Chloe Flynt stood there, her black hair soft and tousled in the sexiest case of bed head he'd ever seen. Her eyes were the most amazing purple-blue, and they gazed at him in the vaguely unfocussed way of someone who's not totally awake yet. He had no idea what—if anything—she was wearing since everything from the neck down was behind the door.

"You should have asked who it was before opening the door," he snarled.

"I looked out the bedroom window," she said on a yawn. "I could see you." Almost as though his sharp advice to be cautious had the opposite effect, she straightened and opened the door fully.

He'd checked her out, the way a single man in his prime always checks women out. He'd sensed a very nice body was packaged in the trendy clothes she wore. But he'd had no idea.

She wasn't a tall woman, but she was exquisite. She wore teeny-tiny girl boxer shorts with the Union Jack stamped all over them and a little white T-shirt with *Rule Britannia* printed across the chest. Her legs were shapely, her breasts small and perfect. Even the tiny strip of skin between the end of her shirt and the beginning of the shorts fascinated him. So white, so smooth.

His gaze returned to her eyes and he found them fully awake now and regarding him with a certain amused speculation. Damn it, she'd knocked him on his ass and she knew it.

"Don't tell me, your bra has the queen on one cup and Prince Charles on the other."

She glanced down at her outfit as though she'd forgotten what she was wearing. "A going away present from a friend."

The sun was against his back, already warm. To his right he heard a bee sounding like it was snoring in the Texas lilac bush he'd planted last year.

"Did you come over to check that my pajamas are patriotic?" she asked.

He realized he was staring and felt stupid, which annoyed him even more. "I came to deliver some mail that came to me by mistake."

He held out the envelope.

"Thank you." She put out her hand but he didn't relinquish the envelope.

"What's going on, Chloe?"

Her eyebrows rose in an incredibly snooty fashion, as though she might call her palace guards to come and have him shot. "I beg your pardon?"

"Somebody stuffs a thousand bucks in cash in my mail slot in the middle of the night, it makes me curious."

"A thousand dollars?" she exclaimed, sounding delighted. "He must have added a tip. How sweet."

For an instant he was distracted by the thought of what her services were and what she'd done to deserve such a big tip.

"Shit," he muttered, then stepped forward so fast his neighbor squeaked when he bumped her with his body, pushing her inside the house and shutting the door fast behind them.

"How dare you. Leave this house instantly," she demanded, small and fiery.

He ducked away from the window and made a dash for the kitchen.

"Are you a lunatic?" that crisp English voice trilled.

"Quiet. She'll hear you." He was in the kitchen, jamming his butt onto a kitchen chair that put him out of window range of his own house next door.

"Who will hear me? Matthew, what on earth—"

"Brittany."

She followed him into the kitchen and looked down at him. "And who is Brittany?"

"My girlfriend."

She looked at him like he was a few cattle short of a herd but she didn't say a word for which he was ridiculously grateful. Explaining Brittany was complicated. Getting more so every day. She was perfect for him in every way. Sweet, cute, sexy, nice and the kind of woman who would make a wonderful mom. So why was he, a grown man who should be getting on with his life, hiding in the kitchen of a neighbor who was probably a criminal.

Don't miss WHEN HE WAS BAD, a sexy
paranormal anthology from
Shelly Laurenston and Cynthia Eden,
coming next month from Brava.
Turn the page for a sneak peek of
Shelly's story, "Miss Congeniality."

The doorbell rang and Irene didn't move. She wasn't expecting anyone so she wouldn't answer the door. She dealt with enough people during the day, she'd be damned if her nights were filled with the idiots as well.

The doorbell went off again, followed by knocking. Irene didn't even flinch. In a few more minutes she would shut everything out but the work in front of her. A skill she'd developed over the years. Sometimes Jackie would literally have to shake her or punch her in the head to get her attention.

But Irene hadn't slipped into that "zone" yet and she could easily hear someone sniffing at her door. She looked up from her paperwork as Van Holtz snarled from the other side, "I know you're in there, Conridge. I can smell you."

Eeew.

"Go away," she called back. "I'm busy."

The knocking turned to outright banging. "Open this goddamn door!"

Annoyed but resigned the man wouldn't leave, Irene put her paperwork on the couch and walked across the room. She pulled open the door and ignored the strange feeling in the pit of her stomach at seeing the man standing there in a dark gray sweater, jeans, and sneakers. She knew few men who made casual wear look anything but.

"What?"

She watched as his eyes moved over her, from the droopy

sweat socks on her feet, past the worn cotton shorts and the paint-splattered T-shirt that spoke of a horrid experience try- ing to paint the hallway the previous year, straight up to her hastily created ponytail. He swallowed and muttered, "God- damnit," before pushing his way into her house.

"We need to talk," he said by way of greeting.

"Why?"

He frowned. "What?"

"I said why do we need to talk? As far as I'm concerned there's nothing that needs to be said."

"I need to kiss you."

Now Irene frowned. "Why?"

"Must you always ask why?"

"When people come to me with things that don't make sense . . . yes."

"Just let me kiss you and then I'll leave."

"Do you know how many germs are in the human mouth? I'd be better off kissing an open sewer grate."

Why did she have to make this so difficult? He hated being here. Hated having to come here at all. Yet he had something to prove and goddamnit, he'd prove it or die trying.

But how dare she look so goddamn cute! He'd never known this Irene Conridge existed. He'd only seen her in those boxy business suits or a gown that he'd bet money she never picked out for herself. On occasion he'd even seen her in jeans but, even then, she'd always looked pulled together and profes- sional.

Now she looked goddamn adorable, and he almost hated her for it.

"Twenty seconds of your time and I'm out of here for good. Twenty seconds and I won't bother you ever again."

"Why?"

Christ, again with the why.

"I need to prove to the universe that my marking you means absolutely nothing."

"Oh, well isn't that nice," she said with obvious sarcasm. "It's nice to know you're checking to make sure kissing me is as revolting as necessary."

"I'm not . . . didn't . . ." He growled. "Can we just do this please?"

"Twenty seconds and you'll go away?"

"Yes."

"Forever?"

"Absolutely."

"Fine. Just get it over with quickly. I have a lot of work to do. And the fact that you're breathing my air annoys me beyond reason."

Wanting this over as badly as she did, Van marched up to her, slipped his arm around her waist and yanked her close against him. They stared at each other for a long moment and then he kissed her. Just like he did Athana earlier. Only Athana had been warm and willing in his arms. Not brittle and cold like a block of ice. Irene didn't even open her mouth.

Nope. Nothing, he thought with overwhelming relief. This had all been a horrible mistake. He could—and would—walk away from the honorable and brilliant Irene Conridge, PhD, and never look back. Van almost smiled.

Until she moved slightly in his arms and her head tilted barely a centimeter to the left. Like a raging wind, lust swept through him. Overwhelming, all-consuming. He'd never felt anything like it. Suddenly he needed to taste her more than he needed to take his next breath. He dragged his tongue against her lips, coaxing her to open to him. To his eternal surprise she did and he plunged deep inside. Her body jerked, her hand reaching up and clutching his shoulder. Probably moments from pushing him away. But he wouldn't let her. Not if she felt even a modicum of what he was feeling. So he held her tighter, kissed her deeper, let her feel his steel-hard erection held back by his jeans against her stomach.

The hand clutching his shoulder loosened a bit and then slid into his hair. Her other hand grabbed the back of his neck. And suddenly the cold, brittle block of ice in his arms turned into a raging inferno of lust. Her tongue tangled with his and she groaned into his mouth.

Before Van realized it, he was walking her back toward her stairs. He didn't stop kissing her, he wouldn't. The last thing he wanted was for her to change her mind. He managed to get her to the upstairs hallway before she pulled her mouth away.

"What are you doing?" she panted out.

"Taking you to your bed."

"Forget it." And Van, if he were a crying man, would be sobbing. Until uptight Irene Conridge added, "The wall. Use the wall."